"If the book's basic theme of survival is a common one, its construction is distinctly unexpected."

—*Atlantic Monthly*

"Journalist Moran takes on a daunting subject—the Holocaust—through a narrow but encompassing focus in this first novel."

—*Booklist*

"Moran . . . subtly explores the way ordinary people, even children, are capable of both good and evil, betrayal and sacrifice."

—*Publishers Weekly*

"Moran . . . is writing about the enigma of a heroic act performed by the most ordinary of people. He rubs our noses in their ordinariness. They are foolish, petty, prejudiced, jealous. They aren't sure why they hide the Jew—himself such an ordinary man."

—*Los Angeles Times*

"This book is a major page-turner."

—*Seventeen*

THOMAS MORAN

THE MAN IN THE BOX

RIVERHEAD

BOOKS

New York

Riverhead Books
Published by The Berkley Publishing Group
A member of Penguin Putnam Inc.
200 Madison Avenue
New York, New York 10016

Copyright © 1996 by Thomas Moran
Book design by Marysarah Quinn
Cover design by Charles Björklund
Cover photograph © Alexandra Bennett/nonstock

First Riverhead hardcover edition: January 1997
First Riverhead trade paperback edition: January 1998
Riverhead trade paperback ISBN: 1-57322-649-1

The Putnam Berkley World Wide Web site address is
http://www.berkley.com

The Library of Congress has catalogued the Riverhead hardcover
edition as follows:
Moran, Thomas.
The man in the box/by
Thomas Moran.
p.   cm.
ISBN 1-57322-060-4
1.   World War, 1939–1945—
Jews—Fiction.   I. Title.
PS3563.07714M36   1996
96-41042   CIP
813'.54—dc20

Printed in the United States of America

10 9 8 7 6 5 4 3 2 1

With deep respect for
Joseph Roth and
Gregor von Rezzori,

and with thanks to
Wendy Carlton,
Jane Dystel,
and Miriam Goderich

FOR ANNEMARIE

Open the second shutter, so that more light can come in.

Goethe, on his deathbed

THE MAN IN THE BOX

I

Why

We're

All Here

1

I'M UP IN THE ATTIC, pushing old thoughts around. I'm rummaging. I'm raising a miserable dry dust and wishing my hands weren't getting so grubby. I'm wishing that I had boxes for everything. If I could put the things I know into boxes, they would all be safely in their place at last, and no trouble to anyone. I'd stack the boxes in an orderly fashion. Then I'd take a good long look, and walk away, and never look again.

During the war we kept our Jew in a box. It was my father's doing. My mother and my grandma begged him not to. Think of what might happen to us, they pleaded. Think of the danger, and for what? My father didn't listen. He would not be moved. He made a plan for the Jew and he kept to it, as long as he could.

Our Jew was very rare. And he was clever. You might think a fugitive would have crept up in the night, flitting from shadow to shadow through the sleeping village like a Gypsy out to steal some horses or children. But midnight creeping would mean roused dogs and sleepless old women peering through the shutters. Our Jew knew this. Our Jew came boldly in the middle of the day, straight up the road during the hour of lunch, when not a single soul in Sankt Vero could be bothered to raise his nose from his soup plate. Even the dogs were under the tables, drooling for scraps. Lunchtime: Everyone safely in his place. This was the natural order of things in Sankt Vero. So the Jew's knock on our back door resounded. It boomed even though it was only a tap. He had come unseen, and by surprise.

He came because of me, because of the thin white scar on the right side of my belly. He'd put it there himself, years before when I was little and laid out on our kitchen table, my father holding my arms and my granddad pinning my feet. The Jew had been one of the travelers who used the Sankt Vero Pass. He had broken his journey, staying the night in the one hopeful room my mother kept in her mild ambition as a *Gasthaus* keeper. He did not exactly have a peaceful sleep in the mountains. There was the matter of the whimpering child in the next room, tossing and drenched with a great fever, tender to the touch everywhere. A troubled child, causing the mother and the grandma, who were sitting up, great worry. Toward dawn, my whimpers turned to howls. Presently the Jew appeared in the doorway, shirttail out of his trousers, hair standing up oddly. He announced that he was a doctor and could he have a look? My mother nodded. He touched my stomach and I screamed and the next thing I knew I was being held down on the kitchen table. The Jew dripped a metallic-smelling liquid over gauze, held in a wire mask that covered my mouth and nose. I was blinking against the fumes and the light for a moment. Then the world vanished. When I came to myself again it was as if no time at all had passed. And a moment later I was throwing up into a tin bucket by the side of my bed. But when I was able to lie back I noticed the cool clean sheets. I felt tape and gauze on my belly. And although it stung wickedly underneath the bandage, I felt emptied of whatever poison had tormented me.

After the kitchen operation, my grandfather used to always say to everyone he'd had to watch the Jew like a hawk in case he'd felt like clipping any foreskins for good measure when he was finished with my swollen appendix. You don't need either of them, my grandfather would say, laughing, but without the one you feel sort of naked, don't you? My grandfather also made a joke of the Jew because he was embarrassed, I think. The Jew, you see, wouldn't take any money for slicing me open, absolutely refused cash or kind. He even paid for his room. When he left the house and headed for his little black Citroën, I was watching from my window. I saw my father walk with him to the car and shake his hand. He held the car door open until the Jew was in and then closed it for him. My father seemed to bear a weight all the rest of that day. I thought at the time that he was troubled only by my close call, not by what the Jew had done.

It was hard to know what to think about Jews, even in those days, before the heavy propaganda and the heavy laws. It was unusual to see one. Our town of Sankt Vero in the Tirol had no Jews of its own. I knew from my schoolbooks (before they were changed) and also from the old magazines my grandmother had stacked and saved in the cellar (before she began burning them for fuel) that there were so many kinds of Jews, as different from each other as a Tiroler is from a Frenchman or a Turk, that it seemed stupid to lump them all together in one group. But people did.

In one of my schoolbooks there was a picture of Emperor Franz Josef visiting his eastern dominions. It was near Czernowitz or some such place that later became Russian or Polish. And in the picture the Emperor is gazing mildly at strange, long-haired Jews wearing long black caftans and fox hats, who have come to pay him homage and offer Jewish blessings—as if Franz Josef needed any! You could tell from his expression that the Emperor was used to this, nothing new here at all for him. But I'd never seen men like this. These long-bearded men looked like Moses, except for their hats with red tails. I doubted Moses had one like that. Yet for years on certain nights—mainly rainy ones—these Jews would visit my dreams and speak to me. Once I woke, I never remembered what they'd said. But I used to imagine that I might visit the East someday and Jews like that would greet me. They would have a musty smell about them and tell me things in broken German.

That was one kind of Jew. I also knew about the poor working Jews in the big cities like Vienna and Linz. They looked like all the other workingmen in baggy trousers and cloth caps, at least in the pictures of the socialist demonstrations. People said most of the Reds were Jews, but you couldn't possibly tell who was a Jew and who wasn't from the photos. Or who was a Red, for that matter, except by which side of the police lines they stood on. I had seen pictures, too, of the rich city Jews at the Mayor's Ball in Vienna—some from families ennobled by Franz Josef—with great bellies and rolls of fat at the backs of their necks. They wore patent-leather shoes just like the rest of the rich Viennese. Only their names in the photo captions gave them away. There were also the mysterious Jews: the eastern ones with red hair and pale-blue eyes, and the dark, stunted traveling tinkers, who were like Gypsies. And there were secret Jews among us, like ours. Who could tell he was a Jew? He was a doctor; he dressed in proper dark suits. He was correct. He looked like any Austrian; there are plenty with his exact shade of brown hair and blue eyes. I have hair and eyes myself just like his. My father had a bigger nose, with a sharper hook. Who was to say this Jew was a Jew if he didn't say so himself?

He said so himself to us when he came back to our house in 1943. He said they had rounded up all the Jews in Innsbruck and were taking them to camps in the East. He said he only escaped because one of his colleagues at the hospital hid him in the morgue during the roundup, and next day drove him to the foot of the Sankt Vero Pass in one of the hospital's ambulances. He walked from there. He had no star on his coat, which had belonged to his colleague, but if anyone had asked for his papers they would have seen at once: *Jude*.

My father became very solemn and told me to leave the room. I did, but I crouched at the landing of the stairs so I could listen to them talk while my mother poured schnapps and made coffee. The smell of the coffee told me that my father considered this an important occasion, for it was very expensive in those days and not made casually. One cup in the late afternoon: that was the ration in a good week, and it wasn't even real coffee, only some ersatz stuff, unless my father had met up with one of the smugglers who brought things over the mountains from Italy. My mother and grandma and I drank tea on Sundays and hot barley water the rest of the time.

The Jew was saying fantastic things about young soldiers, fresh-faced like schoolboys and just as energetic, shoving along old women and little children and everyone with the yellow star down the alleys and streets to the railroad station. There was no shooting, but the soldiers were implacable. Everyone must go, they shouted. Everyone. A long, long train was waiting, with two locomotives coupled in front. There were only freight cars and animal cars, and the Jews were put into them and the doors were locked. The soldiers relaxed then, smoked cigarettes, sipped from their canteens, removed their helmets, joked and teased with one another. The Jew admitted he had not seen these things himself, for he'd been in the morgue. But he had it firsthand from a colleague who happened to be at the station that morning to meet his mother, who was arriving from Melk.

All right, it's a common story of the time. Everyone's heard it by now. Everyone knows these things took place. But in Sankt Vero, then, it seemed unbelievable. When the news arrived in the usual ways, a few days after our Jew turned up, it made many men in our village uneasy. Not over the fate of the Jews, but over the open exercise of such a terrible power. Everyone made jokes about Yids and affected dislike for them, but they did the same with other people they never saw, like Polacks and Italians. They made jokes. But this shipping of people like animals was something new, something excessive. The Emperor would never have allowed anything like this.

THE FIRST FEW NIGHTS, the Jew stayed in the cellar, behind the wood bunker, while my family decided what to do with him. Poor Jew. My parents sent me to bed after dinner, but I went down and sat with the Jew because I knew that from the bunker you could hear everything that was said in the room above. The voices sounded a little hollow but otherwise were as clear as if you were up there yourself. It was my mother who shattered any hope for sympathy the Jew may have had. We must get the police at once, she said. There's no choice. We can't hide him. We can't feed him. We can't keep such a secret. By my father's silence I guessed he did not consider these things obstacles. Now I think he was like a crafty peasant, sure of himself in his own world, weighing only whether the debt he'd incurred was heavy enough for the payment that now seemed to be required. My mother swore it was not, swore it was God's will that had placed the Jew in her house the night my appendix tried to murder me, swore we owed nothing to anyone.

"We offered to pay!" she said.

My father remained silent for a moment. If he had been a smoking man it would have been a time for him to light his pipe and puff thoughtfully on it. "It's a risk, yes," he said at last. "But maybe there's some good in it for us. Something good might come of it in the end."

"A rope around your neck when he's found is all that will come of it," my mother said. "Oh God, why us?"

My father must have got up off the bench near the stove, where he liked to sit, because the Jew and I could hear his footsteps over our heads, back and forth and back again.

"The war can't last forever," my father said. "Even the first one didn't."

"So what? If we're as hungry at the end of this one as we were last time, all the more reason we can't have an extra mouth. He can't stay here. You'll give him a ride over the pass in the wagon and that'll be that, a good deed done and we wash our hands of him," my mother said.

"We'll just say we never knew he was a Jew if anyone asks," my father said. "He's a doctor, come to stay in the mountains for his own health. No one here will doubt me. I'm a veteran."

"But it's on his papers, and we have to see his papers to rent him the room," my mother said, and I thought she had my father beat then. The Jew was breathing more and more slowly, it seemed to me.

"Keep the Jew? Is that what we're talking about? Over my dead body," my grandma suddenly said, as if the enormity of the thing had only just dawned on her.

For hours that night and hours more the next, the various possible fates of the Jew were proposed, argued, discarded. There were schemes. My father was to lock him in the cellar (bad news for me just then) and go for the village policeman. My father was to hit him over the head with a stone and dump him unconscious in front of someone else's house in the night. My mother was to simply order him to leave but give him some money and a clean shirt. My father was to lead him up to one of the remote little barns in the high pastures, where he could hide for a while but must eventually either starve or give himself up. My grandmother was to persuade him that he really ought to go back to Innsbruck, for the trouble had surely blown over.

"I grant you, he did save the child, thank God," my grandmother said on the third night. "But what would your father say, keeping a Jew in the house?"

"Not in the house, ma," my father said. "I have a better idea."

Two days later my father nailed the Jew into a box. This is what I called it, but perhaps you would have said it was a small room, if you had seen it. But I don't think you would be so generous if you had had to live in it. It was at the very back of the hayloft in the barn. My father used old planks he had saved from our demolished pigsty to build a new wall about a meter inside the real wall of the loft. This made a space a meter wide, three meters high, and four meters long. There was no door and no window. One plank, and only one, could be slid sideways a bit. You had to dig beneath the hay to get to it and you had to know exactly how to press it. We passed the Jew his food through that hole. My father also built a tube of two pieces of old wooden rain gutter and ran it down from the Jew's box into the cow stall below. The Jew pissed and shat down this tube. I hated this, since it was my job to muck out that stall. Cow shit is clean at least. I've walked barefoot in it. It doesn't make you gag.

It was dim in the Jew's box even at noon. He could never show a light. It was cold in the winter; there was no heat. He could only see through a few cracks between the planks of the outer wall, or through a knothole into the loft, and only read by what little light trickled through these openings. What a world! Never to see a cloud or a girl, nothing to watch but your own hands in aimless agitation. A few sounds would be your only link to life.

SO THERE IS OUR JEW, who came because of me. But once he was in his box, I became his greatest worry, and my parents' too. I could feel their eyes on me and see certain questioning looks. They were afraid I would tell someone about the Jew, in anger, perhaps, or to make myself important. I did consider this. I often had dramatic thoughts about it. And I kept the idea of betrayal pressed closely to me. Wonder weapons were supposed to win the war. This felt like mine, though I didn't even know why I might need one. I was thirteen when the Jew came, and there was also the worry that I might succumb to the Party propaganda, that I might become patriotic and turn in the Jew in the name of duty. Things like this happened. Children denounced their parents, egged on by Hitler Youth leaders and teachers and their own surging hormones. Gymnastics teachers spread an evil influence in the naturally dank atmosphere of locker rooms. A lot of the worst young Nazis came from those sports clubs. They were overstimulated there.

For me it was a wonderful thing to be feared a little. I took deeper breaths, I stepped livelier. I felt bold. Yet I received no warnings or cautions from my parents or the Jew. Maybe they thought they would put an idea into my head that hadn't occured to me naturally. Or perhaps they thought I was intelligent enough to understand the gravity and danger, and counted on my good sense and family feeling. I did not actually understand the gravity at all; it was a sort of game to me. But I went in terror of my father and was convinced the police hadn't yet invented a torture that would make me give away our secret. So our undoing was of a different order.

I was the only child in the house when the Jew came. I had had two brothers and two sisters. They were next door, their photos in white enameled frames riveted to black iron crosses in the graveyard in front of the church. It was the usual style, with little red glass votives attached beneath the photos, which my grandmother went to light every night, except when it was raining or when the priest did it first. I could see the lights from my room at night. I had the whole room to myself. There were other beds, but they just had blankets covering the mattresses. Mine was the only one with two sheets and a feather duvet. Only my clothes were in the armoire, only my slippers on the floor; only my robe was on the row of hooks. But the thin linen curtains at the window didn't block the red flickering. All I could do was put my pillow over my face, breathing my own warm breath over and over for as long as I could. Then off came the pillow. There was no escape. Sometimes I'd see that red glow and think of hell. I thought it was strange that sacred ground fussed over by the priest and grandma should seem so evil, until I concluded that hell is all there is, in this world or the next. I was about fourteen when this occurred to me. Immediately I felt I was an adult, with a worldview of some sophistication.

My brothers had died of polio. Rolf was ten the summer he died, and I was four. Heinz died the next summer. He was eight. Two years after that my sister Liese fell in the stream that ran behind the village, was pulled out by the blacksmith, and seemed to be fine, but she died a week later of typhoid. She was six, I was seven. The next year my baby sister, Katrin, died in her crib.

I didn't actually see my brothers die. When they got sick they were taken away, down to a hospital in the valley, and when they came back they were already in boxes. I watched Liese die, though. I saw the way she twisted her sheets in her little fists, sweat on her forehead, fair hair all matted. She was so fretful. Then all at once it seemed she cared for nothing in the world and only wanted to rest. She stopped talking then. And something was gone from her eyes. She looked at me, and saw me, but her eyes were flat. When she finally stopped breathing her eyes didn't change at all, they just stayed open, staring in that flat way. I didn't know what to make of this. I couldn't understand where Liese had gone. My grandma's comment about her being with the angels made no sense to me. How could she be there when her body was here? But then I wondered why the body still looked like Liese when clearly Liese was no longer in it. This was a great confusion. My mother got the priest to talk to me about death after Liese was buried next door. But he made it sound as if she were only sleeping under all that dirt and one day would rise up from it, clean and sound.

I understood no better when I found Katrin dead in her crib. I'd gone into my parents' room one afternoon because I liked to look at the little thing and tickle her a bit so she would gurgle, and that day when I tickled her she didn't move. She was blue. I ran downstairs and hid in the cellar. Nearly an hour passed before I heard my mother cry out and then heard my father's scraping footsteps on the stairs. My grandma began wailing: Oh God, Oh God, Oh God. Then I emerged from hiding. My father picked me up when he saw me and whispered in my ear that my little sister had gone away. No one asked where I had been. I felt a great relief. But for years after I would sometimes wake up shaking in my bed at night. I was terrified my parents would discover I had been in their room that day and had somehow caused Katrin to die.

Katrin was so small she did not get her own grave. She was buried on top of Liese. There was no photo of her, just her name in black letters on a white enamel plaque riveted under Liese's.

The weight of these deaths unsteadied my mother. She began to nap at odd hours, starting right after breakfast. She didn't cry much but developed a bright, brittle laugh that seemed to frighten other children. She also started looking past me when she spoke to me. I should have become the axis around which my parents revolved. But this was not to be. My grandma took on the tasks of seeing that my ears were washed, my prayers said, and the covers tucked under my chin each night.

My mother kept more and more to the house. She stopped going to Mass, even on Sundays. It was just my father, my grandma, and me under the eyes of the carved wooden saints and the other villagers. My grandma endured this for three weeks and then sprang into action. She dragged the priest to our house to talk to my mother, and forced my mother to sit still for it. They sat on the benches by the stove, while my father took me for a walk. It was not a success. Perhaps the priest talked about death as he had to me; he was a young priest, maybe a little immature in his judgment, or so I say in hindsight. My mother refused absolutely to attend Mass ever again. My grandma was very ashamed, since this was naturally the talk of the village. Some people said our family must have done something bad—some sharp practice in the store by my father, some sinful indiscretion by my mother—to deserve the beating we'd got from God. The Prechts and the Cammers forbade their children to play with me.

But most of the mothers in the village felt a little sorry for me. There was hot chocolate for me at many houses.

By the time the Jew came, our standing in the village had returned almost to normal, even though my mother still would not set foot in the church. People had more important things to worry about by then, when everything was rationed and young men went away and didn't come back whole, if they came back at all. My father ran his store in the front rooms of our house, he tended the cows morning and night, he drank beer with his cronies after Mass on Sunday. My mother helped in the store sometimes, sorting the ration coupons and doing other light work. After dinner each evening she walked up the road just past the last house in the village and back again. My grandma took care of me and the house. I had school, and my friends, and jobs to do for my father, and the Jew to talk to.

He was my Jew. Oh, in places like Holland they also kept Jews hidden, but I never heard of one like him in Austria. After the war many people claimed they had done some kindness to this Jew or that, but where was the proof? No one I ever heard of claimed they had hidden a Jew for years in their barn or attic or cellar. If anyone had claimed such a thing and it had turned out to be true, the Allies would have printed it in the newspapers and put it on the radio, to embarrass the rest of us. They liked to do things like that, just as they liked to take people out of prison and make them mayors or police officials. I think they felt that we weren't feeling bad enough. We were, though.

TODAY (pick any one between February 1943 and May 1945) the Jew is telling me about tobacco. He misses it so much, the Monte Cristo cigars from Cuba he used to buy at Glock's in Innsbruck, back in the days when his practice was flourishing. After his surgery hours each afternoon, he'd smoke one at the Café Central, sipping a coffee and reading the *Presse*. The Jew is starved for company. He is telling the things he remembers, which, after all, are not filed in alphabetical order. This is how we get, all in one go, from smoking a cigar at the Café Central to the wedding of his daughter at Schloss Mirabel in Salzburg (where they waltzed in the Marble Hall) to the time in his youth as a military surgeon when he'd amputated a man's nose in a tent in the Carpathian Mountains. The nurse, who had handled every sort of mangled flesh in her duties, simply refused to touch it. All at once, the Jew begins to weep. Sigi is with me, as she is most evenings when I go up to hear the Jew talk. She likes to sit next to me on the straw, her head up against my shoulder like a pet (which I'm not allowed to have). We're the same age, but I'm two inches taller. Sigi says to the Jew: Never mind, never mind.

BUT I'D LIKE TO SAY how it was back then, with the Jew in the box. I'd like to explain what happened. I'd like to start with Sigi.

II
What We
Got Up To

2

SIGI ALWAYS WANTS to look her best. She pesters her mother to braid ribbons into her hair. She is always saying, "Do I look all right?" She's always asking me this.

At school she sits in the midst of us but seems to exist within margins all her own. Her pen never scratches or blots, she never drops a book or a ruler, she never has to go to the blackboard and scrawl equations in yellow chalk. She and the teacher have conversations, while the rest of us commit our answers to paper and then furiously erase after a glance at our nearest benchmate's work. Sigi is the only one the teacher speaks to as an adult. Nobody's crazy about this special treatment, but no one feels able to say anything against it, either.

The teacher talks to the rest of us as though we were children. She just doesn't want to know some things. Most of the boys already have to keep a book in hand to hide the erections that surge up suddenly, without warning and for no apparent reason. The boys all pray daily that they will not be called to the blackboard at the peak of a hard-on. Their prayers often go unanswered. Fräulein Mumelter pretends not to notice the bulges in trousers or the awkward, shifty walks. The girls giggle; what else? They can't help themselves, even when Fräulein Mumelter raps the edge of her desk and calls for order. Sigi is above all that. She sits serenely even as some of her classmates are suffering unforgettable humiliations.

Sigi can't be sure, but sometimes she thinks she has the face of an angel. She doesn't. She's as plain as bread. Regular, ordinary, normal. You wouldn't look twice. But she caresses her face in an adoring way, with both hands, when she feels happy. As she grows she blooms, and though her face stays plain, her body becomes a wonder. Already by the time the Jew came you could see this. The men don't know how to talk to her anymore. They move awkwardly around her. And many times they seem cross with her for no reason; she's done nothing wrong ever. We like to take Sigi on promenades, leashed and led, just to watch the men get edgy. Sigi's mother approves of us. She's an idiot. She thinks it is adorable that Sigi's friends always take her along wherever they go. Sigi's mother is grateful to us. She gives us sweets whenever we call for Sigi.

Sigi is the smartest of us all, but you could do anything with her. When she was little you could tell her the Inn was a river of red under a purple sky filled with brown clouds. You could convince her that bulls had three horns. You could say you saw God's face in the moon. When we were older, you could claim the wild men of Borneo ate bones like dogs, you'd read it in the geographical magazine. Always you could get her to touch almost anything—pond slime, a crushed toad, the scab you'd just peeled off your knee. The spring before the Jew came, Peter put a piece of cow afterbirth in a wooden bowl. He told Sigi it was pudding and got her to stick her fingers in and have a lick. "Salty," Sigi said. And for one wicked week that spring, in dim barns I watched her touch several penises masquerading as a cow's teat or a new pet snake or a fresh sausage. Then one day she squeezed and yanked so hard on Kaspar's that it almost came off. He screamed like a pig, and we all ran. He had to stay in bed for two days and afterward walked with a limp for a while. No more dicks were placed in our Sigi's way.

The blind, they say, are blessed in other ways. They get sharper hearing, a finer sense of smell. They become uncanny. They know when you're in the room with them, even if you're still and quiet. They feel vapors in the air, spirits in the woods. They know when an avalanche is trembling above the firs far away. Sometimes they even know the future and can warn you of things. I don't think so. Sigi never got that way, and if anyone could've, she would've. She was so at home in the world. She was light and lofty. I was the sad one, I was the one who didn't fit, the one too easily out of sorts.

Only once in my life did I see Sigi adrift. It was our first communion, we were eight, it was May. Sigi's dress was yellowed, because it had been worn for May communions by all the Strolz girls ever since great-great-grandmother Strolz made it. But it was still the prettiest of all the dresses that day, with real silk lace. She had ribbons in her hair, the way she liked. After church there was lunch and cake. Pabst the gendarme contributed the cheerful wheezing of his accordion, as he always did at any celebration. I danced with Sigi, being very careful of her dress. Kaspar and Martin and Simon ignored Maria and Monika and Evi and ate cake. But when I went for more cake, I lost Sigi. She vanished. No one seemed to notice she was gone. No one was looking for her, no one seemed concerned. I was worried, though. So I looked first behind the schoolhouse, then in my barn. And suddenly I thought of the stream, and the day went bad. I thought of a girl in the water. I started running. I don't think I wanted to get there, though. I think I was afraid. I had to pass Sigi's barn, so I stopped and looked in. She was crouched just in front of the back stall, peeing, her bird-thin shoulders rising and falling with each quiet sob. Her cheeks glistened. She finished peeing, stood up, and leaned against the stall. Her shoulders kept rising and falling. I had no idea what to do. There was dirty straw sticking to the hem of her dress. I just watched her. In the end I walked away as quietly as I could so she wouldn't know I had been there.

The next day she was fine, knocking on my door after breakfast, wanting to go up in the valley where the little waterfall was. We could take her anywhere. We just tied a bit of rope around her waist and led her. Watch out for the rock, Sigi. Step up now, Sigi. One step right, Sigi. Duck, Sigi. Sometimes when we were walking like that she'd bark at us and laugh.

But after our communion, I became very careful with Sigi near the stream. I always gripped her by the upper arm when we sat down on the rocky banks, always placed myself between her and the water, never let her out of my sight.

Sigi is the only one who knows about our Jew. I take her with me to talk with him in the evenings. My father knows I do this, but he's never said one word. He must believe Sigi can be trusted. He's known her all her life, and he believes he has the knack of knowing character. He is very proud of this. "I may not be well educated, but I know people," he often said to my mother, whenever anyone had fulfilled his expectations, good or bad. "I learned this during the war, how to judge a man. You didn't get two chances. Believe me, this is the most valuable skill you can have in life."

Sigi's opinion is that my father is afraid of himself. Nothing else would frighten him, but he would jump at his own shadow. She says her own father was that way, like all the men who had come back from the Great War. They have things within them that they are terrified will come out one day. That is why they are so much gentler with us than our grandfathers are, Sigi says. They don't want anything bad to happen. They try hard to control themselves. The Jew, too, controls himself, she reckons. The Jew more than anyone.

Sigi's voice is a lot prettier than she is. It's a little low for a girl, but it flows through its range so musically. It did make you think of music, her voice. Which was odd, because she couldn't sing at all. The Jew loves to hear it.

The Jew's name is Robert Weiss. We call him Doctor Weiss when we bring him his food. We're very polite. Here's breakfast, Doctor Weiss. Here's supper, Doctor Weiss. No butter today, Doctor Weiss, but surely some tomorrow. And mama says a cup of tea too. Here's my library book, Doctor Weiss. I have to have it back by Thursday, so you have six days. You've got to tell me how it comes out in the end, in case the teacher asks.

The Jew likes to be told about our day while he is spooning up his soup, munching his bread. He wants to know about our hike up the north slopes. He wants to know what we saw.

"Chamois," Sigi says. "A half-dozen of them. We surprised them in the boulders just below the Kirchspitz. It was beautiful up there today, lots of flowers. We brought you some—see them on your tray? And the valley was so green, with the dark pines marching up the slopes."

"Ah," says the Jew. "You saw chamois."

"We almost never get to see any," Sigi says.

The Jew does not know Sigi is blind. Why should we tell him? Does Sigi need his sympathy, if he has any to spare, which seems unlikely?

Sigi doesn't want a lot of sympathy. She feels she gets more than she needs. She just wants to be a part of things. "No one's looking at me," is one of her common complaints. She needs to feel herself in the regard of others. "If I'm in a dark room with no people around, I feel as if I am only someone's dream," she says. "Falling asleep at night feels like dying. I think so anyway. I don't know if I sleep with my eyes open or closed."

The first time I took Sigi up to the box in the hayloft, I expected dark suspicions. I expected a quiet Jew, fearful and discreet. I expected reserve, resentment, perhaps even a sulky refusal to talk at all to a stranger. No! The Jew told Sigi everything, all in a rush, as if she were his best friend, long missed. I felt a little jealous, to tell the truth. He said his name and profession, his military service, the name of his wife, and the name and nickname of his daughter. He described how he'd sliced my belly and saved my life those years ago. Go ahead, Niki, show her the scar, he said.

"I am fifty-six years old," he said to Sigi. "I have seen a lot but not enough, if you follow me. I don't know why things are going on as they are."

"Oh, the wheeling and revolving of things," Sigi said.

"What's that?" the Jew said.

"It's from a hymn," Sigi said.

"Ah," said the Jew. "We do wheel and we do revolve. I wheeled in my career, and later I revolved around my wife and daughter."

"Poldi," said Sigi.

"Yes, my daughter Poldi, nicknamed after my friend Leopold Goldwasser," said the Jew. "My comrade medico, long departed. When Leopold and I finished medical school in 1914, we went straight to the army. We learned to be surgeons. But not in some fine hospital in Vienna or Budapest. No, it was the mountains for us, first the Carpathians and later on the Alps."

"Just like my father," I said. "Only he was a sharpshooter with the Alpine troops."

"Mine too, but not after any medical school," Sigi said. "He was an Alpine soldier too. A Kaiserjäger."

"Naturally," the Jew said. "But do you know we were all dead the instant we entered the army? There was no life in us at all. We were already killed. We were only born, those of us who weren't shot or blown up, when the war ended. That's when we received the gift of life."

"My father said that the day the war ended was the saddest and happiest of his life," Sigi said.

"It could have been. It could have easily been. For me it was only happy, because it meant I could have a life."

"I hope you have had a good one," said Sigi.

"An excellent one. As good as anyone could want," the Jew said. "Did I tell you that my daughter is in America? She left in 'thirty-eight. She was only nineteen; she had just been married. A beautiful girl. She has two daughters of her own now."

"America. I would like to see that place," I said.

"My daughter says the best thing about America is that you never have to carry your papers, because no one ever demands to see them. They leave you alone in America."

"Did your parents go there? Did your wife?" Sigi asked.

"My parents are in the Jewish cemetery in Graz. It is a very small one; it's easy to find their graves. The attendant would show you. My wife . . . she is traveling. Yes, at the moment she is on a journey. I would expect a card from her any day, except that she does not know where I am."

"I once got a postcard from Lake Garda," Sigi said. "My uncle was there and sent it to me. I've kept it pinned by my bed."

Sigi and I are sitting back to back in the straw. I'm thinking about her postcard, how big and blue the lake is, with little red-roofed towns right on the shore. All our roofs in Sankt Vero are a mossy damp brown. They're made of wooden shingles, all ex-cept for the dome at the top of the church tower, which is made of tin. It gleams like silver when the sun hits it. I think the light gleaming on that great lake would trouble your eyes, if you lived close to it.

I said it was time we were going. Sigi took my hand.

IN SCHOOL the next day Kaspar was called to the blackboard in the middle of an erection. But he was so fat, who could really tell? The girls giggled anyway at the way his ass wobbled when he walked. I could see our barn from the schoolroom windows. Ever since the Jew was nailed in, I'd had to make a special effort not to stare at the barn, not to search for signs of his presence. Now I saw Sigi's face turned toward the barn, almost as if she could not only see but see through the thick pine planks to the Jew in the box. This alarmed me very much. I wanted to hiss at her but didn't dare. Then I remembered that no one ever paid at-tention to the direction of Sigi's gaze. Everyone knew it was empty; everyone knew she'd look at a blank stone wall six inches from her face with the same expression she'd have if the whole of the Alps was stretched out before her. When we had lunch, I asked if she knew she'd been staring at the barn all morning. I thought I might have been, she said.

"I was thinking that the Jew will live for a very long time," she said. "But I was wondering if he also feels like he's dying when he falls asleep."

Sigi liked to be close. Once, near the end of the war, I got her to strip for me by telling her I'd let her touch if she'd let me see. She was so pale and perfect. But it wasn't only me who got to see Sigi, who saw me touch her too, though that wasn't part of our bargain. And that was my worst sin. I knew it right away. When Sigi reached out to touch me that night, I slapped her hand away. She called me a shit. She said it wasn't fair. So I lay down in the hay and let her touch, and I actually cried because it felt so nice; I'd never felt anything that nice before, her warm hands. And Sigi kissed where she touched. I wanted to die. The soft way Sigi had with me was a rebuke for every bad thing I'd done.

3

IT'S TOO BAD that Sigi is half an orphan. She lives with her mother in a wooden house with two floors just on the other side of the graveyard from us. Her mother tends red geraniums in window boxes. There are usually some chickens pecking around Sigi's front stoop.

Her father's picture and his little red light are in the graveyard thanks to my grandfather. I didn't mind about my grandfather very much. He was never fond of me, and his jokes were bad. He took a switch to my backside too often. You didn't want to be in the same room with him when he took off his socks. But it was sad about Sigi's father. He was handsome, and when we were very small he used to take Sigi by the arm with his right hand, and me by the arm with his left hand, and spin us around way off the ground. It was like flying. His hands were rough, but you knew he would never drop you.

My grandfather had wanted to save petrol coupons. He was a tight, closed man, a natural hoarder. That was why he and Sigi's father had gone down to the valley in the wagon instead of in the truck. Picking up the dozen sacks of cornmeal was only my grandfather's errand. Sigi's father hadn't needed to go. It was no business of his; he was a carpenter. But he must have felt like traveling. It was a traveling sort of day, soft the way mild October days can be, even in the early morning, when they left.

We actually heard the crash near dusk that day, and within moments saw the men running to where the road makes that first sharp curve on its way down the mountain. School was long over, suppers were simmering, Sigi and I were outside my father's store. I was washing the windows. I put my rag in the bucket of soapy water and I took Sigi by the hand and we ran too. Sigi would always run if I had her hand in mine. I kept her behind me when we got to the edge of the road.

I'm looking down, down the ragged slope to the streambed below. Men are already clambering, descending. Others are rigging ropes and a pulley. I don't want to say anything, but Sigi is insisting. Tell me, she's saying.

The wagon's all smashed, just big pieces of kindling. The horse is bent over a big rock. Its mouth is open and its tongue is hanging out. I don't know how its back could be bent the way it is. Everything's yellow, everything's dusted with cornmeal. They are lying very still, Sigi. They're not moving at all; they look like puppets without strings. The men are trying to pick them up and tie ropes under their arms. They're floppy, like puppets.

"Goddammit, don't bang them against the trees like that," Gendarme Pabst shouts at the men who are hauling on the ropes to raise my grandfather and Sigi's father from the ravine.

"Will you take me home now, please?" Sigi asks. It's exactly what she says every day after school.

It seemed my grandfather hadn't been paying attention. Most likely he had drunk a fair amount of beer in a tavern down below while the cornmeal was being loaded. Perhaps he had even brought several bottles with him to drink on the trip back up the mountain. This was normal. Maybe the reins needn't have been so slack in his hand when a young deer, who shouldn't have been anywhere near the village, leaped out of the trees in front of the horse's nose. But then who would expect such a thing? Who would think that the wagon's left rear wheel, a meter in from the edge of the road, was too close? The horse reared and backed up before the deer. We knew this because the blacksmith had stepped away from his forge at just that moment and actually saw the rearing horse and the fleeing deer. My grandfather, fuddled, must have pulled too hard on the reins, forcing the horse to back up more. The left wheel went over, the wagon teetered for a moment, the heavy sacks of cornmeal shifted, and then they were all falling their long fall.

People fall off mountains all the time. It's the nature of mountains that this should be so. It's nature's doom for those who overreach. Usually, though, it's climbers. Usually it's Germans who misjudge a grip and plunge. There are little metal crosses littering the bases of various favorite peaks, marking where they have landed. The Germans especially have sentimental feelings about this.

Nobody blamed my grandfather. It was an accident, after all. But after the funerals, the words I heard everywhere in the village were "if only." It was if only this, if only that. Even the men who had been in the Great War were saying it. My father was hard hit by the deaths. He had always said we have to take our lumps, we have to take life's kicks in the teeth, we have to face everything. And now he was saying "if only" like the rest of them. I think the if onlys, along with the grief and regret, were all for Sigi's father. He was the center of so much; he was the one everyone depended on to take charge of things. Even Pabst the gendarme deferred to Sigi's father. Nobody missed a sour old man like my grandfather, except for my poor granny. But it didn't even take her long to remove the empty chair from the table and give his clothes to the Winter Relief.

Sigi did grieve. She was weeping hard at her father's funeral—what else would you expect? But when she stooped to take a handful of earth to throw into the grave, our Sigi lost her footing. She slipped. Her dress rode up as she slid into the grave and you could see her panties. They were baggy gray wool. Everyone froze except the priest, who was droning something from his book. Nobody moved a muscle. Sigi was just sitting there on her father's dark coffin. She stopped crying at once. My father reached down with his long right arm and hauled Sigi up. She was dry-eyed. She stood quietly next to her mother, who was absentmindedly brushing dirt off Sigi's bottom, while the rest of us threw our handfuls of dirt into the grave. I spit on my handful, for luck. Pabst's friend from down in Fussing played something so dreary on a dented trumpet.

This was about two years before the Jew arrived. Sigi cried a lot at first, but then she got over it. Within six months she could bear to think of that day and actually try to puzzle it out. She said it's so easy to trace any disaster backward to a beginning. She said any schoolboy could do it. It began when my father decided he felt like traveling, she said, and stepped up onto that wagon. An everyday thing to do, nothing to worry about or consider important. Nothing worth a second thought. The thing you can never know, she said, is exactly the point when the bad bit becomes inevitable. The instant of change, she called it. One of those could happen to anyone, anytime. She didn't want to bring God into it.

"WHAT IS DUE to come to us will come. If not today, then tomorrow," says the Jew, when I tell him the story. He has a small store of these sayings, from which he selects to suit the occasion. He irritates me with his sayings. I feel he isn't being frank. Usually he does most of the talking, but sometimes he claims to want to hear about us. I don't remember how it came up that Sigi was half an orphan, but it did and so I told the whole tale.

But who can compete with a Jew telling tales? Just now, for example, the Jew is about to sacrifice his medical career for love! Imagine that. This could be bad news for me, for it would mean he would never save me on the kitchen table. It could be my instant of change. I'm not sure I want to know how close I came to becoming nothing but a photo and a little red light. But Sigi thinks this is the most exciting thing we've heard so far and urges the Jew to go on. He never needs much of that.

"You have to imagine me a fairly handsome young man," the Jew says. "Is that credible? Can you manage? All right. I am in Vienna, studying like a demon, but really living. I tell you we were living then, the young in Vienna. We never even thought of wars. Life was really golden; we expected such bright futures. I am a student: the most privileged state of life, although you never realize this until it is too late. One is not completely free. I can't have a wife or even dream of one. But one day I see the girl I must have, and—how to say this?—my life begins to spin like the big Ferris wheel at the Prater. You don't even care if you eat or sleep when you're in love like that. You'll walk the streets all night in the rain and be happy, thinking of her."

The girl turns out to be the daughter of a rabbi in Przemyśl. Her name is—what else?—Rachel. This dark Rachel would never be seen unchaperoned in Przemyśl; the boys wouldn't be allowed to get close to her. She'd be watched, guarded. But she's in Vienna, to help out the rabbi's sister, who is ill, and things are different there. She's looking after the household and the children. The rabbi's sister sees no real danger in allowing Rachel to take the children to the parks in the early afternoons, even though she knows her brother would disapprove. Rachel's a good girl, and the parks of Vienna are safe as bank vaults. It's hard for a seventeen-year-old to be cooped up in the house all day. So Rachel graces the parks, most often the very park where medical student Weiss, books under his arm, goes to eat his modest lunch every day it isn't raining.

He sees her. God, how could he not? He manages to attract her attention. For weeks they nod shyly at each other. Finally he speaks to her, and she isn't frightened. Very soon they are falling in love, giddy with its prospect of joy.

Of course, it is impossible.

She's poor, a strict Jew, barely speaks German. Her father wears a caftan and deals in tin kitchenware. He has probably already arranged a marriage for Rachel in Przemyśl, to the son of another rabbi, and is only waiting for her to return from Vienna. Weiss's father is Primarius Doktor of obstetrics in Graz. He does not go so far as to pretend not to be Jewish, but neither does he ever draw attention to it. He makes discreet appearances at the synagogue on the High Holidays and contents himself with modest financial contributions the rest of the time. No Yiddish or Hebrew ever passes his lips. He feels embarrassed by the Hasids, with their curly side locks and straggly beards, whom he sometimes sees hurrying through the streets of Graz in pairs or trios. They remind him of furtive ferrets. He considers himself an Austrian first, just as any Austrian Catholic does. "You see the problem Rachel would be for me," the Jew says.

"My father is my sole means of support," he says. "I have only one choice: I must leave my studies and find employment if I am to marry Rachel immediately. We will get no help from our families. We'll be outcasts. This should be a familiar condition for

Jews, but not for Austrian Jews of my class then. Not for someone like me. It is hard to see how we'd manage, Rachel and I. She
says we'll find a way, but I'm so doubtful.

"There's one hope. I will graduate in ten months. I'll be a doctor, I'll be able to practice. If she'll be patient until then, if she
can manage to stay in Vienna until then . . . So there we are, meeting when we can, yearning for each other when we cannot, always anxiously hoping she will not have to go back to Przemyśl."

Time for Sigi and me to go. We can't stay in the barn too long,
or people will get ideas.

We go down the steep pasture, through the gate, and along
the alley to her back door. Then we go in and sit by the big tile
stove to study. Her only task is to listen to me read a chapter of
our history book, but I have to write a report on the chapter. A
lot of our classmates take turns reading to Sigi, but for me it's always the history.

"We don't have to be detectives to know she didn't have to
go back to Przemyśl. He's already told us his wife's name is
Rachel," Sigi says when my Bavarian troops are riding into Innsbruck and starting to burn things. "Unless of course he lost this
Rachel and married another woman with the same name, for
grief. Or maybe he slipped, calling his wife Rachel. Maybe she's
named something else, but he's still pining for poor lost Rachel."

"A man knows the name of his own wife," I say. "It has to be
the same Rachel. It would be too much of a coincidence otherwise."

"Oh?" Sigi says. "For instance, you could marry another Sigi,
and who would know if you were talking about me or the other
Sigi whenever you said Sigi? I mean, unless they were from this
town and knew us by sight."

"I don't know any other Sigis."

"You might meet one someday and fall in love, just like the Jew. There are Sigis all over the place. There's a lot of them down in Schwaz. My father told me that."

"I've never been there and don't expect to be going."

"You have to admit it's within the realm of possibility," Sigi says.

"I could tickle you right now until you wet your pants," I say, and I don't even have to touch her before she starts laughing and squirming.

"But you do have to admit," she manages, "that it's more within the realm of possibility than anyone marrying me."

"Relax, Sigi. I'll marry you," I say.

"I won't have a husband who will never be able to grow a mustache," she says, and then we're both laughing so hard that her mother looks puzzled at first when she comes into the room with cups of hot chocolate. We settle down. It's only ersatz chocolate. Sigi's mother sees my history book open on the table and pats us on our heads even though we both think we're getting a little old for this.

I HAVE TO READ my history report in class the next day. It's pathetic. I've got my dates for when Napoleon's Bavarian allies were plundering the Tirol all wrong. I've got the wrong Bishop of Salzburg too. Fräulein Mumelter isn't pleased with me at all. She says I'm getting as bad as Kaspar, which causes him to hoot and then blush when Fräulein Mumelter orders him to the blackboard to read his report. He has a hard-on again.

That very day, my mother seemed to emerge from the daydreams she'd been strolling through since Katrin died. She still looked eccentric with that peasant scarf on her head, which was old-fashioned even in Sankt Vero by then, but she had a snack ready for me when I got home from school and sat with me while I ate it. Only my grandmother had bothered to look after me in ways like that since Katrin. Now my mother, who for some years hadn't seemed interested in anything but the weather and what she'd have to wear on her nightly walk, began to ask me questions. What was I studying in school? What was my favorite subject? History? German? Religion? She hoped not. And how is your teacher, Fräulein Mumelter? Is she well-spoken? Did she have on one of her nice white blouses today? Isn't she pretty, don't you think so? Does she ever wear any scent? Did you see her leave school? Did she walk home alone?

Fräulein Mumelter lived in a tiny apartment above the town hall, which had always been reserved for the schoolteacher. This was a mysterious place, reached by an open stairway at the back of the building, which was a few hundred meters down the road from the schoolhouse. No student had ever been known to enter that apartment, either during the three years Fräulein Mumelter had been the teacher or during the tenure of any of the previous teachers. Naturally, we were dying to know what went on in that place, what she did there in private. Naturally, we held discussions in which we speculated. Mostly we tried to imagine her underwear, and how she would soap herself in the bathtub. Kaspar thought she would use a sea sponge, which was an exotic thing for our town. He thought that since Fraülein Mumelter was from someplace far away and bigger than Sankt Vero, she would know about and be accustomed to such things. Simon and I thought it would be an ordinary scrub brush, the kind you could buy in my father's store. Kaspar wondered if she bathed when she was having her period. He tried to get at least one good whiff of her in class every day for a couple of months, to see if there was any apparent change in her cleanliness.

Of course, no old maid or man would have stirred us up like

that, but they seldom taught in a tiny place like Sankt Vero. We got the green girls straight from teachers college, and they didn't usually last long. Fräulein Mumelter surprised everyone by liking Sankt Vero, by staying longer than any other young teacher had. Fräulein Mumelter was twenty years old when she came up to us. She had exceptional breasts for such a skinny woman; we all agreed on that as certainly as eleven-year-olds can judge these things. She had shapely calves too, probably because every Saturday afternoon when classes would finish she'd change into knickers and hobnailed boots and go off hiking, up hunters' trails mostly. She was warned to be careful during the autumn, when the stags were rutting and aggressive. Simon and Andreas and I once tried to follow her, but after a kilometer or so she lost us; we just couldn't keep her pace. Pabst the gendarme, who was one of the few bachelors in the village, frequently invited himself to accompany her on her hikes. She always refused. Pabst would click his heels politely. He remained fond of her and always had good things to say whenever her name came up.

It was three years before Fräulein Mumelter's mystery was violated. It was Simon who did it. He was a crude boy, but clever, so it shouldn't have surprised us. He had, first, access to his father's old army binoculars, good Steiners. He had, second, the run of his uncle Ignatz's sawmill. Now, this sawmill was situated about 100 meters obliquely behind the town hall, near the stream. He was almost breathless when he first reported to us that from the cockloft of the sawmill you could see two windows of Fräulein Mumelter's apartment. The distance was nothing for the Steiners: you could see every detail of the room. You could see the bathtub. He claimed he had seen her naked, big white tits bobbling as she scrubbed herself—with a brush, not a sponge.

What an uproar! What a fracas! We're huddled under the overhang of piles of curing pine planks, and everyone wants to be the first to go with Simon to see this fantastic sight. It was more fabulous than the women from the *Arabian Nights* stories we'd seen in the big book Kaspar's father kept locked in a cabinet. After all, it had only drawings of women, mostly veiled. There's some threats, then some shoving. Finally Andreas winds up punching Kaspar in the stomach so hard that Kaspar has to curl up on the ground like a bug for a while. Then we are able to agree on drawing straws. They don't want to let me draw at first; they don't really consider me part of the gang. So I have to punch Kaspar in the stomach too, to prove I belong. Kaspar becomes so upset he pushes down Erich, the smallest boy, and sits on him until all the straws are picked. Then Simon has to measure them with his ruler. I get the shortest, which means I go last.

We wanted to go all in one night, but Simon said no. It wasn't safe for all of us to be up in the cockloft at once; his uncle might hear us. Anyway, the loft was only a space two planks wide, ending at a small round window. Only two at a time could manage— Simon, since he had the binoculars, and one of us. So we set out a schedule of Sunday, Monday, Tuesday, Wednesday, and Thursday. I got Thursday. The trick was to come up with an excuse to get out of the house and over to the mill around eight. On my night, I just left right after supper and said I was going to Sigi's to do homework. Sigi was out of this entirely. We didn't tell her anything about it.

By my night the others were all raving. They claimed they'd seen everything, absolutely everything. They said they thought Fräulein Mumelter knew they were watching her, and liked it. They said she moved very slowly so they could have a good look, and it wouldn't surprise them if one day they were invited to sneak

up to that apartment, where Fräulein Mumelter would be waiting, nude under her white nightgown.

But there would be no pale spheres for my eyes, no seeing
everything, no languid invitation. At the appointed time, I met
Simon outside the rear door to the sawmill. Scouting right and
left, we slipped in and began to climb the ladders to the cockloft.
They were splintery, not much used. We were within five meters
of our goal when suddenly we saw a dark, bulky figure filling the
entire loft. It was Simon's uncle Ignatz, lying there with the spotting scope he used for hunting, saying, "Oh. Oh. Oh."

I don't believe any of them ever saw anything. The steam from
the bath would have fogged the windows, surely. Surely Fräulein
Mumelter would draw the curtains too. They were just making
it up, what they said they saw.

But I didn't like the idea of Big Ignatz and his Oh. Oh. Oh.
So the next night around six-thirty, when everyone was buried
in his soup plate, I carried a paper bag of shit I'd collected in the
stall under the Jew's box and snuck up into the cockloft. You could
see her windows, and you could see somebody moving behind
the curtains. But it was just a shadowy figure; you couldn't even
tell if it was a man or a woman. I smeared the shit all over the
planks and on the window frame too.

I'm hoping Big Ignatz will crawl right into the stuff, snuffling
like a pig. Let's see how he explains those shit stains to his wife.
But it goes wrong. It's Simon and Kaspar who go that night, fat
Kaspar forcing his way in first, hurrying past the first shitty smells
until he realizes what soft stuff is smearing his hands and arms
and belly. There's Kaspar recoiling with a gag, Kaspar missing his
footing on the ladder, fat Kaspar tumbling down and snapping
his left arm when he hits the sawmill floor.

They have to take Kaspar down to Fussing in my grandfather's

truck, which now belonged to my father. They make him ride in
the open back, because of the smell; it seems he has crapped in
his pants. The Fussing quack, Herr Doktor Durchleuchter, the
very same quack who will ruin me two years later, refuses to work
on Kaspar until the boy has been hosed down outside.

Big Ignatz beats out of Simon, with a birch switch, what they
were doing up there (as if he didn't know himself). Bald, many-
chinned Ignatz makes a show of boarding up the little window
(but leaves one or two nice cracks, I think). All the fathers inter-
rogate all the sons very closely on exactly what they've seen.
They want details. Then the boys are all thrashed, and the case
is closed.

But Fräulein Mumelter, blameless Fräulein Mumelter, has
become established in the village mind as something more than
the teacher. She is perhaps a source of trouble. She becomes a
focal point for all the envy, desire, and tension the village has
to spare.

"Were they really spying on the poor girl?" my mother says
at dinner that night.

"At least Niki knew enough to keep out of it," my father says.

"But she wouldn't be the type to leave her curtains open,
would she?" my mother asked.

"I don't think so," my father says.

"But don't you think her dresses are a little risqué?" my mother
persists.

"Perfectly proper for a schoolteacher," my father says.
"They're all more or less the same."

"So you notice what she wears?" my mother says.

"Not really," my father says. He seems to be talking to his
soup.

Sigi thinks the whole thing is incredibly stupid. "What would they get out of seeing?" she says. "What's so special? They've all seen their mothers' breasts, after all."

"Not lately," I say.

"Idiot," Sigi says.

A FEW DAYS LATER I was looking forward to the late-afternoon religion lesson. Here, I thought, is where Fräulein Mumelter is really going to humiliate Simon, Kaspar, and the rest. Kaspar looks miserable in a huge rough white plaster cast that goes from his shoulder the whole way down his arm. But it's probably more the pain than the shame. I expect some flashing, wounding phrases on the wickedness of prying eyes, the depths of sin, the awful punishments that await such perverts. But Fräulein Mumelter fails to roast the sinners. She acts as if nothing has happened and talks about Lot's wives. At the end, Sigi thinks of something she needs to know.

"What is the legal age to marry?" Sigi asks.

"Have you had a proposal, Sigi?" Fräulein Mumelter says, winking at the class and raising the titters she intended.

"I just wanted to know," Sigi says evenly.

"It's sixteen, Sigi. You have some years to go," Fraülein Mumelter says.

"What about for Jews?" Sigi asks.

"I don't think we need to worry about them," the teacher says.

"I was just curious," Sigi said.

"We have special laws for Jews now, Sigi. Honestly, I'm not even sure if Jews are allowed to marry each other anymore. It's a crime for one of them to marry one of us."

Dinner for the Jew that night is two big boiled potatoes with a spoon of blue-veined cheese. He's always a little sad the potatoes aren't salted enough, but he packs them right away.

"How old are you?" the Jew asks.

"Sixteen," Sigi lies.

"Old enough these days, I suppose." He sounds weary. "Rachel was only seventeen. Well, I'll tell you frankly: we became lovers; you've guessed that, haven't you? It wasn't easy. She had trouble arranging excuses to be away from her aunt's house, and I had to smuggle her into my rooms. My landlady would have called the police if she'd known. We never spent a night together. We simply met for a wonderful hour whenever we could. I would put a single rose in a vase every time she came, and never remove it. The vase was filled completely at the end, dozens of dried roses. There's nothing you can do with them, though. They crumble so easily."

He is crazy about Rachel's coarse black hair, the earthy aroma that seems to emanate from under her skirts. He wants to bury his face in her lap and breathe of her.

This is what he says, these are his words.

I am wondering just how a dark young Jewess would smell. It must be different from Sigi, or Fräulein Mumelter. They just smelled of soap most of the time. I'm thinking a Jewess might smell Oriental, but I don't have any idea what an Oriental smell is. Maybe it's like the incense at church, heavy and smoky. I'm trying to picture making love. I can't quite see how the one thing gets inside the other. It doesn't seem like the angles would be right. The sizes, either. It's just a little slit, after all? Sigi seems suddenly restless, impatient with the Jew.

"So you were lovers for the ten months and then you were married," Sigi says. "She was pregnant, you gave your fathers fits in Przemyśl and Graz, but they got over it."

"We never married, Sigi," the Jew said. "It wasn't to be."

4

OUR JEW has escaped to Italy. He's driving like a madman, as if the police are in hot pursuit. He's wheeling a thirteen-year-old Mercedes, which doesn't belong to him, over the Brenner, down through the Südtirol, and across the Lombardy plain to Venice. He has a young girl with him who isn't his wife.

"The one fling of my life," the Jew says. "The one adventure."

The Jew is driving Sigi crazy. She wants things in some kind of order. She prefers progression. She likes to learn how things turn out as soon as possible, without untoward delay. She especially wants to know what has become of poor Rachel from Przemyśl. But the Jew goes where he pleases, when he pleases, and he is in the middle of his great escape to Italy. It's a few days after Sigi posed her marriage questions to Fräulein Mumelter in religion class.

More and more we're understanding that we have to take this Jew on faith or not at all. There are no checks on him, no tests we can apply. We don't even know anyone who's been to Italy, excepting Sigi's uncle who sent her the postcard from Lake Garda, and he's dead. How can we know if the Jew is telling the truth about the little bribes he paid to the owners of small hotels to ignore the fact that the name on the girl's passport isn't the same as his? Or about how the spring tides bring the canal water lapping into the Piazza San Marco, where the Venetians walk on flimsy bridges of planks? Or about how he and the girl did not leave their hotel for thirty-six hours, no explanation offered, leaving us to imagine what two people could get up to alone in a room all that time. But more and more we're also understanding that perhaps it doesn't matter much. He's speaking of the past, after all, a time mostly before we were even born. Why should we care if he lies a little? They are only lies to himself.

"You couldn't say she was pretty," the Jew says. "Her nose was broad, she had cropped hair, her hips were too slim. She looked a bit like a street urchin. She smoked too much. It was a style then."

He's speaking of the girl beside him in the Mercedes, which he's borrowed from his friend ex-Baron von Trotta. The Jew says there were a lot of types like Trotta around in the twenties: aristocrats who, years after it happened, still seemed dazed that the Emperor was in his tomb and the Empire with him. They lived entirely in their pasts, these men, because the present was incomprehensible—or repulsive—to them. He and Trotta served in the same regiment. This gave them certain claims on each other, he explains. The Mercedes, for example. But never on a girl! No, the girl is his alone. And yes, it's a cliché, but she's a nurse, what else? Everyone understands about nurses and doctors. They go together, they're made for each other. Every nurse wants to marry a doctor, but not vice versa. Hardly. As for me, he says, who else would I know well enough to persuade to make this mad dash with me? Who else would accompany me to a purely imaginary medical conference in Italy? In Italy, so recently the enemy country? Yes, to discuss advancements in the treatment of certain wounds, especially those leading to nerve damage of various sorts. So easy to diagnose, so difficult to treat.

Sigi can't stand that she doesn't yet know who or when he married, that she can't picture who he's left behind for this nurse or how it came to this. The Jew is not inclined to help her over this. Her consternation doesn't interest him; he forges ahead. She wants to pull him back.

Sigi is testy these days anyway. Her mood isn't the best. She's been having bad cramps with her periods lately. She's only been having periods for a year, and she's a little worried there may be something wrong. She thinks bad thoughts. But mostly she hasn't gotten over her anger with all of us, the entire village, really, over the spying on Fräulein Mumelter. This secret peeping is the worst sort of sin, in her opinion. It's a gross violation; it's the most terrible thing that could happen to Fräulein Mumelter, or to anyone. For some reason she blames everyone, not just Kaspar and Simon. She feels the broken arm was less than was due to Kaspar. He should have broken his neck, she says. Although most everyone feels Kaspar and Simon have embarrassed the village and should be punished, most believe they have been, and Sigi's views are considered somewhat extreme.

The whiff of scandal perked up my mother, who had recently become a little overly interested in Fräulein Mumelter anyway. She took fewer naps. She left the house more often. She began to speak again to certain people she had ignored for years; even her cousin Christina, with whom she'd quarreled over my little sister Katrin's christening dinner. Christina had not been seated at the main table; there wasn't room for everyone, after all. Christina felt so slighted that she called my mother a bitch to Aunt Maria, who told my mother, naturally. So Christina and my mother never spoke for years after that. But now my mother was reentering the life of the village, which meant mainly that she once again began to receive and relay gossip.

But that wasn't enough. My mother baked a poppy-seed cake

and took it personally to Fräulein Mumelter's apartment one Sunday after church. She was invited to have coffee, as she knew she would be, and thus gained half an hour to study the teacher. My mother had, of course, met Fräulein Mumelter when she first arrived and had to pay calls on all the parents. My mother had also seen her at several school functions since but hadn't given much notice, I suppose. My mother reported at supper that night that she found Fräulein Mumelter pretty in an overblown sort of way, but too full of herself, a snob, really, and didn't my father agree?

He only nodded.

"Her complexion is a little coarse for a girl so young," my mother said.

"She should rub her face with cucumbers and then scrub with burlap," my grandma said.

"Do you think the boys with the binoculars actually saw anything?" my mother said, looking at my father.

"Most likely not," my father said, shifting slightly in his seat, as if he wanted to get up.

"They say she walks around her place stark naked at night," my grandmother said. "No wonder they tried to see."

"I doubt that, ma," my father said. "It's just a piece of gossip."

"But we don't know what she does in there, do we?" my mother said.

"And why should we? Does everyone have to know what you do in your bedroom?" my father said.

"I don't do anything to be ashamed of," my mother said.

"Of course not," my father said. Then he left the table.

Around this same time my father began to rise earlier and earlier in the morning. I would hear him stoking the woodstove before dawn, before my mother or grandmother had stirred. I would hear him walking back and forth in the kitchen, three strides up and three strides back, while he waited for the water to boil. He seemed wary now when we went together up to the barn, me carrying the Jew's breakfast in an old flour sack. "The worst feeling at the front," he said one day, "was that there was someone unseen, some sniper, who was watching you from afar. You were his anytime he wanted you. You would never know when your moment had come. You would have no warning at all."

This alarmed me. It was something completely new. My father had never, ever, talked about the war.

Now he began to create a mental list of those who might be watching him, those who bore some grievance or dislike or jealousy. There were easily a half-dozen men, and a couple of women too, he decided, who would like to catch him out doing something wrong. He wouldn't say their names, but I knew they'd be familiar ones. There weren't any strangers in the village. Even if none of them suspected about the Jew, they could be watching for some other, smaller lapse: failure to fly the flag on prescribed days, selling rationed goods without coupons, dealing with the Italian smugglers. We must be more careful from here on in, he said. We have to stay alert. I mustn't spend too much time in the barn, I mustn't draw attention to it in any way. It worried me that he felt he had to say this, since I hadn't been doing either of those things. I didn't like to think my father could be nervous, or afraid. He said it was better if Sigi was with me. It looked more natural, the two of us going to play in the barn, than me going there alone.

I want to ask my father why we are keeping this Jew. After the first month, it felt to me as if we had paid the debt for my appendix. I was not sure how you measured these things, but a month's hiding, with plenty of food, seemed fair. Yet the months passed, half a year passed, and there's our Jew, still eating potatoes fried with bacon for his dinner, while my father walks, hunched, as if he were in a trench under an unseen gun.

So I want to ask why. But I don't dare. My father has never shown any sign of feeling obliged to explain any of his decisions. Why should he start now? And if he did say anything, anything like "because it's the right thing to do," how would I know it was true? It could be like the Jew's stories: no way to tell. And it could so easily be the wrong thing to do. We can't know yet how it will turn out. And if he said something like "because the Jew will protect us when the time comes," would that tell me anything? Why would my father think that we might need protection in the future? Protection from whom? Who would reward us for hiding a Jew? Nobody cares about Jews, that's obvious.

And we are winning the war, after all. The man on the radio, Herr Josef Markhoff, says so. He's a man we depend on. When I was nine, we knew this Anschluss thing was real only when we heard about it from Josef Markhoff on the radio. We never saw any German troops; our village was too small for that. But the news came into our house in the old familiar voice, the voice of a good uncle. It was not too deep, but there was a trace of a rumble to it that made you feel always that he was speaking confidentially to you. There was no new note in Herr Markhoff's voice that night; it was very matter-of-fact. And that's how we knew for sure that Austria was now just another part of Germany.

No German soldiers ever did come up to us. The gendarme before the Anschluss was Pabst, and Pabst he remained. The mayor was still the mayor. The day after the Anschluss, my granny starting hoarding lard, sugar, flour, and salt. She put the lard in big tin buckets and kept them in the cellar. "You never know," she said. "We were terribly short in the last war." There's no war now, I told her. And there wasn't, that summer. The stamps and the money were different, but nothing else changed. Except the boys who went to do their military service did not come back after one year as they used to, because that autumn the war with Poland started, and then the war with most of the world.

We have so many enemies. The ones that scare me aren't the Americans or the Russians or the Germans I've never seen. I don't care for the brown-uniformed men, like the ones who were friends of Sigi's father. I don't like what they get up to, the way they bully with their loud voices, the stale way they smell. When you see one of them, you feel just like you do when you pass a very mean dog in somebody's yard: you hope he hasn't slipped his chain.

Three days after the second anniversary of Herr Strolz's death, eight of these men came up from Schwaz in two little tin-pot Volkswagens painted a drab green. They parked in front of the bar, went in, surely had some drinks, and came back out adjusting the belts of their yellowy-brown uniforms, smoothing their hair, putting on their caps. Then they opened the trunk of the first car and took out a big swastika made of dyed red carnations. They marched this fifty meters up the road to the graveyard, put the thing on the grave of Sigi's father, and stood silently for about thirty seconds. Then they marched back to the bar. After a while, Sigi and I went over to look at the swastika. There was a white ribbon, stained here and there by red dye, which said in Gothic letters: "To an old fighter." I read this out loud.

I went to have a look at the photos of my brothers and sister. It was a sunny afternoon, just a little crisp. The red lights weren't lit yet, so it seemed all right. I was looking, and thinking how strange it was to see your dead brothers and sister looking so alive and fresh. Sigi was plucking out a few of the flowers to take to her mother when the brown men came out of the bar. You could hear them belching. One of them saw what Sigi was doing and came sprinting up the road, shouting, "You goddamn brats! Get away from that!" Sigi and I just stood there. We didn't know what to do. It was as if a bad dog had got loose after us. The rest of the brown men stood in the road with their hands hitched at their belts, or leaned against the little tin-pot cars.

The running man seemed younger than the others, not anyone we had ever seen in the village before. He came into the graveyard and grabbed Sigi by the arm. She stumbled. But just then Big Ignatz came through the black iron gate from I don't know where. I don't remember seeing him nearby. He was up behind the brown man quick as anything, throwing a meaty arm around his neck. Big Ignatz squeezed, the man dropped Sigi's arm. I saw the other men start toward the graveyard. Big Ignatz said softly, "She's his daughter," and let go. The man shook himself like a dog, rubbed his windpipe, mumbled "Sorry," and went out onto the road, gesturing to his friends. They stopped and waited for him. He said a few words, which we couldn't make out, and they started laughing. Then they walked back to their tin pots and drove off. Big Ignatz stood with us until the tin pots were out of sight around the curve down the mountain, and then he walked back to his sawmill. He didn't say anything.

Sigi was spitting. "Who grabbed me?" she demanded. "No one's supposed to touch me. I am not supposed to be touched. What did Uncle Ignatz do? I heard him here. Did he take away the one who grabbed me? I didn't hear any fight." She had red dye all over her hands.

Sigi's father and Big Ignatz were the only men in our village who had ever worn those brown uniforms. Ignatz put his away in 1941 and was never seen in it again. There were plenty of war veterans like Sigi's father and Ignatz who joined the Party in the late thirties. Mostly, they said, out of disgust with the Republic and not from any fondness for Adolf and his Germans. Better to be on the inside than the outside during a storm, even if the inside smells like piss. That's what I once heard Sigi's father say to my father. Herr Strolz was always trying to get my father to join. "Lukasser," Sigi's father would say, "the world's a dangerous place. Men like us have got to stick together." And my father would always reply that he gave no thought to politics. Minding his own business was his policy.

"Ah, Martin," Sigi's father would say, as if he felt my father was badly misinformed about how the world works.

Some evenings Sigi's father and Big Ignatz and a few of the brown men from down in the valley would sit around our kitchen table drinking beer. There'd be the sour smell of that, and a cloud of bluish smoke under the hanging lamp, and voices growing louder with each glass. I'd sneak down from my room to watch. In the end Sigi's father and mine would be sitting there, arms slung sloppily around each other's shoulders, slurring each other's Christian names at the start of sentences they never finished.

My grandmother would have to help my father up the stairs, take off his boots, and put him in bed, while my mother pretended to be asleep. Then she'd sweep me into bed too, never forgetting to see that I resaid the prayers I'd said when she'd put me to bed the first time. I don't know how Herr Strolz got home, or what happened to him there. Maybe his wife also pretended to be asleep, and he had to sleep on the floor in all his clothes.

THE MONDAY AFTER my mother paid her call, Fräulein Mumelter embarrassed me in class. Surely it was deliberate. "Niki Lukasser!" she said in front of everyone, first thing, bright and early. "Yesterday your mother brought me a delicious poppy-seed cake, and I have saved a piece for you!" Everyone was looking at me. It was as bad as going to the blackboard with a hard-on. Kaspar was making kissing faces at me. He looked like a very fat fish.

Aside from the bulky plaster cast from his shoulder to his wrist, which was already getting grimy, Kaspar seemed no worse for his fall. It certainly hadn't done any damage to his attitude. He didn't even seem embarrassed in the presence of Fräulein Mumelter. I couldn't have stood it. She was only a little more correct with him and Simon than before. She certainly never mentioned anything about it in class. What could she do? She could see the way things were. Although everyone knew Kaspar was in disgrace, he was also a sort of celebrity. It was quite an exploit, after all, even if you had to say it was disgusting. Everyone in school had signed his cast. Except Sigi, of course.

After lunch break we were all milling around the school door. "Phew. I smell Kaspar," Sigi said. "Kaspar the hog, porky Kaspar, Kaspar the swine." She began snuffling like a pig. It was a good imitation. We all started laughing. Some of the little kids started making pig noises too.

"Ah, shut up, Sigi," Kaspar said. He pushed her with his cast. I thought of Big Ignatz, but I could never get an arm around Kaspar's thick neck. So I ran up and punched him in the nose as hard as I could. He didn't even stagger—he was too big to budge— but blood came rushing out. He started bawling. Fräulein Mumelter came out in a hurry, helped Kaspar to lie down on the grass, and put her handkerchief to his nose. It turned red fast. I was ready for trouble. But she didn't inquire as to how Kaspar had got such a nosebleed, and nobody, not even Kaspar, volunteered to tell her. "I heard you," Sigi said to me quietly. "I heard you do that. It was great."

MY HAND STILL HURTS. But I don't mind much. Sigi is leaning against my shoulder, and the Jew is walking along the Riva degli Schiavoni at dusk, his arm firmly around the tiny waist of his slim-hipped nurse. She is as tall as he is; her hair is almost as short. She's a dark girl. The light is very blue, and the waters of the canal look as black as her eyes. There is a last late glimmer on the huge dome of the church on the island across the canal. They pass the Bridge of Sighs, and his hand slips to her hip. He can feel her bones move. At that moment he is sure he is in love with her and will never go back to Innsbruck. He feels he must stay with this girl in Venice. They will stroll, they will eat *zuppa di pesce* in tiny trattorias they discover in the dim nooks and crannies of the city, they will make love all night. Sigi blushes.

"He's forgetting himself," she whispers. She's caressing her own face.

"Yes," I say, excited, hoping for description, for a telling of the ways of it. There are so many things we are dying to know. But no. The Jew seems to remember who he is speaking to, and that's as far as he goes.

5

I GET UPSET SOMETIMES. I'll be sitting at our old pine table spooning up soup, listening to my parents talk about daily things. It happens then.

You see the moon. Why is it up there anyway? Why am I down here casting a thin shadow under it, feeling the cold night air plunging into my lungs. You see the Jew in his box. My head rattles with these things. Yet my parents speak placidly across the supper table of the number of needles, or bolts of muslin, or cans of peaches, still in stock in the store. When are they likely to be able to get more? My father praises the soup, the same dumpling soup we've had two or three times a week since I can remember. My grandmother, too, needs to report on her day. She was so distracted by an argument between Big Ignatz and some stranger across the street that she almost scorched one of the second-best sheets.

I've got to leave the table. There's a feeling I get that I'm only dreaming my life. It scares me. And lately I'm thinking my father isn't going to be able to tell me the things I feel I have to know. He isn't going to be able to settle me down the way he used to. I never had any faith my mother would.

Mooning and moping, I'm Sigi's little project. She feels inspired to snap me out of it. Distraction is her main method—a new book to read to her, a walk to take her on. But recently she tried a once-and-for-all cure. "Life's a test," she said. "We're here to see how we do. We're old enough now. We've got the choice to do right or wrong, and we've got to do right. That's the point, passing the test."

If that's the point, what's the purpose? Who is giving this examination, and how is it being scored? I have to say I felt let down. I'd higher hopes for Sigi. I found her explanation almost as poor as the priest's. God Has a Plan was the priest's answer to everything, from a toothache to the horrible deaths of three men in a lumbering accident (all impaled repeatedly and in secret places by the jagged spearing branches of a great pine fallen wrong). The priest was proud to say he had never read any philosophers at all during his school years and priestly training, only Catholic religious works. It must have made his work easier: God Has a Plan is no feat to memorize, and it's as endlessly repeatable as Hail Marys.

And if there's a plan, there's no why, why, why?

But then I thought: Just because Sigi doesn't have the answer doesn't mean she couldn't be my answer.

ONE NIGHT Sigi says to the Jew: "We'll never come up here again unless you say what happened to Rachel in Vienna." I'm thinking I would find this a considerable threat if I were nailed in a box all by myself. I'm surprised at her for being so tough with poor Dr. Weiss. He's surprised too. He's silent for at least a minute. His "All right, Sigi" is abrupt. Then all of a sudden we learn he is leaving for the front in the morning, early.

He's known this day would come, he's talked it over with

Rachel, they're agreed they will marry on his first leave, with or without the blessings of their parents. She's turned eighteen. He's a doctor now, and a lieutenant. He's capable. He has means, meager but sufficient to start. Her love has seemed central to his existence. But something has been quietly happening. Her arrivals no longer quite feel like little miracles. He has noticed lately that when they part after a passionate hour together, secretly he is relieved to be alone in his rooms. He has noticed that the smell of her on his pillow lately seems somehow an intrusion.

"Never do it before you're married," Sigi whispers to me. Does she think that was Rachel's mistake? I don't. People do it anytime they can, it seems to me. Just last summer Monika Fischnaller, who lives three houses up from Sigi, had a baby boy, and she wasn't married to anyone. People do it anyway. I'm just wondering what it's like to do it. Also I'd like to ask the priest if he thinks Monika Fischnaller's baby boy is part of a plan. But I won't. He'd box my ears.

"At some point in your lives, you may discover what I mean. It is something you cannot help. You don't want it to, but a feeling slips away from you in spite of everything. One day it's just gone," the Jew says. "I'm not proud of it."

What he's not proud of is this: Rachel invents some excuse to slip out of her house and meet him at the station shortly after dawn. It's a risk, but she has to take it, as she's had to take them all these past six months. She's anxious, naturally. She's wearing her best hat. She is twisting the handle of her purse with both hands. Her eyes are dry, but her lower lip is trembling in a way that's much younger than she is. He reassures her as best he can. He touches her cheek, he tips up her chin and kisses her until the trembling stops. He thinks of other places he has kissed her. He notices his right knee is quaking. He swears he'll write every day.

He never does. Not once. He never replies to a single one of her letters, which swarmed down on him like moths to a lamp week after week for a year.

"I can't say for sure what happened," the Jew tells us. "It wasn't anything to do with the war. For me the war was just a rigorous test of my skills. You could say I exercised in my profession. I became more polished, better and better at what I trained for. You could never say it was a pleasant time, but it was often a deeply satisfying time. It wasn't complicated, psychologically.

"But from the first, Rachel's letters had a bad effect. There was a childish expectation in her tone that was maddening. And a naive confidence as she discussed our future that had me feeling that my possibilities in life were already circumscribed. She began to feel more and more like a burden than a gift."

"You didn't have the courage to tell her? You just never answered?" Sigi explodes. "How could you? What a hateful thing to do."

"I said I wasn't proud of it," the Jew replies. It sounds as if he is talking to an adult.

"You said you can't say what happened. That's because nothing happened," Sigi says.

"No, something changed," he says.

"You made it change."

"Not deliberately."

"There isn't any other way," Sigi says. "Admit you should be deeply ashamed of yourself. You probably should have committed suicide."

"It was a piece of life, that's all," the Jew says.

"You ruined that life," Sigi insists. "You never went to her in Vienna when you were on leave, did you? You never saw her again."

Oh, the silence. Nothing good can come of this, I thought.

"Never," the Jew admits.

"Shit," said Sigi. "I want to go home now, Niki."

Oh, my angry Sigi! She hadn't minded when the doctor ran off to Venice with his nurse. She raised no objections to a wife and child left behind. But Rachel at the station, Rachel writing letters, believing in a future she'll never have— this has really offended Sigi. She's taking it personally. "Who cares about a fling with a nurse?" Sigi snapped. "That's just what men do. They run off now and then. It's normal. But they go back to their wives. Rachel was supposed to be the wife. It was a romance, and he killed it."

"Such an expert for a virgin," I said. Then I wondered if possibly her father had got up to mischief? I didn't know.

"Maybe I am," Sigi said. "Maybe I know how things work."

That was surely something I wished I knew. But it seemed the older and more educated I got, the less clear everything became. As we walked home, I was trying to hold in my mind the picture of the Jew in a tent somewhere, looking at a letter from Rachel in candlelight. He's been operating all day, he's exhausted. Perhaps he's feeling afraid to open it. Perhaps he's putting it in a pile with her other letters, all neatly tied together with string but never read. Then it cartwheeled for me, I don't know why. I saw it all tumble the other way.

"Do you suppose maybe that's just the way he tells it?" I said. "Maybe he did write her every day. Maybe she never answered *his* letters. Maybe when he went to see her in Vienna on leave, she was gone. He's frantic. Has she gone back to Przemyśl? Has she married somebody else? She could have died of influenza and no one would have let him know. She's just gone. Maybe he pined for years. A man with a broken, broken heart."

"Oh, no," said Sigi. She put her fingers to her lips for a moment. "That couldn't be the way it was."

"Probably it makes him feel better to remember it as he tells it. He couldn't bear to tell the truth, if she broke his heart," I said.

"No, I'm sure he broke hers. I have a feeling about it," said Sigi. "It was wicked, what he did to that poor girl. I'm glad if I made him feel bad. And now I think he'll do what we want. He ought to."

SOME WEEKS have gone by since I broke Kaspar's nose. He's speaking to me again. It's almost as if it never happened. But I don't trust him. He and Simon are up to something, I think. There's a revenge in the works. So I'm alert to ambushes and traps. I walk wide around the corners of barns and houses so I won't be jumped. There's never anyone lurking there, but it doesn't cost anything to be careful. Some days I even carry one of my grandfather's old walking sticks.

Winter's coming. There's a lot of snow up top already, but none yet in the village. The hunters come down with a deer every couple of days. My father is trafficking. He's selling venison at the store, no coupons needed. Other times of the year we don't get much fresh meat. It's mostly sausages and bacon, things that keep. But now we're eating venison most nights. My grandmother cooks it in some dark sauce, with dumplings and cranberries on the side. They're like holiday meals, some of these autumn suppers. I'm always hungry. I stuff myself, and my stomach feels hollow already by the time I go to bed. I never gain a kilo.

Once a week or so now my father sends me over to Sigi's house with some pieces of venison. Once a month or so I've been carrying over a sack of cornmeal or flour. "You'll thank your father for me, won't you, Niki?" Sigi's mother always says. Some Sundays we have Sigi and her mother over to our house for noon dinner. That's the big meal of the day, always starting with a noodle soup and then going on to better things—some kind of meat, maybe pig's feet or once in a while tripe, onions and potatoes, and right now of course always venison. We don't get tired of it. My grandma does the cooking. Her mother cuts up Sigi's meat, but otherwise Sigi does fine by herself.

I think Sigi's mother hasn't much money. I've heard talk of a pension, but everyone knows the war veterans' pensions are not much. The men in the village have been complaining about them for years. It's what they mostly talk about in the bar, along with the weather and the conditions of the pastures and whatever scheme the mayor is up to at the moment. "Something ought to be done for the veterans," my grandfather would say almost every time he drank a beer in the evenings. It was like a toast with him. People expected to hear it. We heard the brown men had raised a subscription, but my father said that wouldn't buy more than a winter's worth of potatoes and lard. And Sigi is starting to outgrow her clothes. The sleeves of everything she owns are getting too short. Her blouses are getting too tight across the chest. Fräulein Mumelter has lately been encouraging Sigi and one or two of the other older girls to wear sweaters over their blouses at school.

The newly sweatered Sigi is determined to have her way with the Jew. Next time we go, she tells him straightaway she wants to hear about his courtship and marriage. She sounds so confident. But Dr. Weiss has a surprise for Sigi. He refuses. He says, "All in good time." There's enough force in his voice that Sigi feels unable to push. But he sounds weary too. Or it could be that he's disappointed in us. Who can tell? Maybe we caused him to think about Rachel in ways he never wanted to.

"Remember my father, the primarius?" he says. "You can imagine what that means: strict, disciplined, arrogant. I should actually have chosen another field if I'd wanted a peaceful youth. He never pushed me into medicine. He even thought something in the artistic fields might be right for me. He himself had made the major step, as he saw it. My grandfather had been a haberdasher, not an elegant one, with a small shop in Klagenfurt. But I liked the challenge of medicine. I rose to it. I think my father was even a bit surprised. Then of course came the army.

"The army is just an exaggerated version of a sports team, you know. You want to win at all costs, and when you do win a few times you come to believe you are unbeatable. Which is what makes the inevitable defeat so horrible. But my particular work remained the same whether we won or lost. Sometimes I was even busier in victory than defeat.

"Debridement. I became an expert in that. Do you know what debridement is? Of course you don't. I'll tell you. When a part of the human body is shot or crushed or stabbed or blown apart, a lot of tissue is so badly mangled that blood can't flow through it anymore. It looks like sausage meat before it's stuffed into the casing. But if you simply stuff a wounded soldier's torn flesh back in the skin, he will die of gangrene. So you must cut away all the mangled flesh, toss it into a bucket at your feet. The orderly takes it away and throws it on the rubbish heap. Crows come. That's debridement. I'm an expert.

"Now," Dr. Weiss says, "I'm tired. Would you go, please?"

This is the first time he has ever dismissed us. We've always been the ones to go. It's unsettling. Sigi and I are quiet as we walk home, but I'm getting anxious and I feel sure she is too. I drop her hand and put my arm around her shoulders. It's awkward to walk like this. Our hips are bumping. Mine's bonier and gets the worst of it. But I want her closer. "I think I was too rough," she says just as I get her to her door. "I may have to make it up to him."

She kisses me on the lips, the first kiss ever. "I wish I could see you sometime," she says as she goes inside.

IT'S THE TIME OF YEAR when you know that each fine day may be the last for a long while. November has passed; we're well into December. It's clear and dry now, but who knows for how long? Usually everyone asks my father. Others check the moss on the pines, or the hairiness of the caterpillars, but my father is simply sensitive to the weather. That's his reputation. He is most often correct in his predictions. He foresees storms infallibly. But this year he seems confused, or perhaps just distracted. People aren't getting straight answers from him. Even so, he reads the clouds better than he reads the moods of my mother. He predicted the big Christmas Eve storm, but not my mother's eruption shortly after. Which was a pity for Fräulein Mumelter, who took the force of it.

Ever since the spying incident, Fräulein Mumelter has seemed slightly suspect to some people, as if she somehow bore a responsibility for the bad behavior of Kaspar and Simon. Why something so crazy should be so, I don't know. People are just that way, aren't they? I want to say it was mostly the homely women, the old bags in their thirties and forties, with a couple of kids, whose husbands maybe drink a bit too much and fall asleep early. I want to put it down to envy and bitterness. But it wasn't only them. "They've started to discuss her at the bar," my father said. "That's a bad sign."

My father had recently begun taking me by surprise, showing he thought I was more grown up than I thought he'd noticed. I was pleased when he spoke to me frankly. It made up a bit for the loss of so many of our old ways together. He'd put certain things aside lately. He used to pick me up and squeeze me sometimes, but not anymore. He didn't seem to want to touch me at all. He'd shy like a horse if I put my arm around him or tried to hold his hand. So sometimes I'd just punch him in the arm and skip away. It was a way to show affection, that's all. He'd laugh.

But what he'd said this time made me sad. I was still a bit cross with Fräulein Mumelter over the cake, but I didn't want any of the men to slander or scout her. I liked her too much. I began to think up hard things I could say if I heard anyone doing that, things that would shut them right up. I wasn't very successful. The best I came up with was "You think like a sow in heat." When I snarled it at Herr Dietz the mailman in front of the bar one day (he was elaborately sniffing a letter for Fräulein Mumelter), all the men watching burst into laughter. As did Dietz himself.

The worst of it went on behind closed doors, over supper tables. The parents had no discretion. It was sickening. They'd gossip in front of their children, who naturally would tell all their schoolmates the next day what had been said. It heightened the attention. Fräulein Mumelter became watched intently. None of what was said was very bad. Nobody accused her of anything, nobody could cite an example of bad conduct. It was her "influence": that was the word so many people used. Was she a good "influence" on the children? they wondered.

I never heard my father defend Fräulein Mumelter. He did refuse to listen to talk about her. If someone brought her up in the store, he'd never reply but only speak of the customer's order. If my mother tried to tell at the supper table what she'd lately heard about the teacher, my father would say, "Not in front of Niki, please." That would stop her, although I'm sure she spewed out whatever it was once I'd left the room.

Things were feeling sort of poisonous in town.

Then a thing came along that made everyone except my mother forget entirely about Fräulein Mumelter and her influence. Just when the snow began to fall seriously, Kaspar's revenge began to unfold. It wasn't deliberate, it wasn't directed against me. Yet he managed, without even trying, to get back at me, plus everyone who had ever made farting noises when he sat on the schoolbench, or ever hit him in the face with a snowball, or ever stole his clothes from shore while he was floating in the lake like some small whale in the summer, or ever made, as Sigi had, unkind references to swine.

Are there accidents in life, or does everything have a cause? I don't know how you square that up. But there was a definite cause of our affliction that winter. It was Linde, Kaspar's ugly older sister.

Linde was as skinny as Kaspar was fat. Except for their noses, which matched before I broke Kaspar's, you would never know they were brother and sister. She had legs like sticks, and no bosom that I ever saw, even when she wore a dirndl dress on holidays, when you could see great bulges on everyone who had a pair. She was eighteen around the time the Jew came, and had got a job at a glassworks down in the valley. They made something there for airplanes. Nobody was supposed to talk about it, but everyone said it was bombsights. She lived in a workers' dormitory during the week and came up to the village on Sundays. The men and women workers had separate dormitories. There were curfews. But somebody wanted Linde, stick legs or not, curfew or not.

What she brought up with her one Sunday was a case of crabs so fresh she mustn't have known she had them. And what she did, innocent thing, was take off her clothes and crawl into Kaspar's bed for an afternoon nap. This was her habit. Kaspar's room was on the third floor, and quieter than hers in daytime.

Kaspar went peacefully to sleep in that bed Sunday night.

Crab lice will go wherever there is hair. Kaspar had none on his privates, or hadn't had any last summer when I saw him naked at the lake, and so awoke with lice in his head. But he didn't notice it that day. He didn't stop Simon from snatching his wool knit cap at lunch break and putting it on his own head. This is the sort of thing that quickly becomes a game. Andreas snatched the hat from Simon, Erica snatched it from Andreas, and a couple of others grabbed it in turn. The next day Katrina borrowed Erica's head scarf to run home and fetch a book she'd left behind. The day after that I felt a little sick and used Katrina's hooded sweater as a pillow when I lay down on the schoolroom bench. That evening Sigi had her head leaning against mine as we sat back-to-back in the hayloft, listening to Dr. Weiss. And by the end of the week, one way or another, every student in the village had got lice.

Such suspicion! There was talk of summoning the doctor up from Fussing to check the virginity of some of the older girls. It was feared one of them might have been seduced by a passing stranger, or a soldier on leave. Such interrogations! The older ones had to deny all carnal knowledge. Our questionings were less direct. Had we taken our clothes off in any barns with anybody? Had we touched anybody? Had there been any intimate contacts between girls and boys, playing doctor or so forth? Any wrestling or other horseplay? No, no, no, we said. There was just the game with Kaspar's hat.

Satisfied their children had not been bad, the parents began to criticize the hygiene practices of every other house in the village. Outrage was as thick as autumn fog. All the old grievances and suspicions came billowing forth. People argued in the streets over points of cleanliness. All the mothers accused each other of filthy habits.

But to us, none of the name-calling or criticisms stung anywhere near as much as the kerosene our mothers used to wash our hair and, if we had hair there, our privates. I myself had to stand nude in a tin washtub, with a water-soaked rag tied around my eyes, while my mother scrubbed kerosene into my scalp. She used the brush she normally used on the floors. My grandmother felt she had to supervise the procedure. She suggested using the brush on my privates as well, but my mother decided on a piece of burlap instead, thank God.

Eventually Linde was found out. She'd have been safe enough in Fussing, where she worked. But kerosene didn't do the trick on her. Perhaps she didn't use enough. So she sought help from the Fussing doctor, the one who later ruined me. He dusted her with powder. He also confidentially told our priest about it the next time he was in Sankt Vero. "Venereal crabs," he confided. "Sexual intercourse, undoubtedly." Or so the priest said when he called in Linde's mother and father for a confidential talk about their daughter and what she was getting up to. This visit was the subject of heated discussion around the Hufnagl dinner table. The next day at school Kaspar told everyone that Linde had the crabs, and all the details. Half the town laughed about it. The other half said she was a disgusting slut who ought to be ashamed to show her face in Sankt Vero again. The priest preached a sermon about how everything was part of God's plan. He said it was up to us to draw the lesson from this terrible incident.

It wasn't until spring that certain people started speaking to each other again, though.

ONE SUNDAY AFTERNOON shortly before Christmas, Sigi and her mother come to our house for dinner. She and I sneak back to her house as soon as we're finished, leaving the adults around the table. Sigi wants to root through the big wooden chest where all her father's things have been stored. It's too big to get into the attic, so it's sitting on the top-floor landing, under a window, where there's plenty of light. There's a smell of mothballs when we open it up. They're protecting the yellowy-brown uniform, and also his old army jacket with the medal ribbons above the left chest pocket. There are more than I supposed there would be. On one side there are bundles of papers: marriage certificate, military discharge certificate, school certificate, birth certificate. That's the summary of a man's life, isn't it? Just those four pieces of paper. And there is a small stack of books, maybe a dozen volumes. There's some war memoirs, a Hemingway novel. I see one or two famous old things I've heard of but never known anyone to've read. Sigi wants to snitch one to give to Dr. Weiss. While she's choosing, I spot some photos down deep.

That evening we slip a book to the Jew along with his supper. *"Faust,"* he says, and starts laughing. Then he begins talking about the morning he left for the front. It's clearly something he's been thinking about. He doesn't mention Rachel. He's displaying a set of curious memories: what sort of hats the women wore, how the porters cursed under their loads, the way the engines' steam smelled oily. He's painting us a picture of an important day in his life.

"And I actually had to wear a sword. I had to make myself even more ridiculous than love had already made me." He laughs. Then he goes silent for a moment.

"All right, thank you for listening to me all along. And thank you for the excellent book, Sigi," the Jew says at last. "Now I say to old Mephisto, 'Stop!' "

It goes right over my head. I'm thinking hard about one photo I saw in the bottom of the trunk: Sigi's father in his army uniform, his arm tight around the waist of my mother. It's just the two of them. She looks about sixteen, she curves into him, and she's smiling like the sun.

6

"THE JEW WANTS TO DIE," says Sigi. She's trying to kick horse turds at the barn door even though she's wearing her one good pair of boots. She mostly misses. "All we do for him, and he's ready to quit."

See what can come from one little word? It was Dr. Weiss's "Stop!" that brought Sigi to this. I'd have forgotten all about it. It was just one of those things people say that don't mean much, I figured. But Sigi worried it every which way. I couldn't understand why anyone would want to be nothing more than a photo and a little red light in the graveyard. I couldn't imagine anyone longing for the cold ground. But Sigi could.

Still, she didn't reach her final conclusion on the doctor's state of mind until she'd consulted with Fräulein Mumelter. She'd simply raised her hand in class and asked the teacher what happened, please, between Faust and Mephistopheles. "Niki is trying to read it to me," she said.

"Ah, one of our German treasures," said Fräulein Mumelter, smiling sweetly at me. Kaspar nudged me, hard. "The great Goethe's Mephisto," she said, "promised to provide Faust with whatever marvelous experiences he wanted. Anything at all, without limits. There was one condition, though: when Faust had at

last got his heart's desire, he must call out 'Stop!' And at that moment Mephisto would collect Faust's immortal soul.

"Faust was so clever, so sure he could outsmart Mephisto and
never have to surrender his soul," Fräulein Mumelter went on.
Then she placed her right hand just at the base of her throat, the
way she did whenever she was in the vicinity of a moral point.

"Here it comes," Kaspar whispered.

Andreas smirked. He had a way of smirking that reminded me
of a lizard Big Ignatz had kept for a while in a glass case in the
sawmill office. The lizard was supposed to be from Brazil. It
didn't last a winter.

"No one," said Fräulein Mumelter, looking around the classroom, "can outsmart the Devil."

"What's Sigi up to?" Kaspar whispered to me. "You're not reading that book."

"Sure I am," I said. "Already got to page fifteen."

"Crap," said Kaspar. "What's she care about the Devil? What
do you do with her all the time, really? You ever get her to take
her shirt off up in the barn?"

I whacked Kaspar in the shin with the dull edge of my ruler.
He squealed.

"Are you ill, Kaspar?" Fräulein Mumelter inquired. "Or are you
planning an exciting pact with Mephisto?"

"No, ma'am," said Kaspar. "My leg fell asleep. Pins and needles."

The class laughed. We laughed almost every time Kaspar said
anything, even if it was the answer to a math problem. He wasn't
bad at math. He didn't try to be funny. Nobody could say what
was so amusing, but nobody could keep from laughing. Kaspar
saying "The length of the hypotenuse is twelve" broke us up. But
Kaspar always began and ended as if he were accorded only re-
spectful silence.

So here stands Sigi before the barn in her best boots. The smell of woodsmoke in the air is almost stronger than the manure. The sun's gone, but the first stars haven't appeared yet. The sky's its deepest blue, poised on the margin of night. Things in the distance appear soft at the edges. Sigi's pale, plain face looks almost ghostly. For no reason I can name, I am suddenly afraid of what will become of her.

"He's certainly not got his heart's desire," Sigi says, kicking at nothing. "He was being sarcastic, the way my father said smart Jews are sometimes. 'Stop!' just means he can't stand it anymore. He's fed up."

"Maybe he was just joking around to himself," I say. "He probably thought we wouldn't get it."

"Some joke," Sigi says. "He wants to die."

Sigi has utterly convinced herself that the Jew truly meant it when he said "Stop!" She won't consider that it could have been banter. So she's determined that the Jew must be kept from his despair. He must be diverted from morbid thoughts of self-destruction. She's scheming. Distractions, yes. Keep him absorbed in his own tales. Get him to relive his life in enough detail that he forgets the slow, dull passage of the present. And give him tales of our own, she says. Bring him into the life of the village, help him feel part of it, Sigi says.

"Why should that interest a man like him? He's traveled, he's seen things. Sankt Vero is nowhere," I say.

"He's not traveling now," Sigi says.

I get off to a poor start. I've torn out some photos of the fox-wearing Jews blessing the Emperor to take to the loft. I think they might remind Dr. Weiss of his young days. After all, he once actually saw the Emperor in person during a parade in Vienna in 1915. And since he was on the Eastern Front, he probably saw some of these Jews. I slipped the pages through the hole in the box. I heard Dr. Weiss pick them up, leaf through them. "The silly Yids," he muttered.

"Imagine the arrogance of these people, Niki," he said. "They believed their God would protect them. So proud and so stupid. Silly Yids. Only the Emperor could have saved them. We'll hear no more of them, that's for sure."

Dr. Weiss told us that all those eastern Jews disappeared into Poland or Russia after the First War, when the boundaries were redrawn. He pronounced "Poland" and "Russia" as if they were the ends of the earth. Dark places, primitive, like the Congo or Borneo. Had the Reds tolerated the fox hats and caftans and Shabbat and the old business practices? Had the Poles? Dr. Weiss doubted it. He doubted it very much. No need to mention the Germans.

"What the end of the Empire meant to those Jews was oblivion, though I don't think they realized it. What it meant to us was emptiness," he said. "We no longer knew where we belonged. For years you could never think of the future because you were sure there would be none. With the war over, there was suddenly a possibility of having tomorrows; it didn't matter that food was scarce and things were difficult. But we felt lost just the same. And now, of course, it's oblivion for us too."

Food is scarce and things are difficult right now in Sankt Vero too, I thought. My parents and just about everyone from Big Ignatz to Pabst say so all the time. There's a lot of complaining at the store when there's no sugar or lard. Yet it seems all right to me. I don't feel deprived, or frightened. I have enough to eat, and I sleep warm each night. I think you can probably take more trouble when you're young than when you're older. Possibly it's because you have less to lose, and you haven't had time to become attached to having everything a certain way. Possibly that's why young Dr. Weiss enjoyed his life right after the war. Probably that's why old Dr. Weiss despises it now. Sigi thinks so. She says that's definitely her impression.

THE SATURDAY AFTER Sigi gave Dr. Weiss the book, my father sent me over to the Stocker house with a dozen tins of sardines, one liter of cooking oil, and 250 grams of raspberry jam. I'm always running those kinds of errands. It's my job. Some Saturday mornings Sigi tags along with me on my rounds. She does today. Nobody comes to the door when I knock at the Stockers'. So Sigi and I go around the back to the big storage shed where Herr Stocker keeps his snowplow, his tools, and other supplies. I look in the door. It's very dim in there, but near the back wall I see Maria Stocker. She's fifteen, already out of school for a year. A tall girl nearly all grown up. She's got her skirt hitched up around her waist, she's got one hand inside her blouse, and she's riding a big hundredweight sack of cornmeal like it was a horse. She's sliding lightly back and forth, and the hand under her blouse seems to be kneading. I can see the muscles in her thin thighs contract and relax. "What's up?" Sigi whispers. She can't understand why I'm just frozen there at the doorway, not saying anything. Maria doesn't hear. Her lean bottom bears down on the sack. Her motions become unruly. She lunges, she's insistent. All at once she shimmers, she flutters, she mewls like a cat and sort of collapses on the sack. This looks alarming. I'm about to call out to her, asking if she's all right. But Sigi, hearing her, pulls me back from the door.

"Were they doing it?" Sigi asks when we're safely away from the shed. She thinks it's Maria's mother and father in there; she imagines it's Maria's mother who moaned. She's digging her fingers into my arm. "Did he have it in her? Could you see that?"

I tell her all I saw. She only says, "Ah."

When my father asks why I haven't delivered the goods, I tell him there was nobody home.

Sigi's "Were they doing it?" lingers. It won't leave me alone. It forces me to imagine Mr. and Mrs. Stocker on the cornmeal sacks: a vague sort of image, full of random motions I don't understand. Then I think of Big Ignatz and his Hilde pushing against each other. That's the way it must work, people pushing against each other. I've seen the bull mounting cows, but it's hard to imagine the man's thing sinking deep inside the woman like that. I can see Hilde's huge breasts dangling, I can see Ignatz squeezing them like we squeeze the cows' teats. Then I imagine Kaspar's parents naked, belly to belly, pushing. God, the weight that poor woman would have to bear. The bed would break!

And then I try to think about my mother and father. A door slams shut in my head. I've seen them naked once or twice in my life, accidentally of course, but it's left no trace in my mind. I can't say at all what sort of bosom or bottom my mother has, or what my father looks like. I can't bear to think of him with a big cock standing up, hard. I can't bear to think of my mother wanting that. Even skirting the edges of those thoughts makes my stomach quake and roll. I know they've done it; they made so many kids. But in my mind it's something clinical, a procedure. They can't still be doing it. They can't be loving late at night when my grandma and I are asleep and won't hear. And my mother would never have moaned.

Then I begin to think of my mother as she was in that photograph I saw in the bottom of the trunk. I think of that girl doing it with Sigi's father as he was then. They look fresh, clean, made for each other. Suddenly I can see that girl unbuttoning her blouse, lifting her skirt. I can see Sigi's father, smiling, undoing his belt and unbuttoning his trousers. This I can picture, although just as I get about that far, it begins to feel all wrong. It could never have happened, could it? Was it before she knew my father? No, they always knew each other. Growing up in Sankt Vero, everyone knows everyone. Was it while my father was at the front and Sigi's father was on leave? Were they rivals? Or was my mother of no interest to my father until well after he came home from the war? They didn't marry until 1920. Sigi's father, my mother. I wonder if Sigi knows anything about the two of them, curving so nicely into each other. I wonder if someday I'll do something with Sigi. It wouldn't be right. It would be easy, though.

But as these thoughts circle round, more and more I'm beginning to feel like Kaspar's stupid dog, Bobbi. Bobbi is famous for dumb persistence. Whenever anyone's hosing off his wagon wheels or truck, Bobbi tries to bite the stream of water. But he never learns that he can't get a grip. He leaps at the water again and again and again, snapping his jaws, until he lies down exhausted. I simply cannot clear my mind of Maria's tensed thighs, of the lazy absent look on her face, as if she were dreaming of something wonderful. I'd like sometime to see what she was seeing. Instead, fast asleep in the night, I see her riding her sack. She knows I'm watching, but she doesn't care. She even turns to look at me. She shimmers.

I HAVE TO TELL about Maria, in every wretched detail. I have to say how I got a glimpse of her blond pussy as she rode the sack. I have to describe the way her smooth lean buttocks flexed, the way she surged. I even have to imitate her mewl.

All for Dr. Weiss. I would rather have bitten my tongue until it bled buckets. But Sigi insisted on it. She said we had to go to any length to save him from his sadness. I have to tell the story of Maria. It'll amuse him so much, she said. She swore she'd help me in every way.

"I tried it too," Sigi says as soon as I've finished telling the tale to the Jew.

"Shut up," I blurt. This isn't the sort of help I expected. It isn't something she should say even if it's true, which I doubt.

"I tried it with my pillow last night. I wasn't wearing any underpants. Nothing happened really. I got a little wet down there. Certainly nothing to moan about. I'm going to ask Maria what she was up to."

"Sigi, Sigi, Sigi," the Jew says. "I don't want to know these things. These things are private. You shouldn't speak of them to anyone, least of all to me."

"Yes, just shut up, Sigi," I say.

"But he's a doctor," Sigi says.

Dr. Weiss laughs so loud I'm instantly fearful someone will notice. "I've heard that before," he says. "But now I'm a man in a box, growing older and frailer every hour. The way young girls discover themselves is not something I feel up to contemplating these days, do you understand? These discoveries are something the young should share with each other only."

"I felt like telling you," Sigi says. "I wanted you to know. I hoped you could tell us some things. It's hard not knowing, exactly."

"Everything will become clear to you in time," Dr. Weiss says. "That's the way of the world."

I'D TOLD MY FATHER that the Jew has been asking for something strong to drink. My father gave me a half-liter bottle. I've given it to Dr. Weiss. Now I think I hear him drinking. His

Adam's apple must be bobbing. Do his eyes water like mine when I try schnapps? It doesn't matter. Pretty soon his voice is getting higher pitched and less crisp.

"Here's the way of the world," he says after a while. "I had nothing waiting for me in Vienna when I got out of the army. So I went home to Graz, home to my parents. They had a large apartment on the Jungfrauenstrasse. You should have seen us, me and Mother and the primarius. We were dressed in our best around the grand mahogany dining table, fine silver and good linen, faced with only a small mound of potatoes and turnips, and not even any butter for them. We even had a maid serving this mush. You would have laughed. Potatoes and turnips, night after night, insufficiently."

He laughs.

But life, he says, life always finds a way.

"It's working," Sigi murmurs to me.

There was no post in Graz for Dr. Weiss, ex–army surgeon, during the hard winter and rainy spring of 1918–19. There was no schedule to follow, no agenda for the days. Tuesday might as well have been Friday. Every Austrian city had a Café Central, and that is where Dr. Weiss repaired every afternoon, for one cup of poor coffee, one cheap cigar. There were many other patrons his age, probably of similar background and circumstances. No one ever spoke, no one ever introduced himself. It was the etiquette of former officers in defeat. Every man was permitted to carry his own zone of privacy with him.

In the early evenings, Dr. Weiss would stop by a bar near his parents' house for a schnapps or two before dinner. Most nights there was a girl there doing the same. She had red hair. The rules of the café didn't apply to women in a bar, so Dr. Weiss introduced himself. Her name was Rosi Kornfeld, she was twenty-three years old, and she lived two buildings down from his parents', in a big apartment on the second floor.

"The Orphan," his mother said when he'd mentioned the girl between bites of potatoes and turnips. The primarius more or less snorted. "The Kornfelds. They weren't really our sort. People said he was a war profiteer of some kind. He had a factory. Then he had a heart attack. No one knows where the mother went after that."

The primarius made the snorting noise again but concentrated on his turnips.

"The girl," his mother said, "is too fast for her own good. She'll come to a bad end, I'm sure."

You might have expected to meet a plump, blowsy, easily bruised girl in Rosi Kornfeld, Dr. Weiss says. "But she was fine. She had the most delicate ankles, and long fingers. There were thin blue veins on the insides of her forearms. You could see her pulse at her right temple. No matter how much schnapps she drank, her voice never slurred, though it was always a little hoarse."

"The Orphan said 'yes' when I asked," he says.

Once she'd said 'yes,' every evening after dinner Dr. Weiss would tell his parents he was going to the café to meet his old army friends. But he would never reach any café. He had a standing arrangement at moderate expense with the concierge at Rosi's building. He would tap softly at Rosi's door, softly so the neighbors would not hear, and slip into her arms. The first time he was amazed at the casual way she took off all her clothes with the lights bright and blazing, and then lay down on the sofa. He expressed his surprise. And she said, "But you're a doctor!"

Usually just before midnight, he would tiptoe out of Rosi's apartment, walk softly two buildings north, and climb the stairs to his parents'. He would sleep what he thought was the sleep of the just, or at least the self-satisfied. "There isn't much difference, you'll find," he says.

And here is the way of the world: One evening about three months after the affair had begun, Dr. Weiss slipped into Rosi's, took a willowy girl in his arms, cradled a breast in his right hand, and realized the breast was not one he knew. The girl shrieked. Rosi, lounging on the sofa, laughed. "Robert," she said, "I would introduce you to my cousin, but I see you have already met. Should I leave you two alone?"

"Oh, Rosi," said the cousin. She was darker than Rosi, but Dr. Weiss saw a deepening blush. He apologized profusely.

For two weeks Dr. Weiss is celibate. But then the cousin ends her visit and goes back to Innsbruck, where she is studying architecture. He happily resumes his affair with Rosi, who is studious in love if nothing else. They frolic most nights. They drink wine from the same glass. He is fond of the small pink birthmark on her right hip. It has the shape of a rose, he thinks. "And smells as sweet," he says.

"He's drunk," Sigi whispers.

Three months after the cousin's departure from Graz, Dr. Weiss receives an offer of a post in the surgery department at the Innsbruck hospital. He has to accept. There can be no question at all. Rosi understands. Rosi makes it easy for him. She never talks of marriage, or going with him. She's ready for a change herself, it seems.

The Orphan lets him go without fuss, with best wishes, and with the parting present of a small photo of herself in the nude.

He looks up Rosi's cousin when he arrives in Innsbruck. She's engaged to a young architect. But six months later he meets her by chance in the lobby of the Stadttheater during the intermission of *The Cherry Orchard*. She is no longer engaged, he soon learns. Six months after that he marries her in Innsbruck. Rosi was invited, but she only sent flowers.

"What was her name?" Sigi asks. She's so eager she can't sit still.

"Rachel," says the Jew. "What else?"

"I knew it!" says Sigi.

"But now," Dr. Weiss says, "I shout 'Stop!'"

"Oh, no you don't," Sigi says. "You haven't got your heart's desire."

"How do you know that?" Dr. Weiss says.

"Do you think we're stupid just because we're young?"

"So you know my heart's desire? You understand my deepest longings? You've decided I suffer from Weltschmerz?"

"I know that sitting in a box, smelling your own smell, talking with me and Niki is nobody's heart's desire," Sigi says. "Anyway, you're not old enough to die."

"Everyone's old enough to die," the Jew says. "Everyone."

"But what was it you just said? Life always finds a way?" I say.

"The world's changed. Maybe it's not a world I want to live in anymore."

"Who cares what you want?" Sigi says. "You have obligations."

"To whom? My family is God knows where. Everything's destroyed. Who am I obliged to?"

"Us!" Sigi shouts.

"You presume too much, little girl," says the Jew. His voice has a hard tone we haven't heard before. "Let me disabuse you of some things. I operated on Niki only because I couldn't stand the whining and moaning anymore that night. Otherwise it was just another peasant kid likely to die young. So what? What would that have been to me? I'll tell you: Nothing."

"I don't believe that," Sigi says. Dr. Weiss ignores her.

"Cutting out your appendix was so simple, Niki. I could have done that drunk. In fact I was a little drunk that night, to tell the truth. Slice, slice, clamp, sew, sew—presto! Out with the rotten appendix and back to bed for some sleep at last. I was careful to leave the smallest scar I could, though. Patients always feel better with a small scar."

THE NEXT DAY was the worst of my life. Sleep had only troubled me. I dreamed Maria was naked on her sack and the Jew was sneaking up on her with a scalpel in his hand, saying, "This is what we do to peasant kids. Slice, slice, clamp, sew, sew." I wanted to wake and couldn't.

Then at breakfast my grandma poured some milk that had gone off over my farina. When I complained, she sniffed it and said it wasn't that bad. So I had to eat it. My stomach was sour and smoky all morning. I had no wish for lunch.

We were studying right triangles. Kaspar had already said "hypotenuse" and made everyone laugh. Suddenly Fräulein Mumelter stopped midsentence and looked over our heads toward the door. We all looked too. There in the doorway was my mother. She was staring at the teacher. She looked utterly normal, hair neatly pinned, a sweater draped over her shoulders.

"Fräulein Mumelter!" she shouted. "I know what you are up to, you slut!"

Then she folded her arms across her chest. Kaspar giggled. Otherwise there was silence. Fräulein Mumelter placed both palms on her desk. My mother showed no signs of going anywhere. She simply stood. My ears were burning. My head felt big as a balloon. Then I heard Fräulein Mumelter saying softly, "Niki, would you please fetch your father?"

I didn't want to move. But I guessed I had better do as she asked. I slipped out of my seat and edged toward the door. I was afraid of getting too close to my mother. I felt as if I were approaching some wild animal. Finally I dashed the last few feet, dodging around her. I don't think she noticed me at all. Once out the door, I sprinted to the store.

My father came up to my mother in the doorway of the schoolroom and gently took her by the elbow. "Let's go now, Elisabeth," he said. She looked at him as if he were a stranger, but let herself be turned and walked to our house. My father had me run to Pabst the gendarme and ask him to call the doctor in Fussing, who came up that night and gave her a needle of something. He left a little bottle of pills my father was to give my mother three times a day. She mostly slept for several days. And when she came around to herself again, my mother admitted no memory of what she had done. But everyone else never forgot.

7

SOMETIMES IN BED, white sheet tucked up under my chin, breathing easily, drifting over the border into night, I picture The Jew in the Box. It's as if it were a painting, a piece of art with a title. It simply doesn't seem real. There is a living man, used to walking around in the sun—even used to delving into the secret places of bodies—now trapped and blinded by four plank walls. His world is reduced to a glimpse of Sigi and me through a knothole, if we're sitting in the right spot. I see The Jew in the Box very clearly for a moment, and just when I think I have the meaning of it in my mind, I'm asleep. It never follows me into my dreams.

But Maria Stocker often does, with her bunched-up skirt, her absent gaze. And now, more and more, so does Sigi, but in a completely different way. Maria is turbulent. Sigi is fine. Sigi shimmers differently for me. I wake up eased by Sigi, unsettled by Maria. And there are regular visitors: my father and mother, Big Ignatz, the brown men from Fussing, soldiers I have never seen. I dream also of Fräulein Mumelter. She's recognized me, she's picked me out specially. I can't see her clearly; I only sense that she's naked. But I'm sure no one else has ever seen her that way. She was waiting just for me. We don't touch. She simply shows herself to me, and that's enough. Sometimes I imagine that I write a poem to Fräulein Mumelter, and in front of everyone, she tells me how beautiful it is.

I feel that my dreams are getting out of hand. My grandma says I look hag-ridden. It's harder to recognize myself in the mirror each morning.

And I feel so queer. There's a sense of things going wrong. There's an understanding that all the barriers are down, that there's no safe place. It's the feeling I had once standing at the very edge of a sheer drop on Kirchspitz, nothing between me and an endless fall but my sense of balance and some luck with the wind.

The Jew's no help. He tells me yes, the sky can surely fall. Yes, the worst demons in your mind can appear in person before you. Yes, things more horrible than you can imagine can happen, are even bound to happen, if not to you then to the other fellow. But you have to pretend you don't possess this knowledge, he says. Otherwise you couldn't live a single sane, untroubled hour.

My grandma is after me to pray more often and go to confession twice a week whether I need to or not, just as she does. But I don't feel right telling that devious priest what I ate for lunch, let alone my secret thoughts.

I'm beginning to understand part of why I am afraid. I see something happening to my father. Martin Lukasser is well known as a substantial man. He has heft. He has to be paid the proper attention. Now he hasn't lost any weight, he still works as hard as ever and speaks as well at town discussions. But my father is becoming airy and spare. He is drifting like snow in the wind. His presence is somehow thinner. Any day now, I fear, I will be able to see right through him. I overhear people wondering what is wrong with Martin. Cancer? Let's hope not, they say.

It's not cancer. It's the weight of the world. It's my mother, the Jew, my dead brothers and sisters, me.

So he jettisons the Jew. He acts as if there is no man in our loft. He never speaks of him. If it weren't for me and Sigi, Dr. Weiss would be forgotten and starved. My father looks at me quizzically when I ask for things like schnapps, as if he supposes I want them for myself. Dr. Weiss has become entirely my duty. He doesn't realize on whom he depends.

My father believes very much in the value of good opinions. Nothing is worth more to you in life, he'd said to me many times, than the good opinion of your neighbors. Never do anything, Niki, that will cause people to speak badly of you.

So how must my father feel about my mother, doing what she did? She did the worst: she let the family down before everyone. But I don't hear him reproach her for it. He never says one thing. He's solicitous, anxious to please her and ease her. He's kind. And yet that kindness makes him less formidable to me, in a way I wish hadn't happened until I was older.

Still, my father is not yet so diminished that people feel free to say out loud what they are thinking about my mother. But I know they talk about it at home, over their supper tables. They are saying my mother is raving mad, she's gone out of her mind. But maybe, they're saying, she's not entirely unhinged. Maybe that dog Lukasser is actually having it off with the teacher. She's got the tits and the ass for it, no question.

At school the kids are wary of me for days after my mother's astonishing performance. It's as if I'm infectious with chicken pox or ringworm. No one wants to get near me or talk to me. What would they say? "Hey, Niki, your father find a straitjacket for your mother yet?" "Hey, Niki, are you building a padded room in your house?"

I sit there not paying any attention to my studies, mooning over Fräulein Mumelter even though I'm humiliated to be in her presence. I'm wishing Sigi could move in with me. I'd like to sleep next to her at night. Hearing her regular breathing would soothe me. If I had a bad dream she could hold me. Or vice versa. But Sigi claims she never dreams.

8

THE VISION loosed by my mother of Fräulein Mumelter, un-
bound and amorous, terrified every married woman in Sankt
Vero. They crossed themselves repeatedly. They locked up their
men tight as they could. The bar lost all its evening business.
Wives questioned husbands to within an inch of their lives.
Even Big Ignatz shuffled about like a whipped dog. Innocence
was no defense. They were all found guilty of impure thoughts
at least. My mother had chucked the largest stone into such a
small pond that the bad feelings spread in waves, not ripples.
The men resented my father for failing to keep his wife under
control. They resented even more that my father might have
been the one who got the Mumelter, though some swore
Lukasser hadn't the juice to do it. The wives began resenting
youth, and sex in general.

At first no one seemed to consider that Fräulein Mumelter
might be no slut at all. Only days later, when it became clear my
mother had no memory of what she'd done, and no grudge
against the teacher, did anyone stop to think. Half the town saw
my mother wave and call out *"Grüss Gott"* to Fräulein Mumelter
as she entered the school one morning, and the other half heard
about it before lunch. The words "hysterical fit" began to be

heard, and "Poor Frau Lukasser." But people didn't feel like letting the young teacher entirely off the hook. She was too at-
tractive to let go of. People wanted to linger awhile over the
dubious question of her "influence."

Our Mayor Ausserhofer had a fine nose for public sentiment.
Or so my father said, explaining how he'd been elected five times
with five different kinds of promises. What the mayor smelled
now was disappointment that a scandal hadn't fully ripened. He
knew how to handle this. He called a town meeting.

At seven on the appointed night, parents trooped into the
schoolroom and wedged themselves into our benches. Fräulein
Mumelter stayed in her apartment, naturally. My mother also
stayed home. We students were not permitted to attend, but Sigi,
Kaspar, Simon, Andreas, and I all snitched glasses from our
kitchens. We placed their mouths against the thin wall under the
schoolroom's south window, and our ears against their ends. We
could hear everything as clearly as if we'd been hiding inside in
the cloakroom. As Kurt Cammer (two grades below us) was, and
caught and beaten for it too.

The mayor rumbled and rattled. He danced all around the Incident, as my mother's strafe of the teacher was known, without
mentioning either my mother's name or Fräulein Mumelter's. This
amazing feat was achieved by his substitution of the phrase "and
so on" for the statement of any fact that had been gossiped about.
Which meant he hardly had to say anything at all beyond "the
Incident that occurred" and the fact that anyone who wished to
say something about the Incident should feel free to do so. There
was light applause when he finished.

We heard the priest first. He was so fond of his voice. "I only
want to say one thing. I shall be brief and to the point, no elab-
orate metaphors, so don't look for any; after all, I'm not at the pul-

pit here. I'm speaking not as spiritual adviser but strictly as a friend to this village," he said.

Now he was warmed up. "I have monitored Fräulein Mumelter's religion classes on many occasions. Yes, and I may say with great interest, because after all this is my special area, I don't need to tell you," he went on. "And I have found them beyond reproach. Knowing what I know of her character and personality, I can only presume Fräulein Mumelter's conscience is clear in terms of the Incident.

"And I would like to remind you all," the priest concluded, "that Fräulein Mumelter is not Caesar's wife, if you please."

"She's nobody's wife, that's the problem! That's why she's got her eye on our husbands," snapped Frau Stocker.

"Oh, certainly on yours," said Frau Egger, Simon's mother.

"As likely mine as any other," Frau Stocker said angrily.

"No no no, you've missed my point," said the priest.

"Point is, has she done it with any man here or not?" said Big Ignatz. There was a hissing sound, and calls of "shame, shame" from the women. "If she has, where's the proof? Who's admitting to it? Come on. I don't know any man here she's gone with. If she hasn't, why bother with all this talk? She does her job, don't she?"

"Good for you, squarehead," Sigi murmured. I was feeling fond of him too. Then I remembered him and his spotting scope the night before Kaspar's fall. I spat.

"She did or she didn't doesn't matter, if people think she did. Or would," said Herr Egger.

"I'm bound to say that the lessons have been better since Fräulein Mumelter's been here. I've always found her perfectly proper," said Frau Tscharnigg, Andreas's mother. The whole village knew she was a fine judge of proper. A few years earlier, Tscharnigg sold a piece of land up the mountain to the Power Authority for an indecent price and that winter gave his wife a fox coat for Christmas. The story was she ran around the house all day wearing the coat and nothing else, and dragged her husband back to bed at least twice.

"You see your mom's tits that time? Were they saggy?" Kaspar asked.

"Eat shit, Kaspar," Andreas said.

"She may teach all right, but her skirts are too short," said Frau Stocker.

"Not as short as Maria's," said Frau Tscharnigg.

"She's just a girl!" said Frau Stocker.

"You'd better have another look," said Frau Hutter, the mother of Monika, who was the first in our class to get any pubic hair and showed it to everyone, boys as well as girls.

"Ladies, ladies. This isn't the issue," said the mayor.

"Isn't it? Maria looks like she needs a husband as badly as someone else we won't name," said Andreas's mother.

"What's that supposed to mean, Frau Tscharnigg?" Frau Stocker said.

"This is all a lot of crap," said Big Ignatz. "Nobody's got a shred of evidence of anything. Leave the teacher in peace, for Christ's sake, and put Maria in longer skirts before she gets knocked up. Do the kids learn their lessons or not?"

"Mind your thoughts!" said Frau Stocker.

"They seem to do very well," said Sigi's mother. "Even Sigi."

"Oh, thanks," Sigi murmured.

"Yes, they are quite proficient," said the priest.

"Simon's most proficient at jerking off," Kaspar said.

"Eat shit," Simon said.

There was a lot of talking back and forth about how we were doing. Some parents became a bit boastful about their children.

Nobody claimed a child had got duller under Fräulein Mumelter's tutelage. I could hear Big Ignatz grumbling about proof, and a lot of hissed "shames" apparently heaped on him. "Wash your mouth, Ignatz!" called Frau Egger. Frau Tscharnigg laughed her braying laugh.

The mayor's instincts did not betray him. "I take it," he said, when the noise had settled a bit, "that we all agree the Incident was unfortunate but that there is really no reason for any action? That she is in fact blameless? I take it we would be happy to have her continue in her post? May I see a show of hands on that? Good.

"So she stays," said the mayor after a moment, having managed to avoid saying "Fräulein Mumelter" even once. We heard the scraping and shuffling of people getting up to leave.

"Just a minute, please," the mayor called. "Got something very important in the way of news. I've been informed by the civil defense authorities in Salzburg that the Wehrmacht is sending up a team of spotters to Sankt Vero. Their job will be to watch for planes coming up over the mountains from the south and radio their directions ahead to Innsbruck, Salzburg, and so on. They tell me it's an important job. We've got to billet the soldiers. There will be four or five of them. Anybody wants to volunteer, see me tomorrow. If we don't get enough volunteers, I'll have to allocate based on who's got space."

"Do we get paid?" asked Big Ignatz.

"Of course; a per diem and so on," said the mayor.

There was a lot of muttering about how many marks might make a per diem, and anyway who wanted soldiers most likely wrecking the sheets by sleeping with their boots on? There was more scraping and shuffling as people unwedged themselves and moved toward the door. We took off into the darkness. Andreas and Simon one way, Kaspar another, and me and Sigi round the back and past the barns toward her place.

"I would like to lift up Fräulein Mumelter's hair and press my nose against the back of her neck. I'd like to really smell her," Sigi says as we're walking up to her door.

"Like this?" I say, lifting Sigi's thick pigtail and touching the fine skin beneath. I expect her to shy away, but she stands absolutely still while I sniff. She smells like fresh-made butter.

"Yes, just like that," Sigi says, breaking away and stumbling as she does, so that she winds up falling on a soggy pile of old snow beside her stoop. She looks a little confused, as she always does when she takes an unexpected tumble. But she's laughing when I help her up and guide her right hand to the door latch.

"I can find the latch myself," she says.

"I know," I say.

I stand there watching until she's shut the door behind her. We fed the Jew before the meeting, so I can go straight home once Sigi's safe inside. I go in a hurry, to get past the red lights in the graveyard, which from Sigi's side cast a glow on the piles of skulls and bones in the open ossuary. The bones are taken out and piled there when a family's graves get too full. Graves can only hold so many, you know. In another twenty or thirty years, my brothers may have to come out to make room for my parents. They'll go in the pile like everyone else, though they'll be smaller than most.

I'M JUST AS GLAD to go home instead of to the barn. It's different with the Jew ever since he said he didn't care if I lived or died. I don't much feel like talking to him. He's got too dark, too harsh. Whenever I leave the loft now after taking him his food, I feel a little afraid in ways I never did before. He's taken some of my faith in life. That's what it feels like. He's stolen something I needed.

Sigi says it's just a mood. She says the Jew was drunk when he talked about that slice, slice, sew, sew business in my belly. He's got his reasons to be short-tempered, she says. I can't argue with that. And, Sigi says, he's tried to apologize in his way, or at least explain.

I suppose you could say so.

"Do you know why I was drunk and cranky the night I took out your appendix? Of course you don't," Dr. Weiss said the night after my mother had appeared in the schoolroom door and shouted at Fräulein Mumelter. "I'm drunk on that night every year, and have been since 1917. It's the anniversary of the thing I most regret in my life. The ugliest thing."

In 1917, he said, the soldiers were tired, they were depressed. Some of them shot themselves as a way of getting out of the fighting. That was a risky thing. You could be court-martialed. And no bullet wound is ever safe.

So a soldier shot himself in the foot one night. No, he was not some cherubic-looking Slovenian peasant boy, pining for his cows and his mother. He was a hard case, nearly thirty, who had been in trouble before the war, possibly even served some time in prison. He should have known better than to do what he did.

"It was stupid entirely," said Dr. Weiss. "First, he held the rifle so close there were powder burns all over his boot, the first sign a sniper hadn't got him. On top of that, he didn't shoot at his toes for a clean wound. He fired straight down through his instep. The bullet utterly shattered the foot.

"The fool must have wanted a bad wound, one which would guarantee he wouldn't just be patched up and sent back to the front. He finished his sentry duty somehow before he told his officer he was shot. How he bore the pain I'll never know. But by the time he got to the aid station, that foot was a bloody mess. The doctors there did what they could and sent him back to the hospital where I was working."

The soldier was chained to his bed. Some days went by. It was such a nasty, splintery wound. A court-martial was held, which he attended in a wheelchair. He was found guilty and sentenced to the usual, in seven days, at dawn. "It was believed useful," Dr. Weiss said, "to give the convicted time to ponder their crimes."

The day the court-martial adjourned, Dr. Weiss examined the man's foot during his evening rounds. He could smell the gangrene before he got the bandage off. "It's worse than the smell of death," he said. He told his major that the man would be dead within three days if nothing was done. The major consulted the colonel in charge of the hospital. The colonel ordered that the man must be kept alive, so that he could be executed by firing squad as the court-martial had decreed.

"They told me to amputate his foot." And Dr. Weiss paused. "I did.

"He thanked me for it. He never believed they'd shoot a man whose foot had been cut off. So he lived long enough to be shot. I saw it. He looked very surprised," the doctor said. "Hell, he deserved to be shot; he was a hard case. Still, every year on that night I get drunk. And I suppose I will until I die."

"You could have just refused to do it," I said when he'd finished. Sigi punched me in the ribs. I didn't care. I was still angry with the Jew.

"Yes, you're right," Dr. Weiss said. "I could have just refused." That was all he said.

I felt frustrated. I wanted to argue, I wanted to clash. But later, when I realized the depth of it, I admired him for that silence. And although I still felt bad blood, I was relieved and grateful that he didn't laugh when Sigi raced through every humiliating detail of my mother's fit and how it flustered the women of the village and angered all the men.

"Sometimes when they are under a lot of mental pressure, people lose their connection with the real world for a little bit," Dr. Weiss said. "They're not deliberately trying to ruin anything or embarrass anyone. They literally do not know what they are doing, because they've temporarily lost their ability to see the world as the rest of us see it."

He did laugh like anything when we told him about the town meeting, though. "I would have liked to see this Ignatz fellow in action," he said. "I'm thinking perhaps your Fräulein may actually be a slut and Big Ignatz is the one who knows for sure."

Just like that, he undid the good. It seemed so careless. He'd no need to offend us. But now it was Sigi's turn to get cross. "You don't know anything," she said. "She'd never have anything to do with a coarse man like Ignatz."

"So you say, Sigi," he said. "But you might be surprised."

So smug, I felt like saying. But who's in the box, Doctor? Who's so bitter? For the first time, I began to get impatient listening to the Jew. I began to think that maybe his stories of this and that in Vienna or this and that in Venice weren't really any more interesting than real life right here.

Here, although one day seemed much like another, life looped and twisted and leaped up all around us. Anyone could see it.

My father and Big Ignatz began planning a secret trip over the mountain to meet their Italian friend with all the coffee and sugar. One morning Frau Egger appeared on the streets with a bruised eye. Kaspar and Simon found Maria Stocker in the shed riding the flour sacks, just as I had. They were so excited. Fräulein Mumelter began receiving letters every couple of days from Schwaz. The handwriting looked masculine, according to everyone the postman showed the envelopes to. My mother had suddenly started cooking my father's favorite dishes, like dumplings and sauerkraut, for lunch each day. And pretty soon, Sigi got closer to Fräulein Mumelter than she'd ever dreamed of being. Well, maybe she dreamed of closer things. But she didn't tell me and I don't want to think about it. It's too confusing, what with everything else that went on.

FRÄULEIN MUMELTER pays a call on Sigi's mother one Saturday afternoon. They sit on the bench at the kitchen table and sip ersatz coffee. No cake, though. Sigi and I are perched on the first-floor landing, eavesdropping. There is, we hear Fräulein Mumelter say to Frau Strolz, "a budding problem. Not with school as such, no. Sigi does better than we have a right to expect in that regard.

"I thought we should speak of it confidentially," Fräulein Mumelter goes on. "I'll be brief: it's Sigi's clothes."

"Sigi's clothes," says Frau Strolz.

"They are, I must tell you, too small," Fräulein Mumelter says softly.

"Too small?"

"Sigi, as you know, is becoming a woman. She is developing. To be awfully frank," Fräulein Mumelter says confidingly, "boys in the class are beginning to stare at her chest because her blouses are too tight, and they are also looking at her behind and her legs, because of the short skirts. I've come to ask if Sigi can't be provided with things of a more appropriate size."

Sigi's trying so hard to suppress her giggling that little tears start to leak out of her blank eyes. When they shine with tears like that, it's impossible to think that she sees nothing through them. They look so alive. They are such a pretty shade of green. I think maybe the giggling is a nervous reaction. I think Sigi's mortified to hear herself described that way.

"Well, things are rather hard, Fräulein," Sigi's mother says. "It's not so easy to buy the things she needs. I would like to, naturally, but . . ."

"Frau Strolz, permit me, I understand. But I have a proposal. Surely you have one or two things in the closet that could be altered down to fit her? I myself have a nice woolen dress which has become too small for me. With some alterations, it could easily be made to fit Sigi."

"We couldn't accept that, Fräulein."

"Please. Otherwise it will go to the Winter Relief."

So it's agreed that Sigi will be outfitted. I get my mother to contribute a loden skirt that's spent my lifetime wrapped in tissue in a cedar chest, and some cotton blouses that aren't too badly worn.

Next Saturday morning Sigi's standing in the middle of the kitchen on a big wooden bucket turned upside down. She's wearing a white slip, which has to be clean but looks dingy with age. It only comes to the middle of her thighs. Her pigtail has been pinned up.

Sigi's interested. She wants to look good. She feels the fabrics delicately, she judges the feel of them favorably. She inquires about the colors. She isn't satisfied with "blue." She has to be told it's that certain blue the pools in the stream have on clear days in August when the water level is low. The cuts, too, she can only imagine, though everything feels looser than she's recently used to. "We'll keep it a little baggy in the front," Sigi's mother says at one point, inserting pins here and there. "You're only going to get bigger, Sigi."

"Do I have to?" Sigi said.

"Afraid so," said Fräulein Mumelter. "You'll be pleased, though."

When Fräulein Mumelter is pinning the loden skirt my mother gave, her hands are brushing Sigi's bottom and the backs of her thighs. It can't mean anything; it just happens when you're tailoring clothes. Sigi's slight nipples jut. I can see them pucker the thin fabric of the slip. I can see her face flushing. She begins to twist the slim silver ring she always wears on her little finger.

"Niki, you can't hang around here all morning," Sigi's mother says, not even looking up from the newly altered blouse she's ironing. "Your father will be cross. Get over to the store and make yourself useful."

I feel banished. I should be helping my father, but I don't go to the store. I go into Sigi's barn. Shafts of sunlight make dusty columns, just like they do in church. Near the back there's a big old feed box, completely empty. I decide to see what it's like to be the Jew. I open the feed box, climb in, and lower the lid. It's big enough that I can either sit up or lie down. I lie down.

It's a warming spring day, changeable. It's the spring of 1944. I'm just fourteen. I can't see anything except some very slender streaks of dusty light, which dapple me. I can feel the texture of the wood. It's dry, splintery. There's a smell of straw and oats, slightly toasted. It's not bad in here. It's peaceful. I'm thinking about Sigi in that little slip, and somehow she becomes Fräulein Mumelter in a little slip. I'd like to hold on to this, but I'm drowsy; my thoughts fade one into the other. Then I'm asleep. In my sleep, I'm alone in the schoolroom. I go to the blackboard and start to write, not knowing what I'll write. Suddenly I feel I have the answer to all my problems: with my father and mother, with the Jew, with Sigi and Fräulein Mumelter, even with the war and everything. It's all so simple, one thing follows the other like clockwork, I must be an idiot for not seeing it before. But the moment I awake, it all tumbles back into a mess, and nothing is clear at all.

It takes me a moment to realize I'm in a box. I look at my grandfather's pocket watch. I can just make out the hands. I've only been asleep an hour. I decide I must stay there at least another hour. Within a few minutes my legs begin to twitch slightly, the way they do on nights when you've gone to bed very tense. I feel as if dust and spiders are falling on my face, but there's nothing there when I wipe. My head begins to feel bigger than normal, and I feel small inside it. I can hear the blood surging in my ears. It's too warm. I think: In forty-five more minutes I can climb out and see the mountains rising all around.

But I don't last another five. I shove back the lid, leap out, and run. There's a lowering sky. I can't see a single peak, just rows of dark pines marching upward into the mist. But that's enough. That's better than the damn box.

ONE MORNING there's a notice posted outside the village clerk's office. It starts *Achtung!* as they all do, even the mildest ones, and announces that four soldiers and one sergeant will arrive in the village June 1 and will be billeted as follows:

Stocker: one sergeant
Egger: one soldier
Cammer: one soldier
Hutter: two soldiers

It's signed Mayor Ausserhofer.

So Maria Stocker gets one and Monika Hutter gets two. I'm glad Sigi didn't get one, even though her mother could have used the money. But I'm vexed and fretful about soldiers coming anyway.

The unit arrives in a little green truck that looks like an ambulance. They're going to keep their equipment in my father's storeroom. I watch them unload three big wooden tripods and three leather cases that look like they're for trumpets. But I soon see they hold huge binoculars. They are bigger even than those the U-boat commanders have slung around their necks in photos you see in *Signal* magazine. The soldiers are in uniform, of course, but bareheaded as they work, and it's the haircuts that get our attention. The sergeant's head is close cropped all over, but the young soldiers have their hair shaved only on the sides and back, and left very long on the top. It's a style we've never seen in person before. The boys here mostly have bowl cuts. Within a week every boy in the village who can has convinced his mother to cut his hair that way. Andreas and Kaspar are the first. My mother refuses.

My father is amiable with the soldiers. He even has a schnapps with the sergeant when the gear has been stowed, and unlimbers an old war story or two of his own. The sergeant listens patiently. My guess is that throughout his military career, civilians have tried to tell him about their army days. The sergeant most likely finds them boring but tolerable, as long as they buy the schnapps.

Yet when the soldiers have dispersed to their billets, my father seems agitated. The idea of troops in the village, even a few plane spotters, seems to alarm him considerably. "I've never seen a plane overhead, have you?" my father asks all his friends who drop by the store to get the gossip on the soldiers. "Why do they think we're going to start seeing them now? I wonder. Surely it's too far for the planes to fly."

It wasn't too far, in the end.

I have to report this sinister news to Dr. Weiss that evening. I am worried about telling him we have soldiers here now. He's full of questions. He wants to know about their badges, their equipment, their weapons. Yet it seems that Dr. Weiss isn't perturbed by the soldiers, who after all have no interest in him since they don't know he exists. It wouldn't even cross their minds that he was here, he reckons. "It's the police, not the military, that one always needs to be wary of," he says. "They're devious bastards, every one. They think there's a murderer under every bed, a rapist in every closet."

But then he just has to surprise us.

"Men who fly are insane," he says out of the blue. "They'll do insane things. In normal times they would all be locked in asylums."

"These men aren't fliers," Sigi says.

"Ah," says Dr. Weiss. "But the ones they're here to look for are."

9

"TIME TO MAKE THE TRADE, Martin," says Big Ignatz. He has a low, impudent way of saying my father's name, which my father never notes. "Time to ship the goods over the border."

But we're already over the border, we've already moved the goods. We're in the mouth of a tunnel blasted through a living peak by soldiers in the last war. It's so high we hear faint music where there is no sound at all. It's the emptiest place on earth at night. Not a tree, not a bush, not a stick or a flower. Just pale-yellow stone, so still, just cold air flowing like rivers and streams. And the fugitive shadow of a corvo sailing under the sickle moon.

We can't show a match, or the red glow of a cigarette coal. Any light at all could be seen for miles up here, and there are sometimes border patrols.

There's an Italian with us in the mouth of the tunnel. He's called Gision. His name guarantees he's a northerner, our kind, a man of the mountains, not any macaroni from the plains. I'm here because I can now carry fifteen kilos up and down, nine hours each way. That's fifteen more than my father and Ignatz could carry on their own. That's my value: fifteen kilos. If you measure that in coffee, it's a lot. The Italian has a mule worth even more, I think.

My father has been dealing with this Gision for at least ten years. Big Ignatz has been in on the trade ever since he quit the brown men. It's just a little trafficking, nothing serious. My grandfather smuggled, and he said his grandfather did it too. And so did all the Lukassers back to the first one in Sankt Vero. That would have been in, oh, 1633 or '34, my granddad said. This night we've done the business: Italian coffee and sugar and canned peaches pushed over to us, raw spirits and matches, six sticks of dynamite, and a box of .30 rifle shells Ignatz obtained with his hunting license pushed over to Gision. He's loading his mule. So what does Big Ignatz mean when he says it's time? Why is he squatting there on the cold rock, with his hunting rifle cradled in his meaty hands? He usually carries the rifle only in the autumn, when there's a chance of a chamois on the way home.

"How about a Jew, Gision?" my father says.

It's the shock of my life, my father exposing Dr. Weiss to two outsiders. I want to clap my hand over his mouth to keep him from saying anything more, but I'm stunned.

"Too heavy to carry," said Gision.

"I'm serious. I've got a Jew."

"Good for you. So keep him. What do I want with a Jew?"

"Take him down to a town, that's all. A favor to me."

"Martin, I can't do that. Don't you know anything in that godforsaken country of yours? All our towns are now occupied by German troops. He'd have to stay up in the mountains with the partisans."

"So take him to the partisans, eh, Gision?" said Ignatz.

"What for? What good is he? Another mouth, that's all."

"He's a surgeon," my father says. "Military background. Knows how to treat wounds."

"Ah, that's something. A surgeon," says Gision, leaving the

mule and squatting with us. "A military surgeon, you say. How long have you had him?"

My father explains the Jew's situation, his arrival, how he's been kept since.

"Decent food?" Gision asks.

"Same as we eat," my father says.

"But how long in that box?"

"About sixteen months."

"That's bad, bad. Never outside, never any exercise?"

"No, it's too risky."

"We can't take him," Gision says after a moment.

"Why not? He's a surgeon. He could help you," Ignatz says.

"Help us? He'd die up here in a week. The man's not walked in sixteen months. Do you really think he could keep up with us?"

"Shit," said Big Ignatz. He repeated this at intervals all the way back down the mountain. "We should have tried this sixteen months ago."

"There weren't any partisans to take him to sixteen months ago," my father said.

"And there weren't any Germans in the Italian towns sixteen months ago, either, Martin."

There was the sickle moon above and the ragged trail beneath my boots. I began thinking of killing Big Ignatz. I'd do it up here on the mountain, where it could be made to look like an accident. I was feeling that our Jew had been betrayed, that Ignatz was somehow a threat now to all of us, and that he had to go. I looked for treacherous spots where I might push or trip him into a fatal fall. But he weighed twice what I did, he was solid on the path ahead, he was experienced. He could easily kill me. One-handed, most likely. He'd never even have to unsling the rifle that now rode barrel down across his back.

"You didn't have to be part of this, Ignatz," my father said.

"Didn't I? Once you blabbed you had the damn Jew, you nailed me, Martin. I was part of it whether I wanted to be or not. Ain't that so, Martin?"

"I suppose you're right," my father said.

"Damn right. So don't go faulting me for wanting to find a way out for us."

"No, no fault," my father said.

When we were in sight of my house and splitting up, that goddamn Ignatz patted me on the ass! "Nice going, Niki," he said. It was a lingering sort of pat. I didn't do anything. I just stood there, speechless and ashamed.

But I told myself I'd come down from the mountain different from our try to trade the Jew up among the yellow rock and the rivers of air. I'd come down a step ahead. The world was exactly the same, but my place in it had changed. There'd been a crossing, I felt sure. I could stand in a new way before my father. He'd seen me march for nine hours with fifteen kilos in my rucksack, he'd seen me watch the trading and figure the rates, he knew I was thinking hard about Ignatz and the Jew. He knew I was ready now to question his decisions. He wouldn't be angry. I expected him to see the change as clearly as I did.

I slept most of the next day. Toward evening, before supper, I hung around the store until it was empty. Then I went up to my father and looked him in the face. He was organizing a box of can and bottle openers. It was a little while before he looked up at me. "So Ignatz knows?" I asked.

"Why ask? You saw so, didn't you?" my father replied.

"Since when?"

"Since Weiss arrived, or a little bit after."

"Why?"

"I didn't want to be entirely alone in this."

"You weren't. You had us."

"Yes, but I needed an ally outside the family."

"Who else knows?"

"No one."

"Not even Hilde?"

"Ignatz says not."

"Why didn't you tell me?

"The fewer who knew things the better. Just in case."

"You trust Ignatz?"

"Yes," my father said. "To a certain extent."

"I don't think you should," I said.

"You don't know what you're talking about," my father said. "And that's always an excellent reason to shut up."

I turned and left the store. As soon as I was outside I began to cry, and hated myself for it.

I told Sigi. She was disgusted by all of it, of course, though she did chuckle at Ignatz's pat and even asked if it felt good, little bitch. She made me swear not to tell Dr. Weiss that we'd tried to give him to the Italians. If I was worth fifteen kilos, much less than a mule, Sigi said, then it seemed that on the current market our Jew had no value at all. This was not, she said, something that would cheer him.

So we don't tell him. And nothing changes, after all. Even though there are soldiers in town and a Jew in our barn, we spend the summer the way we always have. I help my father with the store and the cows, Andreas works in his father's inn, Simon goes down to Fussing to work for his uncle the plumber. Only Kaspar does anything new: he goes to work for Ignatz, hauling and stacking sawed timber. But on many days in June and again in August, we all have to help with the haymaking.

"Haymaking?" says Dr. Weiss. It's the very start of the season, not long after our trip up the mountain and back. It's staying light now until after nine, and the sun's glimmering by three in the morning. He can smell the new season in his box. He's got to be restless. He'd give anything to join us in the pastures; I can feel this so strongly. But there's nothing I can do.

"I myself would rather waltz," says the doctor. "I wish I could waltz outdoors. I was enthusiastic, especially after a glass or two of something. I waltzed for hours on my wedding day."

"You were probably dreadful," I say.

"Almost certainly," the doctor said cheerfully. "But I had fun."

"They waltz all night here," Sigi says. "They haven't any choice, really, because the custom is that the bride and groom's bedroom furniture is stolen and put outside."

"They don't do quite that in Innsbruck," Dr. Weiss says. "We didn't have a large wedding, just a dozen or so friends. We went to an inn for lunch after the papers were signed. There was a violinist there who must have been in his eighties, but he was indefatigable. He played and played. We drank new wine. We danced. We danced in the garden under the linden trees. Rachel's breath smelled like ripe apples. Her hand was perfectly cool and dry.

"Our honeymoon was one night at the Schloss Arnstein. We had a suite overlooking the valley of the Inn. I didn't sleep at all. I spent hours at the window, looking at the moonlight traversing the valley. Then I'd lie beside Rachel, listening to her breathe. I watched her face in the moonlight. Her mouth was slightly open. Her teeth were small, very white.

"Rachel pulled the covers over her face when she awoke to find me staring at her. She was a very shy girl in every way, and she stayed shy all through our marriage," Dr. Weiss said. "At first

I tried to break down that barrier. I saw it as a barrier, for a while. Later I realized physical shyness suited her. I don't think I would have understood her any other way."

"How could you understand someone who hides from you?" Sigi asks.

"By not trying so hard to see what's hidden. By concentrating on what isn't and allowing an area of unknown to exist unmolested," says the doctor.

I think the doctor has too much time on his hands. I think he's getting loose-minded. He's losing the surgeon's precision. Sigi says no. She feels he is revealing sides of himself no one else has ever seen, because he trusts us. She's proud of this. And she says she is learning so much. About what?

"About the way men and women are with each other," Sigi says.

"How Jews are with one another," I say.

"No difference," she says. "And about love."

But she doesn't mention me in this. She doesn't even hint. Well, in that case I don't want to hear any more about love. Love's not for me. Already there are rumors about Maria Stocker and one of the young soldiers, a Rhinelander named Alois. If they are meeting, though, we know it's not in the Stockers' shed, because Simon and I have been keeping a lookout there as much as we can, just to see what we might see.

But there are so many hours for mischief, aren't there? There must be a million ways to get up to it. More and more I feel this. I feel the world widening.

THE SOLDIERS are mostly quiet. But they unsettle the village anyway. Really, the soldiers have no interest in us at all, except Alois in Maria, which really can't be confirmed. They keep to themselves. No connections are made. They do their job. They drink at one table in the bar and never say more than a polite "good evening" to anyone else there. No card games, no war stories. Maria Stocker says the sergeant snores like a locomotive.

We'd see them all day when we were haymaking, marching high above us around the bowl formed by the various peaks. They were looking for places to establish their spotting posts. It was not such an easy proposition. The spots must be high enough so that no significant portion of sky was blocked by peaks, but it mustn't be too high or too exposed. Soldiers would have to man the posts even when there were six meters of snow, and they would have to be supplied. I was in the store one day when the squad came in with the big tripod they lugged everywhere and the sour looks of another unsuccessful day. "Goddamn fuck," snarled the sergeant. "This place is shit."

There were perfect places, of course, winter barns set just beneath ridges and cozy as you'd want even in the deep snow. But nobody felt like showing the soldiers where they were. These ordinary barns became a secret nobody wanted strangers to know. They became a way of keeping outsiders outside. The mayor said he was tempted to step in. He owned the bar and was glad of the extra business. But eventually he reckoned the soldiers would drink more unhappy than happy, so he didn't tell them about the barns, either.

We're up at dawn on haymaking days, and the soldiers are out and above before us. They're probably making bitter jokes about peasants as they hike. Sigi always comes along with me. She can't do a thing, of course. She just sits there on the green slopes listening to the swishing of the scythes, the buzzing of the insects. She likes the fresh smell. Some of the littler girls bring her wildflowers, which she must braid into garlands for them. She wishes they wouldn't do this. "It's embarrassing," she says. "It's like some stupid scene in a children's book. The good witch Sigi with the happy mountain children. I'd rather boil them with toads."

At the end of the day Sigi has a stunt she's done since she was small. She lies down, tucks her arms to her sides, and simply rolls down the hill to the bottom. Most of us liked to do that when we were kids. But I tried it once with my eyes closed, just to know what it was like for Sigi, and nearly got sick. I got badly scared too. It felt so out of control, this rolling blind. You had to worry about a rock or a stray pitchfork in the way, and what it would feel like if you hit one.

Sigi hasn't any fear of such things. She is afraid of fire, but not much else. She'll climb like a monkey, and she gets the chance. Once a farmer has half filled a barn, he invites all the kids to climb up into the rafters and jump into the hay, to pack it down and make room for more. I spent days and days leaping wildly from the beams, a handkerchief tied around my face like a bandit's against the dust. I haven't done it the last few years. But Sigi still leaps. Sigi is a most enthusiastic jumper. She'll trust anyone to help her up to the highest rafters and say which way to go. Then she just flies. She launches herself, arms outstretched, with a gleeful shriek that changes to laughter as soon as she hits the hay. "Did you see me, Niki?" she calls. "Did you see me fly?"

Sigi leaps because it makes her world brighter. "All the time everything's a dull brown," she says. "It turns red when I'm flying, though."

Sigi didn't go blind until she was three, so she remembers some colors and the way they made her feel.

This summer Sigi's best time isn't leaping, but lunch. Usually the schoolteacher goes home during the summer. Fräulein

Mumelter did the first two. But this year she stays. She says things about the difficulty of travel, due to the war. So each day Fräulein Mumelter comes to help with the haymaking. She brings her lunch in an old flour sack just like the rest of us. She usually has black bread, a bit of cheese, and a cold potato.

Fräulein Mumelter can't sit with the farmers; it wouldn't look right. She can't sit with their wives and the other women, either, because there's a sort of distance a teacher must maintain. She really can only sit with her students, and mainly she sits with me and Sigi, since we're the oldest. Sigi is delighted. She cups her face in her hands and smiles her biggest smile. She's bursting with questions. She knows there are limits, because after all Fräulein Mumelter is the teacher. But now, in the casual atmosphere of haymaking, Sigi reckons she can take some chances.

She begins at the beginning, but right away loses any idea of when to stop. "Where do you come from, Fräulein," she starts. "Where were you before you came up here? Where are your parents?" And she continues: "Do you have any brothers and sisters? Where are they? And where did you go to school? Have you been to any big places, like Salzburg or Vienna?"

"That's ridiculous," Fräulein Mumelter says. "Far too many questions at once. I'll tell you this: I come from the Burgenland, which makes me half a Hungarian, and you can imagine the rest."

"You had a horse and you loved to drink slivovitz," Sigi said. "You wore folk costumes."

"That's Hungarian enough for sure, but not quite me. I had no horse and did no drinking. I did have a costume for folk dancing, though."

"Your mother taught you," Sigi said.

"Yes."

Sigi lays her hand on Fräulein Mumelter's bare forearm when she asks her first question at our first lunch. Fräulein Mumelter slips her arm away. The second time, though, she doesn't. And then Sigi is lightly stroking the teacher's forearm whenever they talk.

We learn over the days that her father died a few years earlier in a motoring accident. Her mother lived in the house her family had always lived in. She had an older brother, who worked on the railways and lived with the mother. She had a younger sister, who had married a barrelmaker and lived in the next village.

During the first few lunches, Fräulein Mumelter gave brief answers between the tiny bites she took of her food. But day by day she relaxed. "I wore my hair in pigtails until I was sixteen," she said. "I was good at math. There was a boy in the eighth grade who was always pestering me to let him see my math answers."

"Did you?" Sigi asked.

"Once." She laughed.

When she finished her schooling in the Burgenland, she wanted to see something else of Austria, she didn't want to stay where she'd been born and raised. A great-uncle with a post in the education ministry had found her the job in Sankt Vero. She had spent three "glorious" days in Salzburg before coming up. And so here she was among us. Perfectly normal in all regards.

"Did you quarrel with your parents? Is that why you wanted to get away?" Sigi asked.

"There are other reasons to want to see a new part of the world. There doesn't have to be a quarrel," said Fräulein Mumelter.

"Did a boy break your heart?" asked Sigi.

"Lord, no. Why would you think such a thing?"

"That's the only reason I'd run away."

"I didn't run away. I went away for my profession. And I doubt you know very much about broken hearts."

"I break my own every day when I wake up," said Sigi. "I think about who I should be and how I can't."

I could have killed Sigi for saying that. I knew she didn't believe it for a minute. She was usually good about her condition but every once in a while had the devilish urge to see just how sorry she could make someone for her. But Fräulein Mumelter didn't know this. Fräulein Mumelter felt she must offer comfort.

"You're already so good at so much, Sigi," the teacher said. "Who else do you want to be?"

"I couldn't say; it's embarrassing," Sigi said. Then, "Something like you, maybe. If it were possible."

"A teacher? All alone in life? That's not much to hope for, is it?"

"It would be fine for me," Sigi said.

"But you'll do better. You'll find someone who loves you. You'll be married. You can be a mother."

"I'd like to marry. Maybe not to have children, but somebody to love me. If there was anyone."

"Oh, the children too, Sigi. You should have children. You'd be good with them."

"Oh, it wouldn't be possible."

"Surely it would?" said Fräulein Mumelter apprehensively, as if she was about to learn some new heartbreaking fact about the blind girl.

I'm thinking: This isn't the way she feels. This is just what she's telling two students, what she thinks they ought to hear because they're sure to repeat it. Sigi's wrong to think it's anything more, especially considering how she started it all out. But I can see she does. It's all over her face that she thinks the fräulein has a special feeling for her. She hasn't a clue how to hide her feelings. She's radiant as the morning.

I feel like saying, Sigi, get a grip. I hope Fräulein Mumelter will try to calm her down. I'm certain she sees that Sigi is overwrought. All she'd need to do is tell Sigi not to wear her heart so openly on her sleeve. But she doesn't.

Because we're always on benches and the teacher is always a step above us on the platform, we're used to thinking of Fräulein Mumelter as big. But seeing her each day at lunch and in the fields, I realize she isn't much taller than me. Her hands are smaller, but her fingers are longer. She has the thinnest long neck, almost as thin as Sigi's. It's a shock to realize how small she seems. We'd never thought of her that way before.

"Can a teacher get married?" Sigi asks.

"Yes, of course," Fräulein Mumelter says.

"Are you going to get married?"

"What a question! Someday I suppose I might."

"Do you have anybody in mind you want to marry?"

"No, Sigi. And if I did, I certainly wouldn't confess his name to you."

"Well, you probably wouldn't want to stay here once you'd got married."

"Who knows? One place can be as good as another."

WE ARE IN OUR PLACE, Sigi and I, the Jew is in his. Big Ignatz is with his buzz saw and logs, my father is with whatever thoughts he has while he's milking cows, and my mother is in her world, which I have trouble locating. My grandma is in the kitchen, busy with food, keeping life going. Everything in its place. That's good. When everyone knows where everything is, everyone knows what's expected.

The Jew doesn't think it's so simple.

"There are certain obligations in life you'd think would be easy. Precisely because they're so easy, they come to seem insignificant, unimportant. That's trouble, because then you won't do them," Dr. Weiss said.

"When my daughter was born, I was afraid to touch her. Imagine the ridiculous simplicity of that. A father holds his daughter. The nurse offered me this bundle, this little red twisted face in a mass of swaddling, and I refused. I actually backed away, saying, 'No, no thank you.'

"My wife saw this. She laughed and said, 'You won't drop her, Robert.' 'Oh, but I might,' I said, and still refused. Later on, of course, I held my daughter, I fed her, I wiped her ass, I loved her very much. But I don't think my wife ever entirely forgave me that on first sight I rejected the fruit of her body and her labors.

"God, God, the things I regret. The small things loom so large now. You can never make amends, did you know that? Never, really."

What do we care about that? We're still new to the world. We don't owe it anything yet. The nine years that separate us from Fräulein Mumelter are more than half a lifetime to us. We envy her experiences in the world, even though we can scarcely imagine them. She's seen real cities, she's traveled in trains, she's stayed in hotels and eaten in restaurants. She's been to the cinema and real theaters with actors onstage. Perhaps once she had a lover! Sigi loves to imagine what sort of man this lover might have been. We see her as independent, the way we'd like to be someday. We're envious of her future.

"YOU AREN'T LONELY?" Sigi asked at lunch near the end of the haying.

"No more than at home," Fräulein Mumelter said. "You find loneliness hasn't much to do with your actual circumstances. It's your state of mind."

"Do you miss your father?" she asked.

"Sometimes, but less and less," said Fräulein Mumelter.

Sigi has seized the knowledge that Fräulein Mumelter is half an orphan with all her might. It's a sign and a connection, this condition they share. They are in a way twins, she feels. She senses fate in this and thinks what is fated is certain. She becomes convinced that her life and Fräulein Mumelter's are destined to be intertwined.

"They already are," I said.

"More," Sigi said.

"Forever," she said.

10

GREGOR HAAS is a beautiful boy. He's pale as milk. He has thick black hair. He has the same straight nose and dolorous blue eyes as the statue of Jesus in our church. He has the holes in his hands and feet too. In the left foot anyway. The other's gone, along with the leg up to his knee. The stump and the shrapnel holes, along with the ones in his stomach and head, have healed by the time we see him again. But they are surely there.

Gregor left Sankt Vero for the army in 1941, when he was eighteen. He came back once on leave in 1943, and in the autumn of 1944 he came home for good, driven up from Schwaz in an army ambulance and put off in front of his house. The ambulance ground gears and lurched away before he got inside. I saw him there in a weary, lusterless uniform, right trouser leg pinned up, a fresh-looking wooden crutch tucked under his right armpit.

Nobody knew he was coming. His mother wept the instant she answered the door and saw him. He faltered but didn't drop his crutch when she embraced him. He still looked just like our painted wooden Jesus. But I think his mother, leading him inside, sensed straightaway that he was diminished in ways beyond the missing limb. Important things had been taken from him. That's what I saw in his eyes, when my turn came to look into them.

Gregor was the first boy home from the war to stay. A homecoming was never taken lightly in our village, most especially a military homecoming. The custom of Sankt Vero was this: whenever a boy returned on leave or after finishing his service, he and his father went to the bar directly after the first supper at home. All the other men in the town would be there, waiting. The boy was encouraged to tell his war stories, and then the veterans retold their best ones. It had been done exactly this way as long as the oldest men in town could remember.

Gregor never showed up on his night. My father, Big Ignatz, Pabst the gendarme, Stocker, Hufnagl, the mayor, all of them were at the bar. They had a drink or two, they turned the air blue with smoke and stale anecdotes about their own service. They waited. They drank. Gregor stayed home. No one knew exactly what went on at his house that night. Gregor's father spoke in an apologetic way to the men he met in the course of the following day without exactly explaining anything. No one seemed to consider that Gregor may have simply felt shy, or too tired, or too sickly. No, something had to be gravely wrong. Men began to speculate about the severity of Gregor's head wound; don't think we haven't seen this sort of thing before in our time, they said. Some were wondering if the Haas boy had "gone funny." Head wounds, they said, tended that way.

Everyone eventually got the chance to draw his own conclusion. For two days Gregor stayed home. But he came out on the third morning, wearing that drab uniform, and walked from one end of the village to the other, and back again. He repeated the trip in the afternoon, and every morning and afternoon thereafter.

He'd stop and chat with anyone who seemed inclined to talk. So many did that his progress, hardly rapid anyway, became a series of slow jerks, one house to the next. I watched him from the schoolroom windows, talking and then walking on, and stopping to talk again. For a week Gregor made his rounds, until at last most folks were content to give him a simple greeting when he passed by. They no longer detained him but passed judgment among themselves. The results were mixed. Gregor was quite forthcoming about combat and how he had been wounded. He had a manly approach to these matters, most thought. He acquitted himself well. We had nothing to be ashamed of in Gregor. But a few claimed the boy was soft on the Russians, that he didn't hate them enough, that he actually admired them as fighting men.

It was the head wound, no doubt.

Gregor's a ghost to me. He's a strange floating presence I feel I could see through if the light were right. He belongs to the village and yet he's alien. He's there to remind us of something, but no one can think what it is. He somehow violates the rhythms we all depend on. I'm drawn to him. But Sigi scarcely notices him at all.

WE'D BEEN BACK in school a month when Gregor came home, and Sigi hadn't been happy. She missed Fräulein Mumelter. They talked in class, of course, but it wasn't the same. Sigi was deeply nostalgic for the summer, the smell of the hay, the intimate low murmur of Fräulein Mumelter's voice. She actually spoke of the "low murmur," when in fact Fräulein Mumelter was always crisp and open in her speech. Sigi had a picture in her mind, just the way she liked it, and more hope than she could handle. So Sigi was in a state of more or less constant disappointment; every conversation with the teacher now failed to please.

What could one expect in the classroom, after all?

I say this to Sigi. She only shakes her head.

Sigi's pining. She lulls herself to sleep every night thinking of Fräulein Mumelter braiding her hair. She tells me this. It's all Sigi can do these days to talk even briefly about anything else. She only really wants to speak of Traudl. Traudl is Fräulein Mumelter's first name, Sigi's discovered. She loves to say it, loves the sound of it, although she would never dare call her by it. Yet she's bold enough to say "Traudl Mumelter" when she speaks of the teacher to Dr. Weiss. She'll take my hand when we're alone and hold it between her fresh breasts and, with her cheek against mine, whisper, "What do you think Traudl is up to right this minute? Do you think she can tell we're talking about her?"

Fräulein Mumelter of course is no secret to Dr. Weiss. We've mentioned her many times over the last year. How could we not, when we speak to him of our days? Every pupil has a teacher. But Fräulein Mumelter was never really a woman in conversations among the three of us. She was a force, constant but impersonal. She was The Teacher. Now Sigi's making her a creature of flesh and blood, with a voice and a heart and desires. The woman she's creating does not perfectly resemble the teacher I see every day. I'm sure the doctor can sense this too. But he's willing to humor Sigi. Tell me, please, he says one evening when Sigi's been going on about the talks they had in haying time, what is it that makes your Traudl Mumelter so special? Sigi smiles at the way he uses the name.

"She must come from the moon!" Sigi says. "She's not like anyone else. She's very intelligent.

"Of course, she's beautiful, isn't she?" Sigi turns to me. "She'd have to be."

"No," I say. "She's very fat, with a pushed-in face. She looks like a troll."

"I know you're lying," Sigi says. "She doesn't breathe like a fat person. And the way she walks, she's graceful. When she talks I know she's tall and beautiful."

"So you know what you know. Why ask me?" I say.

"Just to check," Sigi says.

"Ah, Sigi, I don't like to disillusion you, but it's very hard to tell anything about people by the way they sound," Dr. Weiss says. "There's no correlation between the beauty of a voice and the way someone looks. Consider opera singers, for example. They are not known for beauty."

"So what?" Sigi says. "She's not a singer."

"But you can only guess what she looks like," Dr. Weiss says. He can't be thinking straight, to be so blunt. Being locked up for so long has clearly rattled his brains.

"Since I can't see her and never will, she looks the way I want her to look. So does Niki. So do you."

"So what do I look like?" Dr. Weiss says.

"You're dark as a Gypsy, you have a hooked nose, and your teeth are rotten. You have a thick, curly beard with lice. You've probably eaten baby flesh. You drool."

Dr. Weiss starts giggling. I've never heard him do this before. It's not like his normal laugh; it's like the giggle of Stumpf, who has a dent in his skull that would hold an egg. Stumpf got the dent in the First War and ever since has been regarded as the village idiot—though he is really quite handy as the blacksmith's assistant. It's only when he talks that he sounds stupid. And of course there's that giggle.

The sound frightens me. I've been warned about such sounds. This is the sort of thing I'm supposed to be on the lookout for. My father wants to know the Jew's condition. My father is more and more anxious as time passes and the Jew remains alone in the box. He's concerned the Jew will break. He wants to hear about anything abnormal, anything out of the ordinary. He wants to know if the Jew seems stable and sane. This is very hard for me to judge. Dr. Weiss has his ways of teasing us when he's cheerful, and holding his feelings in close when he's not. He speaks to us as adults sometimes and as children at others.

It was difficult to judge his state of mind, just as it was difficult to know what would interest him. Sometimes he loved to hear of scandals and unwanted pregnancies and so forth, but lately when I told him how Maria Stocker had been going off privately with one of the young plane spotters, he seemed not to care one bit. The news of Gregor's arrival, though, perked him up as soon as he heard it.

"Amputation is simply the ultimate debridement," Dr. Weiss said casually.

We'd told him about the crutch and Gregor's bumpy gait as he went from one end of the village to the other and back, the talk of Gregor's head wound, that maybe he'd "gone funny."

"You do it when you have no hope of repairing the damage, and know the damage will kill the patient if it isn't repaired. So you just zip, get rid of it, zip zip."

He asked me if I'd seen the stump, and how the flaps were fastened. Flaps? He asked precisely how much is left below the knee. He asked if Gregor has dark circles under his eyes, and does he hunch his shoulders as if he's cold? Does he squint? Do his fingernails look bluish? Any trembling of the hands? Has he a silver plate in his skull? I hadn't seen the stump, of course, and didn't think I wanted to. I didn't notice much of the rest, either, certainly not a silver plate in his head.

"Ah, Niki, you're useless as a diagnostician," the doctor said. "Next time you see Gregor, notice these things and report to me."

"It's awful," Sigi said. "I wonder what it feels like to have something cut off.".

"I could whip off one of your pretty legs in a matter of minutes and you wouldn't even feel much. Anesthesia's a wonderful thing," Dr. Weiss said.

"You're sick," Sigi said. "And how do you know I have pretty legs?"

"You've told me."

"I never have."

"Then I imagine they're pretty. And if I imagine them that way, then that's the way they are," the doctor said.

"But what does it do to you, to have your leg cut off?" I asked.

"I must have lopped off hundreds of legs in the First War. And I found there were three types of patients," the doctor said. He was in his lecturing mood now. "Most felt depressed at first, felt they were less of a man than they'd been, but they adjusted pretty quickly and stopped feeling sorry for themselves. A few remained so bitter they'd actually tear off their dressings at night, hoping to bleed to death. These were mostly double amputees. Then there were a few rare men who were actually pleased. For them the pressure was off forever. They now had an excuse to avoid all sorts of unpleasant things, like strenuous jobs.

"But only so long as it was a relatively convenient loss, like a left hand or a foot. Both arms above the elbow, on the other hand, demoralized everyone. Those were the ones who would really have tried to tear off their dressings. If only the poor bastards could have."

Sigi wanted to know if Gregor was a poor bastard or not.

"Only time will tell us that," Dr. Weiss said.

SIGI'S NEVER ONE TO WAIT.

The light's fading one late-October afternoon shortly before we're due to feed the Jew. Sigi and I are loitering in front of my father's store. The saws in Ignatz's mill have shut down. Gregor's walking by us, on his usual rounds. He's nodding to me as we pass. We weren't friends. He'd been one of the older boys we looked up to so much when we started school. We'd been beneath his notice. He'd already left school when we went into second grade. He'd gone to work at the sawmill. We'd see him around town, or hiking on Sundays. And then a few years after that he'd gone to the army.

"I hear a crutch," Sigi says. "Must be that Gregor Haas, not even saying hello."

"Hello, Sigi," Gregor says. "You've grown."

"Of course I have. Where's your leg? I hear they have legs now that can't be told from the real thing," she says.

Gregor says that it will be some weeks yet before he goes back to Schwaz to be fitted with an artificial limb. Then he'll have to stay for a few weeks of training.

"Training?" Sigi says. "How hard can it be?"

"They're supposed to be a little tricky until you get used to them, these peg legs," Gregor says.

"Does your leg hurt?" Sigi asks.

"Yes, on and off. Sometimes even the toes hurt. Which amazes me, since they aren't there."

"Did you ever try to rip your dressings off?"

"That's a crazy question."

"Do you feel very sorry for yourself?" Oh, Sigi, Sigi, Sigi. I notice my feet seem to be shuffling on their own. I'm wishing I were someplace else, far away.

"Sure. I feel sorry. Angry too. I think, why me?"

"I don't feel sorry for you," Sigi says.

"Not a bit?"

"Why should I? You could've lost both legs. Or both legs and both arms. You could've had your head shot off. Or something else, even worse."

"Even worse?" Gregor starts laughing. My skin's crawling. That laughter could be the start of some murderous fit. He had a head wound after all. But he settles down almost at once.

"How is it exactly that young girls become philosophers?" he says mildly. "With such certainty too. That's what's impressive, that certainty of being right."

"I'll be fifteen soon," Sigi says. She's up to something. I know it, but I can't tell what it is.

"Yes, I see," he says, as if Sigi's given him a rational answer to his question.

"Of course you do, Gregor," she says. "I said you were lucky, didn't I?"

"Not lucky. You said it could have been worse. Is there some sort of scale for these things, a precise way of measuring them?"

"It's a waste of time to try to measure, isn't it?" Sigi says. "You can't trust anybody to be accurate when they're talking about their own pain."

"Sigi, you must become my spiritual adviser," Gregor says. "I'll need lots of help. Everyone at the hospital said so. They liked to talk about the 'process of readjustment.' "

Gregor's smiling at her like this is some joke, but to me his voice seems brittle. I can't remember if he sounded that way before the war. Maybe being hurt gave his voice this quality. It's like cold glass, easily broken.

Sigi quickly runs her long fingers all over Gregor's face, a thing she rarely does. He doesn't flinch. She says, "You can rely on me."

And Gregor nods and goes on his way, the tip of his crutch making a sucking sound each time he lifts it from the muddy path beside the road.

11

IT'S RAINING down rivers. We get drenched between the house and the barn. It's the 593rd or maybe the 601st night we had come to the Jew, bearing the 593rd or 601st bowl of potatoes with bacon, or dumplings with bacon, or dumplings in broth, or potatoes with cheese. Who could be sure, exactly? What does it matter? As soon as this night's food has been slid into the box, a sodden Sigi says, "Do you masturbate in there?" If she had waited a moment I'm certain we'd have heard a man choking on his food. Instead we hear the Jew mutter, "Damn kids."

Anger gathers. Presently the Jew barks, "How dare you! At the very least you should respect my age, even in these deplorable circumstances. Your minds are at the mercy of raging hormones. Goddamn adolescents! You ought to be whipped on your bare bottoms."

Then nothing. Not a curse, not the clink of the spoon on the bowl, no rustle of the straw, not even an audible breath. We don't dare move or speak. We hear only the drenching rain. I'd told Sigi she oughtn't to ask such a question. I'd told her it was bound to be a sensitive matter. But she felt we had to demonstrate we knew how things were for him. He'd given us the clue the previous night. Sigi had judged his words as sad as any could be. "For almost two years now," Dr. Weiss had said, "I have touched no one. And no one in the wide world has touched me."

It was in the air anyway, Sigi reasoned. An epidemic of masturbation seemed to be sweeping Sankt Vero. I suppose it's the type that comes once every generation. It's the first we've known. Some of the boys are claiming they have to do it regularly or their balls will swell up and burst. Of course, this tale about swelling probably wasn't true, but if it was, surely the Jew's balls might be swelling too. Certainly he would do what was necessary to prevent it. He was a doctor, after all. But Sigi just had to know what was up.

Simon's to blame if anyone is. Simon came back from his summer in the valley boasting that he'd learned how to make himself ejaculate. Naturally I had to look this up in the dictionary at school for Sigi, being careful to do it when Fräulein Mumelter was busy on the other side of the room. Sigi's "Oh, it's just *coming*" was loud enough to provoke a frown from the teacher. Sigi made me look up masturbation next. The entry was very vague, no good details at all. Sigi wanted details. She listened closely as Andreas and Kaspar and three or four others reported back to Simon over the course of a few weeks how they'd managed the trick. Finally, one day after school, Sigi pounced. In front of all of us, she demanded proof from Simon. "I couldn't do it with you too near, Sigi. You might get pregnant if you touched it or anything," he said. "Besides, you couldn't see it."

"Niki would see it and tell me if it really happened. If you could actually do it, Simon, you would. So you can't. Probably you can't even get a boner."

Simon is trapped. Simon has no choice.

We gather later that afternoon in Sigi's nearly derelict barn. There's the barn smell: dry wood, dry straw. There are the dusty shafts of light, the slatted shadows, the eager embarrassed faces. Simon's flat on his back, eyes squeezed shut, rubbing his groin. Almost at once a hard-on appears. It's big and pale compared to the thin red dicks of dogs we've all seen, but nothing to a bull's. Simon takes some lard from a tin cup he's brought and smears it on his right palm. He makes a fist around his dick, like it was a pump handle. He strokes up and down five or six times. He makes a little hissing noise. A little creamy liquid spurts from his penis.

"I smell starch," Sigi says. "Is that it? Did he come or not? It was very fast."

I tell her exactly what I'd seen. She seems to consider the mechanics of it for a moment. She wrinkles her nose at the lard. "That's fairly disgusting, when you think of it," she says. There's a good deal of rowdiness. Some of the boys want to have a go at what Simon had just done. But Simon is being miserly with his lard. No one is listening to us. "Girls are much nicer in their ways, Niki," Sigi says. I assume she was remembering Maria Stocker, thinking that Maria riding her flour sack so intently was altogether more sophisticated than Simon's hurried handful of lard. But I learned later she was thinking of something more personal.

Half the boys have their pants off by now. "Queer bait! Jerkoffs!" Sigi yells. They merrily agree, especialy Kaspar, who has finally got some hair on his privates and is showing it off to everyone. "I was thinking of you when I did it. I was thinking of your pussy, Sigi," Simon calls out as we leave the barn. "I'm going to think of Sigi and Niki together. Two girls at once!" Kaspar shouts. "Fat pervert," Sigi snarls.

IT WAS ABOUT ten days after the incident in the barn when Sigi had stopped Gregor in his tracks on the street. Her feat had not gone unobserved. Gregor had scarcely hobbled out of sight when three of the arch-masturbators came hurrying across the street from the sawmill. Simon, Andreas, and Kaspar had been dying to ask Gregor about combat ever since he first arrived home. They talked over and over about his close-combat badge, the one that meant he'd been in hand-to-hand fighting. They figure they'll be in the thick of it themselves within two years or so, and they want to know what it's like. But they'd been reluctant to approach him. Simon and Andreas admire Gregor very much. They want to know what Gregor said to us. Kaspar is dubious. "If he was any good as a fighter, he wouldn't have got so wrecked," he said.

"Nobody can dodge a mortar shell," I said.

"As if you know," Kaspar said.

"Ask Ignatz," I said. "He knows well enough, and he'll tell you if you ask him."

"Big Ignatz," said Kaspar, with a contempt and lack of fear that alarmed me, considering who Ignatz was. Yet there was Kaspar's recently deepening voice, full of contempt. There were other ominous signs about Kaspar. Much of the blubber he'd always carried seemed to be turning to muscle from his work in the sawmill. He was getting taller rapidly. And he was getting more aggressive. He was beginning to be intimidating, no longer the pathetic fat boy we all bullied. Sigi didn't feel this, though.

"You'd shit yourself if you even heard a mortar," she snapped.

"What you do know, girlie?" Kaspar sneered.

"Just like you shit yourself when you fell out of that spy loft and broke your arm," she said.

"I never did!" Kaspar said. He looked so surprised.

"He shit his pants then?" Andreas asked. "Hah!"

"I didn't," Kaspar said.

"Oh, yes you did," Sigi said. "I heard Ignatz talking about it with your father. They were laughing. They said there was a turd the size of a banana in your trousers."

Kaspar was white. "You cunt," he snarled. His arms tensed, as if he might punch her. Instead he spun and stomped off across the street toward the mill.

"You wouldn't know one if it sat on your face, lardass," Sigi yelled after him.

Sigi gets so tough with people. Why is she so bold? Does she believe people are a little frightened of her wide sightless eyes? Or does she count on sympathy to ease the rules of behavior? None of us could get away with what Sigi could. Any of us would have had to fight Kaspar just now. But Sigi always sails on. And now she's telling Simon and Andreas outrageous lies about bloody things Gregor had done in the war, about blowing up dozens of Russian tanks single-handed, about putting bullets in the heads of any survivors. Gregor once even drank Russian blood, Sigi swore.

"You watch, Gregor's going to want to be friends with us now," Sigi said later when we were on our way to feed Dr. Weiss.

"Friends? If your stories get around, he'll probably kill you and drink your blood. Why did you say all those things?"

"So they'll be frightened of him and leave him alone," Sigi said.

"Why should they have troubled him at all?"

"Because he's crippled," Sigi said. "Because he'd be easy to beat, like Kaspar's always been. Kaspar especially would have got after him as soon as he saw a good chance."

"And now you think he won't?"

"I don't think Simon and Andreas will let him. It would of-fend their sense of honor toward a war hero to let anything bad happen," she said. "Meanwhile Gregor's going to be our friend, even if he is old."

I didn't feel able to make any exciting plans based on that. Sigi'd been wrong in her schemes before, though failures never seemed to hurt her confidence one bit. She was always up and ready for the next thing. Sometimes I felt I was just trotting beside Sigi like a puppy. I felt she was the one who made things happen. And in a way I was content. In the evenings in the loft, she'd slip her body close to mine, and touch me, and sometimes even kiss me on the lips. I hoped one day she'd touch my tongue with hers. That was my modest ambition.

THESE SMALL THINGS meant more that fall than before. That fall there was a parting of the ways in our group. We no longer saw Simon and Andreas and Kaspar every day after school. When they weren't working, or masturbating, they were laboring hard to insinuate themselves with the four young soldiers who were supposed to be spotting planes. Maybe there were some military variants of masturbation, who knows what got passed on in barracks in those days? Maybe they were looking for hints of what their own lives might be like soon, for at sixteen they'd be bound for the army too. The four privates seemed to enjoy having some cadets around to admire them and perform small errands. In return, there was the spectacle of Simon and Kaspar and Andreas, outside the bar, awkwardly smoking cigarettes they'd mooched from the soldiers. The sergeant always spit when he passed them there on his way for a drink. The sergeant, who was old (maybe thirty), wore a close-combat badge like Gregor's and would have nothing to do with any of them. The sergeant only talked to Big Ignatz and my father.

It's feeling a little lonely for us. We feel a bit left out. Then Gregor's waiting outside the schoolhouse one afternoon. If he has heard the tales Sigi told, and if they have angered him, there is no sign of this that I can see. He's standing there, listing slightly to the right on his bright crutch, and there's a wan Jesus smile on his face when he spots us. When I tell Sigi who's there, she grins and calls, "Hey, Gregor. Walk to the bridge with us, won't you?" To me she whispers, "I knew it."

So we head down the road toward where the torrent curves. There's a bridge of bolted wooden beams there, with a good view of the Kirchspitz and the lower valley. People often met to talk there. Sigi's in the middle, holding my hand. My head's above Gregor's shoulder, hers is below. He looks over at us every few steps.

"You've got a very big mouth, Sigi," Gregor says.

"So they say. But it's well intentioned," she says. She's taken the first blow pretty well, I think. She sounds confident.

"That's your opinion. You've no right to one in this case, though."

"In this case?"

"Me. I'm the case. You should have kept your damn big mouth shut."

Sigi's feeling anxious now. I can tell by a faint twitch starting on her lower lip. "I didn't mean any harm. It wasn't disrespectful."

"It was shit, whether you meant it to be or not. You've embarrassed me before the town. You better shut up about me."

Sigi's mortified. I know her so well. She has her lower lip tucked under her front teeth, she keeps plucking at wisps of hair that have escaped her pigtails. She looks as though she is staring at her feet, which is what I'd have been doing if I'd told the stories. We walk on.

"I like this time of day, just before dark," Gregor says as we near the bridge. He's milder now, as if his anger's already used up.

"It's the blue time," Sigi says softly.

"Can you see that?" he asks.

"No. Everything's always brown. Morning, noon, and night. But the evening always feels blue."

"Do other things feel like colors?" he asks.

"The obvious ones. Sunny days, yellow. Rainy days, gray. A birthday feels bright red."

"Bright red?"

"Just a notion I have," Sigi says.

"She's full of notions," I offer. I'm ashamed to feel how much I want Gregor to look at me. "She swears she can tell when the moon's full because she feels lighter, like she might float into the air."

"My grandma would never wash her hair under a full moon. She thought it was very bad luck to do that," Gregor says.

"It's worse than bad luck. It's inviting death into the house," Sigi says.

"My grandma never said that," Gregor says.

"Maybe she didn't want to frighten you," Sigi says.

"It doesn't take much to frighten me, that's true," Gregor says.

"I don't believe that for one minute," Sigi says.

"Did you like it in the army before you got hurt?" I ask.

"I liked some of it. I admit I liked to blow things up. It's very exciting. It's like being a little boy with not only permission but encouragement to be as bad as you please. You can be so bad. You can be bad until you make yourself sick if you want. But you never imagine that day will come. You never imagine that one day you might be the one to get blown up. It's always going to happen over there, to them. When it finally happens to you, it's quite a shock."

"I was shocked when my father got killed," Sigi says. "The shocking thing was how stupid it was, that accident. It seemed too stupid and silly to kill anyone."

"Exactly, exactly. That's the way it always is, too stupid and silly. A bad joke, really. You could almost laugh if it wasn't so painful," Gregor said.

Sigi's lower lip comes out from behind her teeth. It looks plump, pink, and kissable. She begins to smile. She turns her face up toward him. Gregor's staring down the valley.

"So, Sigi," Gregor says. "Here's a bargain. We'll get together sometimes, and I'll tell you what it's like to have a hole in the head and a missing leg, and you'll tell me your blind girl's philosophy. You've got plenty of that, don't you?"

"I'm not sure there's enough to waste on you. And who cares about missing legs?" There's the old Sigi, back again.

"You might find the details intriguing," Gregor says.

"Flaps and things? No. A hole in the head, though, that might be interesting. Do you have hallucinations?"

"Not really."

"Too bad. I'd like to hear something firsthand about halluci-nations."

"I've something better," Gregor says. "I have been to the other side. I can tell you about that."

"The other side?"

"Where the dead go," Gregor says.

"Ah, they go to the graveyard, and that's that," I say. Things are taking a very uncomfortable turn as far as I'm concerned.

"Yes and no," Gregor says.

"Did you see anybody we know over there?" Sigi asks. "Did you see my dad?"

"You don't actually see anything. You feel the presences. There was no one close that I knew. It was in a field hospital in Russia. I was very close to death. The leg and the stomach were nothing. It was the head. My brain was swelling. It was going to kill me if they didn't cut out a piece of my skull to give it room.

"There was a moment during the operation when I felt I was truly dead. It was like lying down in the middle of an ice field up in the mountains. You don't feel especially cold at first. Or maybe you're already numb. You can't move. But you're going mad with thirst. The thirst is the purest agony you've ever known. You'd do anything for a cup of sweet hot chocolate. You would sell your soul for a cup of chocolate. Then you realize you have nothing at all to sell, and no one to sell to anyway. And you realize no one will ever, ever bring you that drink."

"NOBODY'S BEEN to the other side, because there is none," says Dr. Weiss when we're talking about Gregor that night. "When you are close to death, you brain takes steps to protect itself. Your body starts to shut down. Your brain sends comforting signals to itself. You may think there is a loved one who died before you, come now to guide you. You may think you see a great light, the welcoming light of heaven, perhaps. It's nothing but chemicals in the brain."

"That's not proven. If it was, there'd be no religion anymore," Sigi says.

"Nothing's proven. But if you see enough death, you know what's what. Not once in my experience was it good, or even dignified. Although several times it was merciful. There was a young

nurse, no more than twenty-three, who was wounded in the ab-
domen very badly by shrapnel. She was just ripped wide open.
The worst piece had torn apart her rectum. That is the most
painful injury anyone could have; drugs can't even ease it. Only
death could stop that pain. So I did what I had to do: I stopped
it for her."

My heart starts jumping in my thin chest. It's banging into my
ribs. Breathing's hard. I feel like I have to pee but nothing comes
out. There are times like this when the Jew casually turns the fair
world into a horror, even worse than Gregor did that afternoon.
There are times I feel I must tell someone what I've heard from
the Jew. I've got to get it out. But I'm forbidden to speak of him
in our house. I can mention him only when my father and I are
outside, out of earshot of anyone else. My father only wants brief
reports on the Jew's behavior, nothing more. He seems to think
that if we never speak of him in the house, the house will remain
safe. I think my mother and my grandma talk secretly of the Jew,
but only when my father isn't around. So I try once or twice with
my mother. She seems eager at first—it's a little conspiracy just
between us, after all—but then it's as if some shutters close behind her eyes. She doesn't see what I'm trying to say. Maybe it's
too frightening for her. And she tells me, Stop! Your father
wouldn't like it.

So there's no one but Sigi, and no one but me for her. It gives
me a special claim on her that I like. But what can we do for each
other when the weight of knowing what we do becomes more
than we can bear? Can we pass some of the weight to another?
Can we find someone to share it with us?

Sigi's ready for Fräulein Mumelter. She wants to be en-
veloped in the beautiful teacher's calm, she wants to be com-
forted. She wants now to give up our secret, to let Fräulein

Mumelter help carry Dr. Weiss. We don't mention this idea to my father or to Big Ignatz. They would certainly forbid it. Sigi's sure we can trust her. I'm not. It still worries me that even Ignatz knows. And I'm thinking somewhere in the bad part of my mind that Sigi only wants to do it as a way of getting closer to her Traudl.

But we do need help, I think. Ever since Sigi asked him about masturbation, Dr. Weiss has gone moody on us. We have to do most of the talking, and when he does speak he sounds seedy. If a man who wasn't locked up said some of the things Dr. Weiss now says to us, I'd be afraid. I'd go to the gendarme, probably. It's sort of medical, and then again it isn't. Out of nowhere once he suddenly asks Sigi if she bleeds regularly each month, if she has cramps, if her breasts get tender. Once, he asks me if I like having suppositories inserted. We don't know how to answer, but we're too shocked to rebuke him, either. Still, he seems to know when he has gone too far. He never says anything so direct again. But he becomes absentmindedly brutal—as he was in telling us about the poor nurse—or sometimes seems distracted by strange yearnings and odd ideas he oughtn't to admit to us.

"You know," he says one evening, maybe the 610th or perhaps the 653rd, "I was dancing with my daughter on her wedding day, and a thought came into my mind completely unbidden. Dancing, I realized for the first time that she had a woman's body, and I found myself wondering if she was still a virgin. It seemed such a medieval thought. What could it matter? What business of mine was it? Yet I felt this great curiosity about what she might have done already with Erich, her new husband. But my mind revolted. I could not picture her naked beneath Erich, performing the sex act, though I could easily picture her mother together with me. Sex is a natural enough thing. But something comes between a father and his daughter in these matters. I felt so ashamed of my thoughts I almost couldn't complete the dance."

"I don't believe my parents ever did it naked," I say. "It's hard to believe they ever did it at all, looking at them. I don't want to think that they did."

"You prefer to believe you were brought by the stork?" Sigi says. "They probably still do it once in a while. When I was little and could still see, one night I saw my father bouncing on top of my mother. They were both naked, and he was squashing her breasts. But she was kissing him and raising her hips up and down. She seemed to be liking it."

"How long after that night did you go blind, Sigi?" Dr. Weiss asks.

"About six months or so," Sigi says.

"And the reason?" Dr. Weiss asks. "Were any psychological possibilities discussed in your treatment?"

"No," Sigi says.

"Why not?" the doctor asks.

"It was measles," Sigi says. "Niki had 'em and gave them to me. Just worse, I guess."

"Measles," he says. "God, God. Damn lucky you didn't go deaf as well. Many kids do."

Sometimes the doctor is so blunt and rational I'd like to shake him silly. But more and more now that's an exception. More and more he's drifting, he's vague, he's only a notion of himself, as on the dance floor with his daughter. I ask him frequently if he has a fever or feels unwell. He seems surprised to be asked and swears he never felt better.

Of course, he's lying.

Maybe Traudl Mumelter would be good for him. Sigi is dreaming of this. She sees us as a sort of happy family in the loft.

It doesn't occur to her that Fräulein Mumelter might feel only horror or revulsion at this arrangement. She thinks Traudl will save Dr. Weiss.

But before Sigi can make that connection, she inadvertently makes another: Fräulein Mumelter and Gregor.

Little good will come of that, my mother says when she finds out. And for once my grandma agrees.

12

SIGI'S NO LARK. She could scuff the smoothest lullaby. So it is only by way of a mild municipal connivance that she and I and Simon are chosen to be the Advent singers in Sankt Vero that December. We'll have to have costumes, we'll have to practice, and for several nights we'll have to hurry shivering from house to house, exposing our thin talents to people gathered warm in their glowing doorways. They'll give us a few marks or pfennigs for the church, and possibly a small cup of hot cider or chocolate when we've finished our miserly work. I'd rather beg for the money; it would be so much quicker. But that is not the custom. So we'll sing.

"Why on earth did they pick Sigi? Or you, for that matter," my mother said. It was the priest, the mayor, and the teacher who'd done it. "Only Simon can sing at all. What could they have been thinking of?"

Any fool could see, I felt like telling her. They wanted to do something nice for Sigi, a sort of Christmas gift. But it never did any good to explain things once my mother had formed her opinion. She was the type who always knew for sure she was right. She only ever pretended to accept anyone else's version.

Another year I would have been eager. Another year I would

even have felt honored to be chosen, for there was a certain pres-
tige attached to Advent singing. But I'm too edgy these days. I'm
in no mood for the old-time ways, because the old times seem to
be fading so fast even the old men can't save them, with their
weakening, wandering memories. We've finally heard panzers
rumbling and growling down in the valley, on their way to somewhere. Just the other day I saw a flight of silver planes so high
they were almost silent, exciting the soldiers so that they shouted
into their radios. Allied bombers, heading north for Salzburg or
Linz, they said. Things are happening finally. Things may happen to us.

I've never really been the anxious sort before. I'm only afraid
of the usual. I worry one day I might suffer some everlasting mor-
tification in school—an uncontrollable attack of diarrhea, for instance. I secretly fear our house will burn down one night, and
worry something bad will happen to Sigi when I'm not around
to help her. I'm terrified of avalanches in the spring. Other than
that, I'm only afraid to have my photo taken. Because that's the
first step toward having your picture on a black iron cross in the
graveyard.

Gregor has a little 35mm Voigtlander, and he's always trying
to take our photo. I refuse absolutely. Sigi loves it. She never
leaves her house without looking her best, and so she's ready
whenever Gregor wants to take a snap. He likes to stand her in
front of buildings with closed doors and shutters, dead center. He
has her look straight at his voice, so that when you see the photos it seems Sigi is looking at you. Whenever he has a new batch
he'll hobble over to Sigi's place, and we'll sit in the kitchen and
look at them together. They're all the same really: blind girl,
blind buildings. I tell Sigi which building she's standing in front
of, so she can imagine the scene. She always asks if her hair looks

all right. Gregor always says her hair is beautiful, even when it looks straggly and windblown around her plain face.

So Gregor can lie too. Why not? That just proves he's like all the rest of us. It doesn't make him bad. Why should I be surprised? Everybody lies. It's usual. Sometimes it's kind.

I wish someone would tell me a lie that would ease me a little. I have this sense of something gathering that will soon change everything I've ever known. I try to understand the apprehension: maybe it's the Jew, maybe it's the war. But I can't make any connection. The dread that harrows me is independent of anything I see or know. It's a sort of haunting, I guess. I see things in my head, just before I drift off to sleep. My eyes snap open, but there's nothing, just the usual red flickering from my window.

Why can't I know what's waiting for us?

Naturally, no one wants to take such fretting seriously. Who wants the burden of someone else's foreboding? "It's your time of life to go all sensitive," my grandma says. "It'll pass." My father is kind but only says I'm getting too high-strung when I try to speak of it with him. He makes me chamomile tea some evenings and slips a bit of peppermint schnapps into it. "It's no good to think long or hard about what might happen to you in life," he says. "Just get on with it, day by day. Do your best and see what comes."

I suppose that's sensible. But how sensible is a man who keeps a Jew in a box for almost two years and can't say why? Isn't it just the sort of thing someone would say when he has no idea anymore how the world turns, when he's lost the knack of ordering his life? When I say to my father, "What if the worst should happen?" he only looks at me sadly and says, "But, Niki, it could always be worse."

Gregor says the same, more or less. He says there are no limits. Considering his history, he probably knows. He goes further. He even thinks he may already be dead.

"Suppose all this—you, Sankt Vero, Sigi, my missing leg—is only some kind of strange afterlife. Suppose it is what happens to us instead of heaven or hell," he says. He's met Sigi and me after school, as he frequently does, and we're walking down toward the bridge. There's plenty of snow, and the sun's low. Ignatz's sawmill is roaring. I wonder if he's still trying to spy on Fräulein Mumelter from the cockloft. I still feel creepy whenever I remember the way he fondled my bottom with his meaty hand the night we tried to give the Jew to the smugglers. Pabst the gendarme is outside the bar, glancing from side to side to see if there's anyone who'll notice him going in. Without thinking, I suddenly look back, and I see my father in the fading light, walking toward the school, where Fräulein Mumelter is probably still marking papers. I turn to keep an eye on Gregor, never letting go of Sigi's hand.

"Or else I'm in a coma in a hospital somewhere in Russia, and my brain is creating this world," he says, waving wildly at everything around him and nearly swatting Sigi in the head. "It isn't a dream, mind you. You don't dream in comas. What you see is indistinguishable from the real . . . until it vanishes. Then there's nothing and no sense of the passsage of time, as there is in sleep."

"If your brain is creating me, why don't you give me my eyes back?" Sigi says. "While you're at it, why don't you get Fräulein Mumelter to adopt me. I'd rather live with her than at home. I'd love to snuggle up in her place and not come out till spring."

Gregor laughs. "Yes, I should. I'd like to be God for a while. The things I could do!" He suddenly drops his crutch in the snow and hops a good ten meters on one leg, almost as fast as I could run it.

"The head wound," I whisper to Sigi.

"Must be," she whispers back.

"People think it's the head wound," Gregor gasps when we catch up with him and hand him his crutch. He's having trouble getting his breath. "If I say anything radical or peculiar, they use that to understand. They make an excuse for me. But they're wrong, of course. It's actually a little problem of the mind, a psychological thing, a case of the mind from time to time trying to grasp things it cannot. It's not my lightly damaged brain. Oh, no. There's hardly any brain missing at all. Less than a teaspoonful, the doctors assured me."

This notion actually makes me feel giddy, makes my vision seem to waver strangely. Who, I wonder, is fooling who about what's real and what isn't? How could you actually have two separate things in your head that sometimes disagree, or work at cross-purposes? Trying to think of mind on one hand and brain on the other makes me anxious in much the same way that thinking about my dead brothers and sisters does. Nothing so close should be so separate. And there seems no possibility of any answer. Hope leaks from my heart. And I never was a nervous type before, you know.

"A TEASPOONFUL OF BRAINS," Sigi says that night when we're on our way to the loft. "There's no telling what could be in that teaspoon. The phases of the moon, your love for your mother, all the geometry you ever learned, maybe your ability to see colors. God, maybe sex!"

"It would depend entirely on precisely where the teaspoonful came from," Dr. Weiss says when we've reported to him. "There are plenty of places in the right or left lobe where you'd never miss that amount of tissue at all if it was pretty cleanly cut away. On the other hand, there are plenty of places where a missing teaspoonful would make you an idiot, or kill you."

"We know Gregor's no idiot, and we know he's alive, even if he isn't quite so sure himself," Sigi says.

"Feels a bit unreal sometimes, does he? Not so unusual in survivors. Does he hallucinate at all? Hear voices, perhaps? How's his attention span? Does he ever stammer or talk incoherently?"

"No, none of those things, as far as I know," I say.

"I'd like to have a talk with Gregor sometime," the doctor says.

"That's forbidden," I say.

"Yes, I'd like to give him a complete examination. No doubt the surgeons in the field did decent work, but you always need to follow up."

"Maybe we could, if he swore never to speak of it," Sigi says. She hasn't given up on her idea of bringing Fräulein Mumelter to the Jew, and now she wants Gregor too.

"Yes, do that," the doctor says. "And notify my nurse that I'll need her help."

"What nurse? This is crazy," I say. "You don't know what you'd be risking."

"I know exactly what I'd be risking. And I swear to you Niki, after almost two years in this box, I do not care any longer what happens. I would be relieved if anything happened. Lately I've been dreaming of my wife. I know she's dead. And I know I'm not alive. Not as I am. So what does anything matter?"

I'm not entirely surprised to hear this. Things have been getting bad with the Jew for weeks now. There's an odor coming from the box that's almost enough to make us puke. He hasn't washed in over two months. Once or twice a week I'd always brought a bucket of hot water and some soap, and he took a sponge bath. I brought him clean underwear on those days too.

It was never pleasant for him in the cold weather, having to come out from the thick cocoon of blankets and strip off the layers of clothing to wash, but last year he did it without complaint. He seemed grateful for the chance to be clean. But this year he's different. He pushes the bucket of water back out when I try to slide it into the box. He won't take the clean underwear or any clean clothes, either. I don't know how to argue with him about it. I don't want to say how he reeks. He must know it. He must be able to smell himself. Or maybe it's crept up on him so gradually that he doesn't notice his awful acrid stench.

Sigi's had enough, though. The last few times she's been here she's held a handkerchief over her nose and made all sorts of repulsive faces.

"I'll tell you what matters," she snaps at the Jew. "What matters is that you smell like a corpse. You've become disgusting. We better bury you before the whole town smells you rotting. But we can't because you're not dead. So why don't you slit your wrist on a nail? There must be nails sticking out in there. And then we could bury you and get it over with."

The most wretched, wrenching sound I have ever heard comes from inside the box. Dr. Weiss is sobbing so violently I fear his lungs will rip. I put my fingers in my ears. It sounds worse than death. It sounds as if all the sorrow in the universe were in this one small stinking place, pressing unmercifully down on us, crushing us. I need to flee. I take Sigi's hand to lead her down from the loft, but she jerks away.

"Just wash, will you?" she shouts. "I'm sorry, damn you, I'm sorry. But think how we feel. You're our Jew, and we have to save you."

Save? Is that what we're doing? Or are we killing him in the slowest way? We leave then.

On the way home I'm thinking I can hear the Jew howl, but

it's only in my mind. I'm thinking: Everybody has connections, but ultimately you're on your own. You don't have to read any German philosophers to know that. The Jew has his life, such as it is, and we have ours. That's the way it is. That's the way this lonely world goes. It spins and each day's new. And we're the Advent singers, so action has to be taken. Costumes must be made. We can't devote all our time to the Jew and his misery, can we?

SIGI'S MOTHER can't afford much wood, so it's usually chilly in her kitchen. But on the next night, costume night, she's made it cozy. The tile stove is specially stoked, and we don't have to wear our coats and gloves. Sigi's excited. She's sitting warm as toast on the bench behind the table, smiling. From time to time she hugs herself, in that way of hers. She's wearing her best blouse and a good wool skirt that used to belong to Fräulein Mumelter. She's made an effort because it's our Traudl who is coming over to help with the sewing. I wish Sigi wouldn't care quite so much for her. Sometimes when I think about the two of them, I get that feeling where you're so sorry for yourself you want to cry, but you just can't manage to make yourself burst into relieving tears.

But anyway I'm pleased when Traudl comes in. I like to think she's here for me too, even though I know it's more for Sigi that she's come. She's wearing a pretty green cardigan over a lighter-green sweater, and a loden skirt. Her waist is so small it's hard to believe she's as old as she is. She has a smile for me, and when she sits at the table she's warm and I can smell her clean womanly smell. She asks if I've finished my paper on Andreas Hofer yet. We're studying Napoleonic times in the Tirol. I don't think Napoleon ever came here himself, but his soldiers did, along with those Bavarians. Hofer was against them. They caught Hofer and killed him. He's a patriotic hero, Fräulein Mumelter said in school. But once you've said that, what else is there? So I haven't finished my paper, I'm sorry to say.

"Think of heroes as real people," Traudl tells me. "Imagine them simply living, having buttered bread for breakfast or shivering when they go out on a cold morning. They live like all of us, but when the time comes they do something extraordinary. Maybe that capacity is within all of us, don't you think?"

"Like Gregor," Sigi says.

"Gregor?" Traudl says.

"The Haas boy, with the missing leg. Shot up in Russia," Sigi's mother says. "A brave boy, with a medal. But a head wound, you know?"

"Ah." Traudl nods.

"*Grüss Gott* to all," calls Gregor, as if on cue. He hobbles through the door, bringing the cold fresh smell of snow with him. Under his left arm he's got a bulging package wrapped in brown paper and tied with string. It's my costume. "Good evening, Frau Strolz. Hey, Sigi; hey, Niki. And you must be Fräulein Mumelter, whom Sigi and Niki never stop talking about."

I'm so embarrassed that for a moment I want to kick Gregor's crutch out from under him.

"I hate to think what they say," Traudl says, standing up and reaching to shake hands with Gregor before she sees that's impossible. But she's full of grace. She takes the package from under his left arm and then shakes his left hand with her left, all as smoothly as if that's the way people always did things.

"I've seen you outside the school some afternoons, going off with Sigi and Niki," she says.

"They keep me out of trouble," he says, nodding at his crutch.

"You don't tell them war stories, do you?" Traudl says.

"I do my best to never even think of war stories," Gregor says.

It's funny to watch the way Gregor's eyes keep sliding away from Fräulein Mumelter's face. Her eyes follow his to see what's so interesting about the dark corners of the room or the backs of his hands.

"We have to tell him what news we've heard on the radio. He never listens," Sigi says.

"As they always say in the newsreels, 'For the fallen, the war is over,' " Gregor says, trying to imitate the deep, solemn voices of the announcers. "Consider me fallen."

"I don't see how we can do that, when you stand there at attention. Take off your coat, sit down. Have some coffee," Sigi's mother says.

Gregor, studying his one booted foot, says he has to leave right away; he's so sorry, but he can't really stay. "And where do you have to go?" Sigi inquires. "Do you have a girl waiting for you? All the prettiest girls are right here, except for Maria Stocker, and she's taken."

"Sigi, hush," her mother says.

"It's true. Everybody knows she goes off with that soldier," Sigi says. "She'll probably be pregnant any day now."

"It's not for you to talk about," Fräulein Mumelter says.

But Gregor decides to sit and is soon sipping bitter ersatz coffee while I try on the dark-blue cape that was wrapped in the paper package. It's an old postman's cape Gregor's grandfather used to wear. I'm to wear it for Advent, with a hood attached. Sigi's mother is doing the attaching, using a piece of an old blue wool blanket my grandma found in one of her trunks.

Sigi's to be the angel, Simon and I her heralds. Naturally she has to wear white. Her communion dress is much too small now.

So Sigi's mother has brought out her wedding dress, smelling heavily of camphor, from the trunk where it's rested for twenty years. Sigi isn't quite as tall as her mother, so it has to be hemmed. But with a few tucks in the waist and some letting out of the darts in the bosom, it will fit her perfectly. Traudl is doing the fitting while Sigi stands on the bench. She's doing it over Sigi's clothes, because Sigi would freeze if she wore the dress outdoors without warm things under it. I remembered the other time I saw Sigi getting fitted for clothes. I wished I could see her that way now, wearing only a thin slip. Traudl's long fingers are almost brushing Sigi's breasts as she loosens the darts. I look at that, and then I look at Gregor and see his eyes are fixed on Traudl's concentrating face.

"You left town before I arrived, I think," says Traudl, not taking her eyes from her work. Gregor looks away at once.

"Bad luck for me, I think," he says. Sigi cocks her head at that.

"Bad for all the boys who had to go to the army," says Frau Strolz.

"Of course," he says. "You're right."

"Dad always said it was a duty and an honor to serve," Sigi says, a little too tartly for my liking.

"So it is," Gregor says.

"So what are your plans now, Herr Haas?" Traudl interrupts.

"Maybe I'll go back to school. Be a student. I could move to Innsbruck and sit in cafés. The government will pay."

"Ah, the government," says Frau Strolz. "Between us, they aren't so good about pensions. You can't count on them the way you used to."

"Well, we'll see what happens," Gregor says. "I don't expect they're accepting many students just now."

"But what will happen with the war?" Traudl asks.

"He doesn't know anything about the war," Sigi says. "He only knows what we tell him from the radio."

"I know no harm will come up here," Gregor says. "Here we're perfectly safe."

But I know shy Gregor can lie.

The truth I really want is what goes through his mind in bed at night. What does he see just before he falls asleep? And what does he think when he first opens his eyes in the morning and sees where he is?

13

THE JEW was suddenly obedient to Sigi. He was like a soldier in discipline. As if under her orders, he accepted the bucket of hot water the very next time I brought it. He washed thoroughly and changed into clean clothes. He even requested a few fresh-cut fir boughs to sweeten the sullen air in his box.

We had to burn his old underwear.

Then the next day he slammed his wrist against the point of a nail and pulled sideways as hard as he could. You'd think he'd know precisely the mortal spot, being a doctor. But a nail is not a scalpel, or even a razor. And his strength perhaps was not what he thought it was. He failed. All he got was a deep puncture and a ragged rip leading out of it that missed all the main veins. We only knew what he'd done because I saw the bloody rag on his wrist that night when he reached out for his food.

My father left everything up to me. Sigi could sew by touch. With fishing line from my father's store and an embroidery nee-dle, and with Dr. Weiss directing her from inside his box, she managed a passable closing of the wound. But I saw her flinch every time she had to pierce the skin with her needle.

The infection came at once, and almost succeeded in doing what the Jew's crude *Selbstmord* surgery could not. Fever possessed him entirely. We feared lockjaw and hideous death. There was so little I could do. Every morning and every evening I unbandaged his wrist, poured pure alcohol over the cut, followed with a swab of iodine, and rebandaged it with clean cotton. It was a gross, gaping wound that turned yellowish at the edges, but it didn't smell bad. I could tell the stage of his fever just by the heat of his hand. After a few days it began to cool, and a pitted black scab that looked ominous but that he said was a good sign soon filled the hole.

Sigi felt wretched. She'd rock on her heels and keen softly while I changed the bandages. At least she did until the third or fourth day, when, his fever lowering, the Jew growled, "Shut up, won't you, girl? Stop that god-awful wailing. You aren't sitting shivah."

In the end it was just a nasty cut. In the end the Jew seemed to recover himself, as if committing the act had been enough to ease him. He didn't brood on his defeat. But the disordered state of mind that causes a man to push his wrist onto a sharp nail alarmed us all, especially my father.

"You've got to keep him placid, Niki," my father said. "You know him better than anyone else. So it's up to you."

"How? Tell me how. I don't control him. I can't do anything," I said. My left knee started to jitter up and down, just as it does when I take exams. I felt angry at my father for heaping this on me, and hopeless. I wanted to cry, but I didn't dare.

"Be normal, that's all. Keep things normal. If he starts raving, remind him of things you know about his life. Bring him back to reality." When my father speaks like this, I feel as though I am hearing him from very far away.

"His reality's nothing but a dirty wooden box," I said.

"One that has saved his life. He mustn't forget that. And

you've got to remind him of his good memories, to give him a hope for the future. He must still have a little hope, no? Maybe of seeing his daughter in America one day?"

How could I say? It was so impossible. How was I to know the pitch of the Jew's despair? Did he ever feel like remembering his love affair in Venice anymore? Did he ever dream of using his skills and scalpels again at the Innsbruck hospital? Or was everything in his past a wasteland now? Did he want a woman at all? Who could know?

Three days after the bandages came off Dr. Weiss's wrist for good, I had to report that he was demanding to be turned loose. He said if he wasn't let out of the box he would scream until the whole village heard him. He said we had one week to set him free.

THE SNOW HELD the pale-blue tints of night when my father, Big Ignatz, and I started up into the mountains the next dawn. It was illegal to hunt at that season. But Pabst the gendarme? Blind as Sigi, the moment a tenderloin of stag appeared on his desk. Known to wink broadly and joke about the weather. No early riser who saw us tramping off armed would think it at all unusual. My father and Ignatz had their rifles cased and slung over their shoulders, but I don't think my father even bothered to pack ammunition. We ascended through meadow and forest for three hours. We climbed up into one of Ignatz's hunting blinds of badly weathered gray planks, flimsy as a child's tree house but as isolated as anyone could want. They began to nip at a flask of schnapps and discuss, as my father said, "our Jewish question." I was wishing I hadn't any part in this. I was wishing my father had left me home in my snug bed, like a child. I wished he would just take care of things.

"Impossible, Martin. Impossible and stupid. We can't let him go," Ignatz said. "Even if we could smuggle him down to the valley unseen, the fool'd be caught in a day. And they'll want to know where he's been all this time. Oh yes, they'll be so fucking curious, those pigs. They'll get the answer within an hour. They've got their methods."

"The bastards," my father said. "So letting him go is out of the question. Sweet Jesus, Ignatz, what choices do we have? He's going mad, I think."

"Keep him quiet by ramming some sense into his head," Ignatz said. "Or kill him."

"What?" said my father.

"We take him up the mountain at night. We find a nice crevasse. One to the head with my ice ax, and he's gone. In the crevasse for good. The body would never be found."

"Never," my father said. He'd turned so pale.

"For sure, Martin," Ignatz said reassuringly, as if my father's response had been a question, not a statement. "Listen to me. We tried something; we failed. The Jew's cracked up. It's his own fault. We can't do any more. We're not responsible."

"Did I hide him so we could kill him? What are you thinking of? Damn you, I have to save his life, not end it."

"The bastard's going to give us away!" Ignatz said heatedly.

"So be it, if it must be," my father said.

"Nothing must be," Ignatz said.

"Leave it alone now, Ignatz," my father said coldly.

Ignatz smiled. "Of course, Martin," he said. He sat sipping schnapps while my father and I climbed down from the blind and followed our tracks home through the softening snow.

IGNATZ COMES DOWN next day with a gutted deer over his shoulder. He has the beast dressed, and a piece has reached

Pabst by late afternoon. From Sigi's window I can see Pabst with his package, brown paper turning slightly bloody, walking hurriedly home past the cemetery. We're up in her room, supposedly doing homework. In an hour or so we'll have to go feed Dr. Weiss. But just now Sigi's lying on the bed, with her legs bent up at the knees and spread as wide as can be. She's grunting and moaning and holding her bulging stomach. Then with one hand she pulls a doll down from under her sweater and out between her legs. I can see her underpants. They're white with little edelweiss embroidered here and there. Her best pair, I think. "That," she says, "is how they're born. Comes out the same place the dick goes in. It must stretch an awful lot."

"Something you have to practice, is it?" I say sarcastically. I've been trying to explain the Jew's ultimatum and Ignatz's proposed solution while Sigi's been having her baby, and I'm cross.

"Now's the time to bring Traudl to meet him. That will snap him out of it," she says, sitting up on the edge of the bed and holding the doll to her breast. She still gets some thrill out of calling our teacher by her first name.

"Suppose she won't, Sigi? Or suppose she informs on us?" I say. "We don't know where she stands on Jews."

"She'd never tell, even if she doesn't like them," Sigi says. "She loves us, you know."

"That's ridiculous," I say.

"No, it's true. I can tell by the way she touches, and the tone of her voice. Haven't you noticed how differently she speaks to you and me than to any of the other kids? She's good too. She'll want to help."

I'm looking at Sigi sitting there on her bed, almost a woman but clearly still a girl—pretending to nurse a doll she's just pretended to give birth to, still with a crush on her teacher. I feel half crazy. I hate my father for all this. It isn't right what he's done, to take on something so serious and then lay the weight of it on us. I curse him.

"Don't be so hard on him," Sigi says. She's unbuttoning her blouse and is really going to put that doll to her nipple unless I shout at her to stop. I do.

"This is real, Sigi. It's a life, it's all our lives," I say. I'm surprised that she obeys me and puts the doll down. I wonder often if anyone hears me anymore.

"Yes, our splendid lives. Yours, mine too, they go day by day. Every day something new and wonderful. One day your father did a very worthy thing. He decided it was right. We decided to help him. Bravo for us."

"I don't feel I had any choice," I say. "I don't feel I gave you one, either, once I told you about it. But I'm afraid my father lost his nerve almost as soon as he built the box."

"Never mind that now. We have to get help. I say we need Traudl. If you know another way, say so."

I didn't. And I don't remember a moment in my life when I've felt more nervous than I did lurking outside the school with Sigi next afternoon, to intercept Fräulein Mumelter when she left for home. The plan was to explain our problem to her as we walked, so we wouldn't be overheard by anyone. Waiting, I racked my brains for a way to begin. I know I can't say, "Fräulein, we have been keeping a Jew in a box in my barn for two years and now he demands to be let out. What should we do?"

It sounds insane. When I try it out on Sigi she laughs hysterically.

But that is exactly what I say to Fräulein Mumelter as we're crunching through the snow. She's silent; she nods from time to time. Then she invites us up the stairs to her apartment. We've never been there before. No one we know has been there. Sigi is squeezing my hand as we enter. Her palm is sweaty.

It's only a single room with the usual knotty-pine paneling. There's a faint smell of cinnamon, cloves, and lemon peel. Angling out from a corner, instead of being placed flat against the wall like every other one I've ever seen, is a big pine bed. It's heaped with down quilts and pillows, all in white cotton. Sigi, usually so good at navigation, bumps into it, probably because of its unusual location. "So this is where she sleeps," she murmurs, patting the down. Next to the bed there's a pine armoire. Sigi strokes that, as if she'd like to open the door and tunnel into the clothes, just to breath their scent. Traudl is busy putting wood in the stove and then putting an old cast-iron teapot on to boil. She tells us to sit: there are two wooden chairs around a table so old and stained it's almost black. The chairs have colorful blankets, the red-and-black kind we use on our Haflinger ponies, draped over their backs. The only other thing I notice is a small framed print on the far wall, a famous one even I recogize: Gustav Klimt's *The Kiss*. They glow there, the little lovers, in their golden robes.

Traudl brings us cups of mint tea. She pulls a stool up to the table and sits with us. Sigi sighs. "It's just as I imagined," she says, holding her cup with both hands.

Traudl ignores the remark. She says, "I want to be certain I've got it right. One, you have a Jew hidden in a secret compartment in Niki's barn. He's been there two years, never once been out, and no one knows but Niki's family, Sigi, Ignatz, and now me. Two, this Dr. Weiss is at the end of his tether. He's tried to kill himself, and now he wants to be let out, even though he must know for sure that's the end of him. He must also know dreadful things will happen up here when he's caught. Do you think he cares so little?"

"Hard to say," Sigi says. "He's changed so much. There was something fatherly about him at first. Then he got odd for a while. But now you never know. Some days he says almost nothing. Once in a while he'll still banter with us or tell a story. Sometimes he's so obscure we don't know what he's talking about. It's like he's talking to people who aren't there."

"Like to the dead, maybe," I say.

"And you think having a new person to talk to will help him?" Traudl says.

"He says he doesn't believe there's a world outside anymore, or if there is it's a terrible one, evil everywhere. He says he must go out and witness," I say. "I'm not sure what he means."

"I'll come tonight. I'll meet you at the barn an hour after dark. And we'll see about your Jew," Traudl says.

I'm so shocked as we walk down the stairs from Fräulein Mumelter's place that what Sigi is telling me scarcely registers. "You know, Niki," she says, "this is very odd. But it was as if Traudl knew what we were going to tell her. It was as if she knew about the Jew."

"Ah, that's impossible," I said. "She's just a very cool and calm type."

"I didn't hear any surprise at all in her voice. Her breathing didn't change, either. And I don't think she's all that calm," Sigi said. "I think she's very deep. I think there's a lot she keeps deep inside her that might be shocking to us."

My thoughts are elsewhere. No one must know what we're about that night. It's dark by four. An hour later I'm shivering on the blind side of the barn from the village houses. I hear Traudl and Sigi slipping through the snow before I see them. I open the little back door, not the big one out front that the cows use, and up we go into the loft. It's cold, but the hay smells good. There's no greeting from the box, though Dr. Weiss must have heard us on the ladder. No light can ever show from the Jew's box, but I'm allowed a paraffin lantern, since I'm supposedly up here doing chores. I light it. It gives us all the strangest shadows. They almost dance; they're thin like Death in the medieval etchings I've seen in books.

"We've brought someone to meet you, Doctor," Sigi says.

"I'm not receiving company at the moment. I'm dead at the moment," he says.

"Then imagine your soul's young and handsome and has left your smelly old cadaver and is about to meet an angel," Sigi said.

"With my luck, a bloodthirsty avenging Christian one with sword and fire," Dr. Weiss says. "Couldn't I at least meet a kindly Jewish angel, come to save me from you monstrous children?"

"Who in their right mind believes in angels in these times?" Traudl says. Her voice sounds deeper than it ever did in class. "All you'll meet tonight is a woman, almost twenty-four, reasonably intelligent but without a university degree. I'm the village schoolteacher."

"And my two guardian delinquents presumed I was in need of some lessons. Philosophy, perhaps? A bit of religious instruction? I think not. You may go."

"You need some lessons in politeness, it seems to me," Traudl says. "You are obnoxious. I've given you no reason to be. And that's not the sort of man I was told you are."

"Fräulein, I am not sure I'm a man of any sort anymore. I have been buried here for two years. Prove to me we exist."

"How?"

"Move just to the right of that post, the one with the old bridle hanging from it. Then I can see you through my knot-hole."

Traudl moves. She stands very straight. She looks healthy and strong and vital even in the harsh light of the lantern.

"Now," she says, "you see me as I am. I can even see a little of your eye. Does that make anything more real?"

"It would another time, perhaps, but not at this moment. I indulge myself with this idea of shifting realities, of passing over into the world of the dead, when I am feeling especially sorry for myself. As I am tonight."

"Who could blame you for that?"

"Anyone. Everyone. Because almost no one could imagine what it's been like in here all this time. No one could not understand the horror of it. No. I shouldn't say horror. That's too much. I'm safe here, after all, I'm well fed. Call it . . . numbing, or deadening. The only reason I have any sanity left at all is the fifteen minutes each day I talked with Niki and Sigi. The other twenty-three hours and forty-five minutes I live only with my own mind. I've found its resources aren't inexhaustible. This has proved a shock and a disappointment. I've apparently overestimated myself for years.

"I've also found that bad things, terrible things I've done, happen to be some of the clearest images my mind presents for contemplation. It's a sophisticated sort of suffering, wouldn't you say? Sort of suprareligious punishment, something even Dante missed, and he had a fine eye for suffering."

"As a Jew, you can't mean any of that. There's no Inferno for you," Traudl says.

"True, but I'm a Germanized Jew through and through, over several generations. These wild and furious Christian ideas leak into us, no matter how vigilant we are. It seems to me that I am indeed being punished, for reasons or sins I am being shown daily."

"Anyone would feel bitter," Traudl says, "unless they're the type that accepts even gross suffering as part of God's plan. Which I personally think is crap."

"I'm thinking I like your attitude, Fräulein. I'm thinking also it makes a nice change from morbid self-absorption to see a pretty girl."

"Ungrateful man," Sigi says. "Fickle Jew."

Dr. Weiss laughs. "Yes, Sigi."

"So why are you here, Fräulein?" he asks after a moment. "That it's risky goes without saying. My presence is the great secret in this town. What are your intentions? Will you betray me? Or release me?"

"I can't do either. I felt I ought to come, after hearing your story."

"Pathetic, yes? You wished to witness true pathos for once in your young life," Dr. Weiss says.

"You've no idea what I've seen in my young life," Traudl snaps back.

"But still, you've come out of pity," Dr. Weiss says.

"Would you expect anything else? Don't scorn that, Doctor. You are pitiable, and you know it."

"I do, and I hate it."

"I won't come again without your permission. With your permission, I'll come when I can to talk, to bring you a book now and then, to try to help you occupy your mind. And maybe to give Niki and Sigi some relief from you."

"You think I'm hard on them?" he asks.

"Certainly you are sometimes too much for them," she says. "Though I doubt you can help it."

"So you'd come, each time feeling sorry for the old man in the box?"

"Yes. Naturally. But perhaps a little less as time goes on."

"I think my time has just about run out," Dr. Weiss says. "I simply can't bear this much longer."

"But it can't last much longer, can it? The war is going so badly, I think. They're even admitting the Russians are in East Prussia and the Americans are at the Rhine. This thing has to end."

"No," Dr. Weiss says. "Almost everything we've seen in the past eight years has been unprecedented. Perhaps this will be something new under the sun too: a perpetual conflict. The thing that never ends. It will go on and on for generation after generation."

"I don't think so," I say.

I don't know what I'm talking about, of course. It's the sixth winter of the war, but what's that to us? There's Gregor and his missing leg, all right. But otherwise all we see are flights of tiny planes once or twice a week. Supposedly they cross our Alps to bomb Salzburg and Vienna. To us they look like toys, shining in the blue sky.

"Gregor says the German Army is beaten but just hasn't realized it yet," Traudl says.

"Gregor? Ah, the wounded boy. You'd have to allow for some pessimism with wounds like his. And soldiers of the line don't always grasp the big picture," the doctor says.

"When do you talk to Gregor?" Sigi demands of Fräulein Mumelter, almost as if she were speaking to an equal.

"We've had tea at the inn, Sigi. We've walked down to the bridge," Traudl says.

"He didn't tell us," Sigi says.

"Is it his duty to keep you informed of everything he does?" Traudl says.

"He's our friend. We made friends with him," Sigi says. "I let him take my photograph."

Sigi, Sigi, Sigi, please don't talk, I think. "It'd be a poor world if we were forbidden to have more than a certain number of friends," I say.

"Maybe not. It depends on things," Sigi said. "Intentions and so forth."

Traudl looks at Sigi and smiles. "I'd say Gregor is a young man with only good intentions," she says.

"Good for who?" Sigi says. Then she starts laughing at herself, a gift of hers I envy very much for the way it eases awkwardness of all sorts.

"Why don't you bring Gregor up here sometime, and we'll all be friends?" Dr. Weiss says.

"Too many people coming and going. Someone would notice. Someone would tell," I say.

"Just a thought," the Jew said. "I have a little story about friends, or lack of them. I had a patient once, an elderly lady. I was called to her apartment when she died by her maid. She had no family that I ever met, but she seemed to be very well fixed. Her apartment was spacious, full of good furniture. There was no one there but the maid, and a great green parrot who appeared to live on a perch in the old woman's bedroom. The parrot was an amazing creature, very bright-eyed. And he could speak beautiful German. They learn from what they hear, you understand. This parrot kept saying 'Nobody loves me, nobody loves me in the whole wide world.' "

"That's the saddest thing I've heard," Traudl says.

"No, it isn't. It's nothing against what we already know of these times. It won't even register on any scale of sorrow and misery, if the full truth of these times is ever revealed," Dr. Weiss says. "It will seem like a joke in comparison. And I say this knowing my own experience will seem like a joke too."

Leaving, in the moonlight, I see Traudl's eyes are glistening. But no tears glide down her cheeks. Perhaps they flowed later, when she was alone in her white bed. That's the way it usually is with me.

I LIKE TO BE ALONE in Sankt Vero in the evenings. I love to see the warm yellow lights in windows resist the deepening dusk. I like to walk through the town, thinking of this and that, watching the white plumes of my own breath. That's what I'm doing on Saturday, a few evenings after we took Traudl to the Jew. I've just dropped off Sigi, and I'm passing the sawmill, quiet now that the week's work is done. It's dark except for a half-open door, and just inside, there stands Big Ignatz. Usually at this hour he'd be in the bar with his new buddy, the sergeant. I don't like the idea of them together, for reasons I don't exactly understand. I like it less that my father sometimes joins them. Ignatz beckons to me as I pass. I turn toward his door.

Big Ignatz is so strange. He has massive arms and shoulders, a thick neck, a square scarred head. But he has lips like a girl's, and the big soft brown eyes of a fawn. He looks like one of nature's terrible mistakes, embittered and menacing. He opens the door a bit more so I can slip in.

"The Jew's quieted down?" he asks.

"Yes, he seems better, I think," I say.

"Clever of you, Niki, to distract him," he says.

"What do you mean?"

"I think you know."

"I don't."

"What you do up there, you and Sigi. Fooling around."

"We just feed him and talk."

"Sure you do, Niki. You know, Niki, I wouldn't tell about the Jew if my life depended on it. Your father's my comrade, after all. And hell, my life depends on silence too. The swine would tear me to pieces if they found out. But I could tell you some juicy things about your pretty Mumelter, true things you would hardly believe. For a small price."

"Price?" I ask. I'm feeling sweaty under my arms.

"You wouldn't pay anything. You'd like it," he says, suddenly putting his meaty hand between my legs. I'm too shocked to move for a moment. I begin to tremble. He isn't grabbing me tight, just lightly stroking me, so as he leans forward to kiss me I'm able to spin and slip out the partly open door.

"I know all the secrets, Niki," Ignatz calls. He sounds so confident, so sure of himself.

And it was that voice, more than the touching, even, which sickened me so. I couldn't eat, and my grandmother wondered why I was so fretful. I went to my room as soon as supper was over and climbed into my bed, still completely dressed. There was no sleep for me, though. I watched a full moon arc over Sankt Vero, turning the snow bright and shiny as the little tin ornaments we put on our Christmas trees. From my window I could just see a sliver of our barn in the distance. The weathered wood looked silvery. Hours must have passed. Then I heard my father downstairs in the kitchen, fixing his coffee. He always did that around three-thirty, much earlier than most anyone else in town. He said he liked to take care of the cows as early as he could, to free up the rest of the day for the store. I heard him leave the house. Soon I saw him appear before the barn. And I saw Traudl Mumelter come up out of the shadows and take his hand. I turned to face the wall at once, and wondered at the nature of dreams, or the way a mind could play tricks, until my grandma came to wake me for church.

I felt a bile rising within myself all that silent day. I could scarcely speak. I wanted so much to sleep, but not to dream. Sigi urged me to come over after dinner, and we lay together on her bed, as we often did. I couldn't tell her about Ignatz, or about Traudl and my father. I was beginning to believe already that I had never seen them. I said I was upset because my father had yelled at me for no reason that morning in the harshest way. Then suddenly I was weeping, weeping, and Sigi held my head against her soft breast. Never mind, she said, never mind. Then she kissed me over and over.

AND ADVENT came to its end. The Jew was no longer demanding his release. He was looking forward to Traudl's visits. Sigi, Simon, and I weren't so bad as we had imagined. Simon carried us through; he had a nice voice.

We had finished our last carol, we had sipped our last cup of chocolate, we had turned away from the last bright doorway and walked into the peaceful darkness of Sankt Vero's last Advent night. Then we were ambushed.

They jumped us from behind a wagon, scarves wrapped round their faces. Did they really expect we wouldn't know them? You could smell they'd been at the schnapps. Andreas and one of the seventeen-year-old soldiers, who was supposed to be watching for planes, grabbed Simon and wrestled him down. Another soldier kicked my legs out from under me. I hit the ground so hard I lost all my wind. Then he sat on my chest and held my arms. Kaspar—formerly fat and laughable Kaspar and now strong and heavy Kaspar—lumbered around Sigi, who stood still as a deer. "Blind bitch," he said. "Blind bitch." I saw him grab her around the waist, lift her off her feet, and plunge her into a pile of snow.

Then he bundled her dress up around her waist and very rapidly buried her legs and belly with snow. "Too ugly to fuck," he said, looking down at her. The others let Simon and me go. Simon took a swing at Andreas, but the soldier punched him hard in the stomach. Simon fell to his knees, retching. My soldier kicked me in the knee and ran away. Sigi lay perfectly still, but I could hear her crying. I limped over and brushed away the piles of snow and pulled her dress down. Then I helped her stand. Poor Simon was still crouched, holding his stomach.

"I'm going to murder Kaspar in cold blood," Sigi hissed.

Some words are best not spoken. Some words should never be heard.

14

OF COURSE, we never saw the letter that betrayed us. They don't have to show you things like that. They don't even have to show any sort of warrant or order. The people in uniform can do just what they please to the people who aren't. But we knew there had been a letter. Just after New Year's, on a dreary thawing day, a squad of troops came rumbling up from Fussing in a big canvas-roofed truck. They crowded into my father's store with their rifles unslung and their bayonets fixed. With them came Pabst the gendarme. A sergeant with a chapped face and watery eyes who couldn't have been more than twenty-five told my father he and his men were going to search our property.

"May I ask the reason?" my father said.

"No," the sergeant said. "We've got our orders. We start now."

There were twelve of them: the hard sergeant and eleven boys. They were younger than Gregor. Four of them went all through the store like vandals, pulling out drawers and breaking boxes, crawling under counters and into cabinets. One kept giggling. The others went up and down in the house, opening every door, every armoire, every pantry, cupboard, and bureau, looking under every bed, pushing boxes around the attic, stabbing coal piles in the cellar. After a lot of clattering and slamming of doors and the grating of hobnailed boots on wooden floors, the sergeant, who'd been sitting on the steps smoking cigarette after cigarette, judged the commotion had been sufficient to flush out the prey. He blew a whistle, and the soldiers came clattering back to him. Then they marched off behind him to the barn.

They were all from the city. You could tell from the finicky way they stepped around the horse shit and mud puddles but plowed right through the flat stinking cow plop. They moved inside the barn like awkward girls at their first dance lessons, fussily using their bayonets to lift the tops of feed bins and fertilizer tins and poke around in bales of hay. "This means trouble, Martin," Pabst whispered to my father. As if that wasn't obvious as hogs' balls. But my father just glanced at Pabst and smiled. He stood there outside the barn door, looking like he should be smoking a pipe. Looking as if there was nothing in the world out of the ordinary about having a squad of Wehrmacht soldiers heaving hay and straw around your barn with bayonets and banging on the walls with the butts of their Mausers. Only if you looked at the back of his neck, and saw the short hairs there standing up like a scared dog's, would you know anything bad was under way. Me, I had to pee so bad I kept hopping from one leg to the other.

"Christ, man, let the brat go piss, why don't you?" the sergeant snapped at my father. But I didn't want to leave. I felt I had to be right there, that as long as I was there everything would be all right.

After they'd finished the main floor of the barn, half the squad clambered up into the loft, while the rest stood around the sergeant. They were going to light cigarettes when my father shouted, "No smoking in there. It'll go up like a torch, with all the straw." The sergeant lit up, anyway, but then herded his charges out the door before they could. They looked liked schoolboys sneaking a smoke before church on a Sunday morning. "Christ, fuck!" said the sergeant, catching the heel of his boot in a flat patty of cow shit he hadn't noticed. "You peasants live like pigs. Shit everywhere you look. This could be fucking Poland."

"*Ja,*" my father said. "But it's a life."

"A pig's life," the sergeant spat.

"That's what we thought when we took the Veneto in 1917 and saw the way the Italians lived," my father said. The sergeant squinted at him briefly, then looked back to the barn.

Up in the loft the soldiers were pounding on the walls. The new wall that formed the Jew's box looked like all the others. The wood was just as weathered. Making it, my father had covered all the fresh-cut edges with a mixture of sawdust, tar, and paint, so they looked old and half rotten. You couldn't tell it was false, looking at it. He'd built it solid. We were pretty sure there'd be no hollow booming if they tested it with their butts. But please, oh please, let the Jew keep his nerve, and his silence. The soldiers were yelling at each other, criticizing each other's personal methods of pounding, probing, and tossing things around.

"God in heaven," the sergeant sighed.

A little trickle of urine ran down my leg, but I managed to shut off the flow. And then a thought from some lightless place seemed to detonate in my head. I could see myself suddenly running up to the loft and pointing out the Jew's hiding place. The soldiers would be excited. Some would pat me on the back and ruffle my hair, while the rest beat down the wall. I imagined the excitement, I imagined seeing the Jew's face for the first time in years, imagined him blinking like some dumb crippled animal as they brought him out into the pale daylight.

Then I saw the Jew and my father and me tied up and tossed roughly into the bed of the army truck, beaten now and then with rifle butts by the soldiers sitting on benches along the truck's sides. In Fussing, they'd put us in a freezing dungeon. They'd torture us with rubber hoses and electric shocks. We'd be given only a moldy potato to eat, and then we'd be taken out to the courtyard and shot by teenage soldiers, who would probably spit and feel wretched afterward. I only hoped they would hit my heart and not put bullets in my face.

I began to pray. I'd stopped years before, when my prayers were never answered. But now I tried hard. Not the written prayers or the ones the priest insists that everyone memorize, but my own private dare to God to prove Himself by keeping them from finding our Jew. There was so much shouting and pounding coming from the loft. But at last a corporal came down and shrugged his shoulders at the sergeant. "There's fuck-all up there, Sergeant, but hay and rat shit," the corporal said. "It's bare boards and straw, you couldn't hide a sausage."

"Another fucking wild-goose chase," the sergeant spat. "Somebody's got a hard-on for you, Lukasser. You've pissed somebody off for sure. Maybe you got some people in the black market who don't care for your way of doing business. Or maybe you messed around with the wrong woman. None of my business. But I'd watch my back if I were you."

The sergeant paused for a moment, then ordered his men to the truck. He looked my father in the eye. "In the Veneto, eh? Whereabouts?" he asked.

"Sacile. Shot through the chest, October '18," my father said.

"Christ," the sergeant said. His men were pulling themselves aboard the truck, chaffing and shoving. "You didn't hear this from me, Lukasser. But somebody wrote my boss that you were hid-

ing a Jew up here. Anonymous, like always. I didn't believe it myself. You damn peasants would never stick your necks out like
that. Too damn shrewd.

"My dad was killed at Vittorio Veneto in '18," the sergeant
added. Then he turned on his shit-encrusted heel and strode
over to the truck. He climbed in up front beside the driver and
looked straight ahead. The truck coughed, then ground off down
around the curve toward the valley.

It was all over in an hour. Pabst the gendarme stood by my
father for a while afterward, looking like a dog who knows he's
done something to displease. Only after the truck pulled away
did I notice the faces at every window nearby. I saw arms reaching out to pull the shutters closed again. Sigi and Gregor were
standing just across the street. She was holding his left hand. I
saw him bend his head toward hers, and then she waved and
shouted my name. I ran over. Almost everyone else in town remained inside. The place looked quiet and closed, almost aban-
doned or as if everyone were hiding. There wasn't even a sign of
Ignatz at the mill.

But to me it felt as if the world had just opened itself up. I
wasn't bound by gravity. Oh, I was full of the tale. I babbled every
intricate detail to Sigi, not forgetting to mention the way my father ordered the soldiers not to smoke in the barn and how he'd
impressed the sergeant with his military record. I did it again that
afternoon to Fräulein Mumelter. I felt victorious. Even to Dr.
Weiss I made foolish boasts of how my father and I had saved him
by being so steady and cool with the troops, who had somehow
been transformed from pimply boys to serious soldiers. I forgot
all about peeing on myself in the barnyard.

My father bore all the weight of that day. I think he was
shaken to his bones, as if he had finally been shown the crush-

ing enormity of what he was up to with this Jew-hiding. The hair lay down on the back of his neck, he smiled, but a tic began tugging sporadically at the left corner of his mouth. He stammered slightly at supper that night. He issued new orders. Only I was permitted to feed the Jew. And I wasn't allowed to stay to talk anymore. When I said that was pointless, he cuffed me on the ear.

How we stood with the town after the search changed even more than it had when my mother made her unforgettable appearance in Fräulein Mumelter's classroom the year before. I caught odd, fearful looks from most of the kids at school. They were afraid to speak to me; probably they'd been told by their parents to avoid me. There was no business in the store for some days, until people began to run out of things and had no choice. But they seemed hurried in their purchases, not inclined to chat.

My father never speculated on who might have informed. At least not to me. And after a few days, enough tension left him that I was able to resume old routines, taking Sigi and Fräulein Mumelter with me to see the Jew. But I looked at everyone suspiciously. I mostly suspected Ignatz. I thought he'd told the antiaircraft sergeant who was his drinking buddy. Together they wrote the anonymous note to the commandant in Fussing. Nobody would dare put his name on a denunciation, for fear of falling under suspicion himself. I figured Ignatz must have thought he'd get entirely clear of the Jew affair that way.

There was another thing. Ever since that night in his office, Ignatz looked at me in a way that made me feel I had no clothes on. I don't understand how he did this, but I felt stripped naked. I hated it more than anything.

I figured Sigi and I would have to take care of two people now: Kaspar and Ignatz.

Sigi and her mother don't care what the town does. They never shun me. I'm over there every day after school, up in Sigi's room, sometimes reading the lessons but other times just talking of this or that. Sometimes Sigi lets me comb her hair. It's so thick and heavy, her neck's so thin. Sometimes she trails her hands over my face when we talk. She hardly ever does this to anyone else. She says it's to see me. I don't flinch even when her fingers get near my eyes. It makes me feel like I'm special. Once in a while for a joke I'll bite one of her fingers, gently like a puppy. "Bad," she says, laughing.

TWO SATURDAYS after the search, Gregor invites Sigi and me and Fräulein Mumelter to have coffee and cake with him at the inn in the afternoon. The coffee's ersatz, but the cream is real, and so is the *Möhnstrudel*. Gregor is treating because he's just got his first pension money. He also says he's had a letter telling him to report to the hospital at Schwaz at the end of February to get his artificial leg.

"Are you scared?" Sigi asks.

"I liked the hospital, actually," says Gregor. "It was warm, for one thing. You could really relax. No one expected anything of you. A little pain seemed a fair price for such luxury.

"Home is better, of course. After army life, the best thing in the world is to wake in the morning between clean sheets," he says, "and suddenly realize there is no danger anywhere. You can lie there safely just as long as you like. This is tremendous. And clean underwear every day. Clean socks. A warm coat.

"But Schwaz should be easy. They just have to fit the leg, and then I have to spend a week or two learning how to navigate on it. I'll be glad to get rid of my crutch."

"Will you get a girlfriend then?" Sigi asks.

"You think no one's interested in me as I am? Too damaged?" Gregor smiles. "I don't have a lot of competition in my age group just now, you know."

"I didn't mean it like that. Just if you had a leg, you could take a girl dancing and things," Sigi says. Her ears are flushing pink, something I almost never see with her.

"Lots of girls don't care to dance much anymore," Fräulein Mumelter says. "Good talk, companionship, understanding, these are the important things. Best of all is a shared dream, no matter how modest."

"Who could dream anything but modestly nowadays?" Gregor said. "The best we can hope is that we all survive these years, that there'll be some kind of life for us when the war is over."

"Some kind of life," Sigi says. Her eyes are bright, but her voice is sad. "Alive, in this little place, among people we know. Is that it?"

"Wouldn't it be enough, Sigi?" Fräulein Mumelter says, touching her on the arm.

"I want very much to see something of the world before I die," Sigi bursts out. "I want to have some experience—I don't know: to swim in the sea somewhere warm, to fall in love with someone who'll marry me, to hear someone talk in a foreign language or eat some foreign food. Just to know for sure there is something beyond these mountains and this snow."

"Even with the world as it is, you might have those things one day," Gregor says.

"Doesn't anyone else but me get tired of waiting for 'one day'?" Sigi asks. "Everything my father ever promised me was 'one day.' "

Gregor and Fräulein Mumelter are looking at each other so intently I feel embarrassed to be witnessing it. They're clearly unaware of anyone else's regard just at that moment. And suddenly I see Traudl again stepping out of the shadows at four in the morning to take my father's hand in silvery moonlight. Then I wonder if Gregor isn't up to something himself with our Traudl. I can't bear thinking of it. It ruins everything. I hope Sigi isn't feeling what I am. I take her hand in mine, her soft, familiar hand with the short, chewed nails and the little bump on her thumb.

Damn Gregor. I almost wish he'd never come home.

"AND NOW," says Dr. Weiss, an old man preening, "you would like to hear the story of my life, *nicht wahr?*"

"No, I would not," says pretty Traudl. "I've heard enough from Sigi and Niki about poor Rachel in Vienna and the nurse in Venice and the other sordid details. You're a dog, Dr. Weiss. You've taken advantage."

The Jew laughs. I think he's pleased.

"What I want to hear is the story of your wife," Traudl says.

"Your wife," Sigi says.

"She's dead," Dr. Weiss says harshly.

What's Traudl done? He'd seemed so pleased to have the company when we'd come, which is not always his response. Maybe he was happy with the brilliant day, the shafts of sun pouring through the cracks in the walls. "Let me have a look at you," he'd said, so we all posed by the post where the old bridle hangs. "Charming," he'd said. Then we sat in the straw.

"Dead," he almost whispers. His voice blighted, forlorn.

"You have no proof of that. You only know she was taken to

a camp. You've every reason to hope you'll meet again, when it's all over," Traudl says.

"In my heart I know she's gone. They've killed her," the doctor says.

"Tell me," Traudl insists.

"We met . . . God forgive me, I can't remember when or where we met," he says.

"I can," Sigi says. "You just grabbed her by the tits in the dark living room of your girlfriend's apartment, thinking she was your girlfriend. You were embarrassed when your girl switched on the lights and you found you were molesting her young cousin. Later you moved to Innsbruck, where the cousin lived, and wooed and wooed her. You remember."

"Of course I do. I remember so many things she said to me, jokes we shared, arguments, what she wore to certain balls, the way she smelled in the morning. But what frightens me is that I can no longer picture her face in my mind," Dr. Weiss says. "Oh, dear God."

"What color is her hair?" Sigi says.

"It's black, with beautiful threads of silver waving through it," the Jew answers.

"Her eyes?" Sigi asks.

"Oh, brown. But an unusual brown, with reddish-gold flecks. I always loved . . . " He trailed off.

"What about her nose and lips?" Sigi inquired.

"I know what you're trying to do. . . . " He pauses. "Her nose is a medium nose, neither large nor small, neither extremely straight nor curved. Her mouth is wide, but her lips aren't full. She has a brilliant smile, though, and when she's cross, little creases at the corners of her mouth."

"And her body?" Sigi asks.

"None of your business," the Jew says indignantly.

"Well, you told about Rachel and the nurse without our even asking," Sigi says.

"But this is my wife we're discussing," the Jew protests, and as he hears Traudl chuckle he begins to laugh himself.

"Yes, you've caught me out. I have in fact described hips and bosoms. But suddenly I find I have reformed. I'm a gentleman, I'll say no more."

"But you loved her up, didn't you?" Sigi says.

"Oh, indeed I did. She was so lovely."

"How do you share a life with someone?" Traudl asks.

"You don't plot a course, exactly," the doctor says. "You marry. You find yourself by custom in the same bed each night, in the same rooms of the house each day. You are thrown together. You discover, happily, certain areas in which you harmonize. You discover others which are not so pleasant. As you make these discoveries, you adapt. And soon enough you have a history together, a joint memory of things. Then you are really a couple."

"What about a child?" Traudl says.

"If the marriage isn't strong, children can break it. If the marriage is sound, children are a . . . not a joy; that's inadequate. They seem to be actually a fulfillment, even when they're noisy, tiresome, and nerve-racking, which all children are."

"So you hold your wife and your daughter in your mind even through all of this nightmare," Traudl says. "They've not left you at all, isn't it so?"

"Yes."

"It's not my wife's face I can no longer picture," he says after a while. "But she's like a photograph, lifeless. Where has she gone? That's what I can't see. My mind will not accept her annihilation. If she's gone, I have gone with her, for all that I am was shared with her. So I cannot accept this, while I still eat and breathe. It is unacceptable, although it may be true."

"Thank you for telling me," Traudl says. "Don't give up hope yet."

EVERYONE IN THE MOUNTAINS knows better than to kick a rock down a steep treeless slope. Kick the wrong one at the wrong time, and you may start half a mountain tumbling down. Try telling this to a blind girl, though. She won't get it. An avalanche to her is just a lot of noise.

A few days after our talk with Dr. Weiss about his wife, Sigi starts to kick rocks. She wants to hear the rumble and the roar.

The first: She whispers to Andreas that Kaspar's soldier friend—Otto's his name—is telling everyone that he makes Kaspar suck his cock anytime he wants. She says Otto's told everyone from me and Simon and her to Big Ignatz and my father. Andreas doesn't really believe it, but Sigi is so sincere. She makes it sound as if everything bad, even the last Advent night, is forgotten, just a joke after all, and that she's concerned for Kaspar. So Andreas, doubtful still but worried, straightaway reports to Kaspar. We see him the next day with a split lip. "What happened?" Sigi asks.

"I told Kaspar what Otto's been saying, and then naturally I asked if it was true. And I got punched in the mouth," Andreas says. He shook his head. "It must be true, then."

Kaspar could not walk down the street with Otto anymore. He tried it once and everyone stared at them. One farmer whistled. Kaspar's fury was almost visible. He seemed to swell with it, the way a toad does when it's cornered and afraid. And then one day Ignatz laughed at him and called him a queer. Kaspar's judgment was so impaired that he threw a punch. I saw this, right outside the sawmill. In a split second Kaspar was knocked on his ass, both eyes bruised and blackening fast.

"Next time, I fire you," Ignatz said. He was laughing as he looked down at the boy.

15

ON A GOOD DAY you could easily forget that Sigi was a blind girl. I did once. It wasn't a tragedy. There was an accident, that's all, some hard luck for my carelessness. As the Jew said, the threshold of sorrows and miseries had been much raised in our times. Sympathy was scarce. It had become very stiff to qualify as one of the truly wounded. Even Gregor was a borderline case. I was nothing.

It was a good day, a beautiful January afternoon with a bright sun in a dark-blue sky, the way summer ought to look but rarely does. We never minded the cold at all on a day like that. We'd walk until the sun had gone. Sigi had picked up a sturdy pine stick from a scrap pile at the sawmill. She was tapping along home very nicely. Then, with more grace and accuracy than you'd think a blind girl could have, she was swiping at the icicles that hung in ragged rows from the eaves of her house. She loved the crystalline sound the icicles made as they shattered. It was pretty to see them fall, changing in the light like prisms. I forgot she couldn't see. I stood too close. I looked up. She hit an icicle nearly the length of my arm. It plunged down into my left eye.

There wasn't any pain. There was only a dazing jolt. I closed my eyes for a moment, I took a step back. I felt a little outside myself, and I could hear icicles smashing far away. Sigi was saying something, but it was only an echo in my head that made no sense.

When I opened my eyes I could see Sigi with my right eye, but in the left there was only a curtain of dark red. I could not see through it. I tried to wipe it away and saw that my hand was thick with blood. But the red curtain remained.

I thought then that I had better go home.

"I'm going now," I said.

"Why are you going?" Sigi asked.

"Got something in my eye," I said.

I wanted to hold my hand over my eye, but when I did, something felt loose and flapping. I couldn't bear that feeling. So I went home with my hands in my pockets and found my grandma in the kitchen. "God in heaven," she said. She took a clean linen towel out of the dresser, folded it, and pressed it gently over my eye. She sat me down on the bench and put my hand on the towel, telling me to hold it in place. Then she went to get my mother, who was upstairs, taking a nap.

When my mother came down, wrapped in a robe, with her hair all tousled, she ran to the store as soon as she'd seen me bleeding there and screamed at my father, "Get the Jew! Get him now!" Lucky for us there were no customers just then.

My father hurried into the kitchen, wearing his canvas apron. He took away the towel, and although he made an effort to smile, his eyes narrowed with shock. "Not so bad," he said. But now I knew better. "Get the Jew, get the Jew," my mother was saying. It was almost a chant. She had a rhythm going, and her voice moved up and down the scale like a monk's. "Get the Jew, get the Jew right now. Hurry and get the Jew." My grandma was holding her by the arm, saying, "Hush, hush. There, there." It sounded to me as if she were talking to a baby. I wished my mother would calm down.

"Martin, you must do something," my grandma said.

"The Jew can't help, that's for sure," he said.

"Why not?" my mother screamed. "He's a surgeon, for God's sake."

"Yes, he proved that once, didn't he?" my father said.

"And saved Niki's life," my mother said.

"I don't need reminding," my father said.

"Get the Jew in here now!" my mother shouted.

"It can't be done, dammit, " my father said. "Some people must have seen Niki coming home with that bloody eye. If they see Niki tomorrow with the eye all neatly bandaged, who will they think did it? Will they think you or I suddenly became doctors? What questions will they ask? How shall we explain?"

"I don't care—who cares? Just get the Jew," my mother said.

"Niki has to go to Fussing," my father said carefully. "Niki has to be treated by the doctor in Fussing. And everyone in town has got to know this."

"No! No! No! The Jew's got to help. He's got to fix this thing right now!" my mother said. She'd started crying, which surprised me, for I didn't think she cared so much for me.

"The Jew doesn't exist," my father said. "There is no Jew. There never was a Jew. The nearest doctor is in Fussing, and I'm taking Niki there now."

My father ran out to get Pabst the gendarme. My grandma took away the blood-soaked towel, and while my mother shrieked, she placed a new one over my eye and tied it there with a piece of kitchen twine. We were rattling down the mountain in Pabst's gray Volkswagen in no time. The exhaust smell was making me giddy.

"Well, well," said Dr. Durchleuchter, the Fussing quack. "Well, well, well. Nasty piece of work. How'd you do it?"

"An icicle," I said.

He started laughing. "You should know better than to walk under them on a sunny day."

"I do know better. I just forgot for a moment," I said.

"I don't think you'll ever forget again," the doctor said. "Martin, hold Niki tight now."

Then he poured an icy liquid over my eye, which burned worse than any pain I'd ever known. But it didn't wash away the red curtain. Soon through the burning I felt the pricks of a needle, the tugs as the thread was pulled through skin. My father was behind me, holding my head still with his hands over my ears.

"Niki should stay here for the night, but tomorrow you must go to Schwaz. A surgeon really ought to have a look at that eye. What I've done is just patch it up for the trip," the doctor said. Pabst drove back to Sankt Vero, bearing this news. I slept in the examination room, and my father slept in the chair behind the doctor's huge, disordered desk. The doctor gave me some pills, which made me feel quite dizzy. The next thing I knew, it was morning.

"Goddamn, what sort of a butcher did this? Did you get the kid a quick sew at the vet's, Herr Lukasser?" the surgeon at the Schwaz hospital said. He immediately took a pair of scissors from a chrome tray of instruments by my side and cut the stitches. "Ah, now I recognize the fine hand behind this. You've stopped at Fussing, haven't you?"

I was lying on a white metal bed, squinting my one good eye against the bright light overhead, which turned the surgeon's face and my father's into silhouettes. The red curtain still covered my left eye. But now I actually saw stars, or at least bright flashes of cold white light, when the surgeon probed around the wound with his fingers. His fingers were cool and gentle. "Let's talk, Herr Lukasser," the surgeon said, taking my father by the arm and leading him out of my field of vision. There was a nursing nun standing next to my bed, with her arms folded over her bosom. But she smiled at me. "Don't you worry," she said. That's when I began to be afraid. The surgeon came back with my father and said, "We're going to have to put you to sleep and do a little work, Niki."

I woke up after the operation in a big ward filled with kids. The ceiling must have been six meters high, the windows four. There were white metal beds under each window, at least the few that I could see. I had a stinky, curdled taste in my mouth, as if I'd eaten bad cheese. My sheets were crisp, my pillow firm. It was comfortable. Then I realized there was a strap across my chest. My head was strapped down too. I felt a kind of panic, which receded when I found that I could at least move my arms, as well as my legs. "Don't you dare!" said the first nun who came by to check on me and saw my experimental motions. "You mustn't try to sit up or make any sudden movements with your head. You'll go blind if you do. Do you want to be blind? I don't think so."

I couldn't argue; the idea was too shocking. Blindness hadn't even occurred to me. I concluded she had only been trying to scare me into good behavior. Nuns were often like that. I forgot about her threat. But as the day dragged on I went mad. It was horrible lying there, unable to move or to do anything about the devious itch that came and went along my spine. I could hear the chatter of children. The large room was filled with wonderful light, but I could only see a small portion of it with my one good eye. I felt small stinging spasms in the other, under the thick bandage that covered it.

But the worst came at night, when the nun dozed off in her chair. A thin, pale girl two beds down from mine, who appeared to have nothing at all wrong with her, slid out from under her covers like a snake. She came over to my bed and began tickling my feet. I stood it as long as I could, and finally I shouted. But the thin girl made it back to her bed before the startled nun could discover the source of the commotion.

I'd been there about a week when one morning I saw Sigi come walking tentatively into the ward, with Traudl and Gregor behind her. She was wearing her best dress, and there were blue ribbons in her hair. Traudl saw me first. She took Sigi by the hand and led her to my bed. Sigi felt around until she found my hand, and then she raised it to her lips and kissed it. "Oh, Niki," she said. There were tears in her eyes. Traudl and Gregor looked so solemn.

I was suddenly afraid. "I'm not dying, am I?" I asked.

Sigi laughed and placed the palm of my hand against her cheek.

"Where did you get a wild idea like that?" Traudl said. Her smile was so beautiful.

"From the gloomy way you all looked," I said.

"People are always like that when they visit you in the hospital," Gregor said. "They're worried. They don't know how to behave: they don't want to act too cheerful, in case you are feeling really low that day. When I was first wounded, my best friend came to see me, and from the look on his face I was almost sure I was already dead."

"You're doing great, Niki," Traudl said. "They say you'll be home in a week or so."

They had ridden the bus down from Sankt Vero just to see me. I felt so pleased, there was a warm feeling in my belly. They had gossip to tell too. Kaspar apparently had made himself friend-less. He'd fought with Andreas again and with Simon. The young soldiers wouldn't let him near them anymore. So he went to school and then to work in the sawmill, where Big Ignatz just smirked at him, and otherwise was seldom seen outside his house. Everything was normal at school. My mother was behaving nor-mally, for the most part. Gregor's own visit to Schwaz, for his new leg, had been postponed, so he had hobbled to the end of the ward to have a word with one of the doctors.

As soon as he was gone, I asked how our Jew was doing. I had been worried.

"Our friend is fine." Traudl said.

"He says he misses you," Sigi added, "and he sends his best wishes."

Sigi never let go of my hand.

I LOST ALL SIGHT in the left eye. The surgeon told me himself just before my father arrived the following week to bring me home to Sankt Vero. He wanted, I suppose, to give me time to get used to it, time to bawl before my father saw me. It could be worse, I told myself. I wasn't going to bawl in front of anyone. It could almost always be worse. Haven't I heard just that a hun-dred times, over and over from everyone for years? Wasn't it a known fact that sympathy was scarce? But I could still hate it, and I did. Bitterly. I was furious.

All the what ifs of a lifetime, even a short one like mine. What if Sigi hadn't blindly swung at that particular icicle? What if I hadn't been standing right under it? What if we had gone directly to the hospital at Schwaz instead of stopping at Fussing? Go fur-ther: What if Sigi had never got measles and gone blind? Further still, why not? What if there was no war and Gregor still had his leg? What if there was no Jew in the box. And what if there was no Ignatz, no sawmill, no Pabst the gendarme, no parents, no school, just me and Sigi, all on our own, snug and secure in an empty village stocked with plenty of food? What if we could do just what we liked? And what if Traudl appeared one day to stay with us, and we were all happy and content? What ifs . . .

They are all so slight, so weightless.

During the drive up to Sankt Vero in Pabst's Volkswagen, my father says something I think is very stupid. He says, "It's important not to let this get you down. Try not to feel sorry for yourself." I'd hoped he would have come up with something better than that. But I'm so glad to be home I cry, even though I had sworn I wouldn't. I get around the house just fine; it all looks exactly the same, except the distances are a little off. I look in my mirror and I tell myself I wouldn't mind so much being blind in one eye if that eye were as bright and lively as Sigi's. But I've got a red twisted scar, an eyeball that's shriveled like a prune. I have to keep the lid closed, and it still leaks tears much of the time, which is a nuisance and embarrassing.

Who's going to love me now?

There's talk of a glass eye someday. The best in the world were made in Jena; before the war anyway, my father says. But I ask my grandma to make me an eye patch. She sews me a fine one out of a black silk mourning band. We've so many of those in our drawers, one or two will never be missed.

THINGS WENT TO POT while I was laid up in Schwaz, of course. No one was able to manage as smoothly as I had. My father was forced to take over the task of feeding Dr. Weiss. And Dr. Weiss had grown cranky. He didn't like having his food shoved wordlessly through the slot into his box, as if he were a prisoner in solitary confinement. He tried to start polite conversations with my father, to no avail. My father only grunted in reply. Then the Jew tried to start arguments. He criticized the flavor and aroma of the potatoes one night, implying they were rotted. My father made no comment. Another night he spoke of the awful roughness of the Tirolean dialect. Still nothing. He did get some response by saying that the Croatian regiments were better combat troops than the Tirolean Kaiserjäger in the Great War. "What a load of horse manure," my father replied. "The Croats squealed and ran like pigs. I saw it with my own eyes." But he refused to be drawn farther.

Finally the Jew tried religion. "You know, don't you, Herr Lukasser, that you Catholics are nothing but barbaric idol worshipers. No better than the niggers in the South Seas. Always bowing and scraping to those vulgar statues. Mary . . . virgin indeed."

"Jewish garbage," my father replied. "You poor Jews persist in thinking you are the chosen people no matter how many times God proves that he hates your guts."

"Hear, O Israel," Dr. Weiss said.

"What will it take to drive that damn superior notion out of your heads? How many pogroms and anti-Jewish laws and relocation lagers? You think God permits this, perhaps even causes it, because He's so fond of you?"

"You must think a bit more deeply than that, Herr Lukasser. The relation of the Jews to their God is a covenant. There are obligations indeed, which the Jewish community does not always live up to. When we fail, when we disobey, we suffer the consequences. It isn't much different from the Catholic idea, except in the fine details, is it?"

"But we can be absolved of our sins," my father said.

"And so can we, if we are sincerely remorseful. We must only atone."

These conversations went on night after night while I was in hospital. Eventually the two of them concluded that there wasn't much fundamental difference between the ways Catholics and Jews experience God. There was always a personal relationship with Him. That was simply the way the world worked, the way God was active in the affairs of the world every day. You got your chance to be good or bad.

The schism was over the afterlife. It came down to the problem of dead bodies, in fact. Dr. Weiss maintained that only the souls of the dead were immortal, while my father believed that there would eventually be a day of resurrection, when all immortal souls would be rejoined with their bodies.

"That's a disgusting idea, when you think of it," Dr. Weiss said. "All those skeletons in your graveyard are going to suddenly become pretty young girls again one day, after moldering among the worms for a century or two?"

"Scoff if you want. But we'll see who's right when the time comes."

So they argued and disputed, even called each other a few names. But it was barroom philosophy, the entertaining kind, not debates meant to end in victory or shameful defeat. And against all my father's wishes and intentions, he had made a new friend by the time I got back to Sankt Vero.

"Herr Lukasser, tell me one thing," the Jew said one evening shortly before my return. "For two years you and I have scarcely exchanged a word. You've sent your child to me instead. You've had children look after me. So I would like to ask you: Why did you never come yourself?"

There was a long silence. At last my father said, "I did not want to know you. It was better if you were nothing but the Jew in the box."

"But why?"

"Suppose I had liked you? I'd have worried myself to death. It was easier to think of you as an object, something stored in the barn."

"I see."

"I didn't want to know your story, your opinions, your likes and dislikes, your happinesses and sorrows. It would have been dangerous to regard you as a man like me. It would have been harder to conceal you then. I felt I mustn't care at all about you. That way you'd be safer. So I sent Niki to do what was necessary."

"Forgive me, but it's strange to me. You risk your life and your family's to hide a Jew, and you don't care to know the Jew. I find this unbelievable. Suppose I was an awful man, the worst sort, not at all deserving of being saved?"

"Who was I to judge? You saved Niki knowing nothing of me, of my character, my politics. So the time has come along again. And I do what I believe I should do. Even if you were an awful man, I would like to say that I would have done the same."

"Herr Lukasser, don't be offended: If I were a Christian, I don't know if I would call you simpleminded or saintly."

"Bah," my father said. This embarrassed him. He said he thought most people would be inclined to do the right thing, as long as they thought they could get away with it.

This is the way the Jew told it all to me, when I took over feeding him again. First he asked all sorts of questions about my accident, about the surgical procedures. He made me lift my patch and put my blind eye to the knothole so he could see. "That doctor in Fussing ought to be taken out and shot," he concluded.

Then he told me all about my father and him. I assume it's accurate, but I can't check. My father never mentioned any conversations with the Jew. He never even dropped a casual word, like "That Jew, he isn't such a bad fellow." He never called him Dr. Weiss. He never said one thing.

16

BEFORE THE MONTH was over, some daring Wehrmacht bureaucrat found the means to do away with patient Gregor Haas at the Schwaz military hospital, which everyone knew was about to burst at the seams with newly wounded from all three fronts.

He simply scratched Gregor off the list. Easy as that.

And they sent, by regular post, a large package wrapped in heavy gray paper to ex-patient Gregor Haas in Sankt Vero. The postman complained of its awkwardness, as if he were angling for a tip. He got none. Inside those layers of rough paper was an artificial leg in the old Great War style. It wasn't modern, it inspired no confidence in its technology. It might even have been used. It seemed a clumsy, imperfect thing. There was a deep wooden bowl on top of two steel rods, which were attached with swivels to a piece of carved wood that looked exactly like a shoemaker's last. With it, folded in the bowl where the stump was supposed to fit, was a handwritten page of instructions on how to use the leg.

Gregor was laughing, playing with the leg, putting a sock on the shoemaker's last, which wasn't even varnished. It also turned out to be two sizes larger than his real foot.

Whoever heard of getting a leg in the mail? The idea of it

seemed funny at first. What a joke! But then the carelessness of it began to seem sickening. Everyone in the village felt it. The disdain and indifference hung over us all like bad odors from the slaughterhouse on a windless August day. My father said the mailed leg made the antiaircraft sergeant extremely nervous. "It's a pathetic damned army that can't take care of its wounded properly," he heard the sergeant say.

It disturbed Big Ignatz the most. "We're screwed now," he said at the bar one night soon after the arrival of Gregor's leg. "We can only pray that the Allies get here before the fucking Russians."

"That's defeatism," said Pabst the gendarme, as if his feelings had been hurt.

"Goddamn right," said Ignatz. "Get used to it, Pabst. You're going to be hearing a lot of it, if the Russians don't just shoot you because you're in uniform."

"That's not going to happen," Pabst said.

"The hell it won't," said Ignatz, "just as soon as they finish raping all our wives. There's nothing those pigs wouldn't do."

That my father would repeat such things to me seemed a signal of important changes. Presently there were other signs of disorder. The electricity frequently went out for hours at a time. There were fewer and fewer trucks traveling through the Sankt Vero Pass. There was no gasoline anywhere, coal was impossible to get, and all sorts of foods were in short supply, even if you had the ration cards for them. The shelves of my father's store were practically empty. The high little silver airplanes flew silently over us almost every day, and the spotters sometimes couldn't radio their sightings because there was no power.

When there was power, the radio boomed with Beethoven and news bulletins. The word we heard most often in the news was "sacrifice." Every battle now was only that, never a lightning

assault anymore, or a panzer breakthrough, or a great encir-
clement.

But it's just the radio, I tell myself. All these years it was only
the radio.

SIGI'S GOING to be fifteen soon, at the end of February. I've
got to get her a present. I've got one in mind: a bird in a cage; I
think she'd like the singing of a bird in her room. It would be so
cheerful in the morning. Of course, there's no place to buy a bird
in Sankt Vero or even in Fussing. You'd probably have to go all
the way to Innsbruck to find so much as a canary. But there is my
uncle Friedl. He's got a cellarful of birds, all sorts. He catches
them with old-fashioned homemade wire traps, mostly in the
spring when they're flying north from Africa or wherever they
spend the winter. His mission is to breed them, but he's seldom
successful, since he almost never catches a matable pair. He
doesn't let many people see his birds. And you've got to be there
during daylight hours, for he'll never disturb them at night, when
they're sleeping. Friedl was a pilot in the First War; he crashed
near Trieste. Before I was born, people spoke of him the way they
did of Gregor at first: It must be the head wound, eh? But during
my life Friedl's just been considered a bit eccentric, with his birds.
Sometimes he lets one or two go, just to see them fly away. But
he's never actually sold one to anyone before.

My plan is to go to Uncle Friedl one or two days before Sigi's
birthday and try to buy a bird that sings at least a little. I'm hoping he'll agree. I don't have much money, just the bits I've saved
from what people sometimes give me when I deliver things from
the store.

I've noticed I've been getting larger coins since I've been wearing my eye patch. Everyone seems a little afraid of me, in fact, almost as if I were contagious. But mostly everyone is nice. Even Andreas goes out of his way to talk to me during lunchtime at school. Kaspar's the only one who's ugly about it. He calls me Cyclops, he tells me how hideous I am now. Andreas and Simon tell him to shut up. He stalks off by himself.

Nobody has to know that I cry myself to sleep almost every night, do they? It isn't any of their business.

Something else has changed since I've been gone. Gregor is waiting outside the school most days. But most days not for me and Sigi; he only says hello and chats with us for a few minutes. He's waiting to walk with Fräulein Mumelter. Sometimes we see them going to the inn for coffee. Sometimes we watch as they climb the stairs to her place. It's hard for Gregor, but he manages. He never stays more than an hour. He knows people would talk. My mother does anyway, all the time. Mostly at the supper table, telling my father exactly how long Gregor stayed at the apartment that afternoon. My father just looks at me and shrugs his shoulders. I feel very close to him then. We know if we're patient my grandma will change the subject and my mother won't resist the way she would if my father or I tried to do it.

Sigi practically has to bite her tongue to keep from asking Traudl what she and Gregor are up to, though. I can see her straining against the impulse. She's dying to know. She's more than a little jealous too, though of whom I'm not sure. It's obvious to me in her tone and her movements. She seems to regard both Traudl and Gregor as her own. She doesn't like it one bit when they get together without her. Yet she seems wary of Gregor, more shy. And she rarely speaks of him anymore when we're with Traudl or visiting Dr. Weiss.

Traudl comes with us most evenings now when we go to feed

Dr. Weiss. We keep him as up-to-date as we can. We tell him every scrap of information we can get. About the lack of food and electricity, about the planes. He seems particularly upset about Gregor's leg. He'd like to see him, see how the leg fits or if it's simply unwearable. But the whole situation is a positive sign, he says, small as it is. There are always signs of the times, he says. Throughout history great events have announced themselves in advance, but only to those who took the trouble to notice, to heed even the slightest hints and indicators.

"The war is almost over," the Jew says. "Germany is finished."

But after our reports, Traudl likes to talk about the doctor's life, in the good days before the war. He seems to go a bit dreamy when she draws him into the past. He sounds sad and wistful, but not devastated as he did often before. Something about the way Traudl leads him into these memories makes me feel uncomfortable. But Dr. Weiss doesn't seem to resist. I sit there and watch her face and body closely. I pretend she's an actress in a play. I've never seen a play, of course, but I imagine this is what it must be like: characters talking, making gestures, conveying emotions.

"Did you have a long engagement, Dr. Weiss?" Traudl asks one night.

"Shorter than her family would have wanted." Dr. Weiss laughs. He's in a good mood despite a dinner of only potatoes and onions. "The truth, I don't mind saying now, is that we were very naughty, pretty Rachel and I. You should have seen her in those days; she really glowed. I was a healthy young man, what could I do? I applied all my worldliness and experience and seduced her. She became pregnant."

"Before you were married!" Sigi says. "And you a doctor."

"What's that got to do with it?" Dr. Weiss says.

"Well, you should have known to be more careful, that's all," Sigi says.

"You will find one day, Sigi, that knowledge and reason are never, ever, a match for passion. You too will lose your head."

"Not me," Sigi says. "I'm having none of that nonsense."

"So Rachel tells you one day, I'd guess a little apprehensively, that she's pregnant," Traudl says. "Be honest now: how did you react?"

"With joy. I hugged her and swung her off her feet. I marched her right into her family's parlor, where I announced to her father and mother that we wished to advance the date of our wedding immediately.

"They were not pleased. They protested over her youth, the unseemliness of hurry. Then I suggested to them in the politest terms that if they did not allow the wedding to take place within a matter of weeks, they would become grandparents at a very inconveniently short interval after our marriage."

"And?"

The Jew laughs and laughs. "They were well bred; they saw at once they were defeated. They accepted the situation with grace and were kind and generous grandparents to our daughter. Rachel's father in particular was extremely proud of the little girl. On Sundays he liked to dress himself up and take her for walks all over town. I can still envision that tiny girl with that tall old man walking slowly under the chestnut trees that lined the streets of Innsbruck."

All through this I'm watching Traudl—the way her chest moves when she breathes, the way the tip of her tongue occasionally brushes her lower lip. She can't seem to keep her hands still. The light from the lantern hits her face in such a way that I can see tiny golden hairs on the edges of her ears. And now her eyes are filling up. It's anyone's guess whether she's going to be able to stop them from overflowing. She places one hand over her heart and inhales deeply through her nose.

Poor blind Sigi missed out on so much that night. All of the real drama was on Traudl's face. Expressions raced across it the way shadows of clouds sometimes dash up our valley on windy days. My one eye was quite a blessing, I knew. But sometimes it felt like a burden too, because now I was constantly worried something would happen to it. My fear made me as shy with my face as a nervous young horse. I was always alert; I flinched if anyone touched my head. I didn't even let Sigi put her fingers near my one good eye anymore when she wanted to feel my face.

A FEW DAYS before Sigi's birthday, it's time to make the trip to Uncle Friedl's house. He lives a ways up the valley, behind and above the rest of the village. I take my grandma as intermediary. I've already discovered my black eye patch gets me a certain amount of special consideration, but I don't want to rely on that in such an important matter. Uncle Friedl is the eldest son of my grandmother's eldest sister. It's a stronger connection than I have.

His house is spotless. There isn't a mote of dust or a thing out of place. He looks at me as though he doesn't exactly remember who I am. Yet he takes us down scrubbed pine steps into the cellar, where a great ceramic stove keeps the temperature summery. I'd expected lots of little cages, but instead three-quarters of the place is simply screened off with chicken wire, and within it birds fly, chirp, hop, and flutter between a few small trees that've been stripped of bark and leaves. My uncle looks contentedly at his flock. I'm a little disappointed; all the birds are shades of brown and gray, with just little hints of blue and yellow splashed randomly about. I expected more color, bright golds and brilliant reds and blues.

"Why's Niki want a bird?" Uncle Friedl prefers to address my grandma.

"It's Sigi Strolz's fifteenth birthday. They're best friends. You know Sigi—she's the blind girl."

"Whose father was a damned SA man," Uncle Friedl says. "Isn't that right? A real rough-and-ready Nazi."

Until Uncle Friedl said it out loud, I'd never really thought of Sigi's dad like that. I'd seen him many times strutting around in his uniform, but he and his friends never got into fights with anyone in the village. He was always nice to us.

"Doesn't matter, I guess," Uncle Friedl says. "After all, your husband killed him. So I guess your old man amounted to some good in his life."

"Frido, you be quiet now," my grandma says. "Show some respect for the dead."

"You think they require any? They're all off having a good time somewhere, everything forgiven, laughing at us who are still back here, worrying and afraid."

"Uncle Friedl, what about a bird for Sigi?" I venture.

"Good eye patch," Friedl says. Then, to my grandmother, "Do you think the girl could keep one well?"

"She's a good girl," my grandma says. "She'd take good care. She's Niki's best friend."

Uncle Friedl goes into the cage and stands very still for a while. Some of the birds flutter to the corners, their little eyes shining and alert. But a few land on Friedl's arms and shoulders and head. There's a small bird sitting fearlessly on a bare branch near Friedl's right hand. He gently seizes it, leaves the cage, and puts it into a small wooden box with a few air holes bored into it. He says to me, "You must carry him home under your jacket, so he doesn't get a chill. You must tell Sigi to cover his cage each night with a square of flannel. He'll eat seeds and dried fruit. Make sure he has plenty of water. And here's a cage," he says, handing me a lovely old thing shaped like our church. It was made of wood and brass, with a little sliding barred door of brass and a beautifully curved stick inside for a perch. "It's a type of finch," he says. "He'll sing for your Sigi every morning and every evening, and mind his manners the rest of the day."

He wouldn't let me pay. He wouldn't even look at my outstretched hand with the tiny bunch of rumpled paper marks in the palm. He just shooed my grandma and me up the stairs and out of his house. I'd have run home, I was so excited, but I had to keep pace with my grandma. She wanted to hold my hand. She felt that being half blind, I needed some aid, but I wanted to clutch the bird box to my belly with both hands. She carried the cage all wrapped up in her scarf so no one who saw us would know what we were about.

Two nights later, we're at Sigi's house for her birthday. We've had coffee and a cake my mother made with almost the last of her sugar hoard. Sigi and I have taken the bird to the little room off the kitchen, while the parents and my grandma sit by the stove, having a glass of schnapps. Sigi's cooing and whistling at the creature, who cocks his head at her but doesn't reply. Then I see her shoulders shudder a little. I know she's crying. I think maybe she's touched by the gift. The idea pleases me.

"I have to confess to you," Sigi says. "I let Gregor do it to me."

"What?" I say. I have a great hollow feeling all of a sudden, although I can't credit what I've heard.

"I let him stick his thing in me," she says, still facing the bird in the cage, keeping her back to me. "In fact I made him do it. He didn't actually want to."

"Jesus, Sigi," I say. "That can't be true."

"It was when you were in Schwaz. I was thinking no one was ever going to want me, and I had to find out what it was like. I thought I might not get another chance. So I made him do it."

"You couldn't have made him," I say.

"I asked him, and he laughed and said I was a little girl. So I lifted up my sweater and put his hands on my breasts. He said I had beautiful breasts. Then I touched him between the legs. He still didn't want to. I had to beg him."

"The bastard—he took advantage. And you? You're no better," I say. "What about us?"

"What about us?" Sigi says. "We never knew a thing, really."

"You do now," I say bitterly.

"It wasn't what I expected. It wasn't great. It burned very much. It only made me sore down there. It was like it wasn't even happening. Except for the burning, I could have been dreaming it."

"Just shut up. I don't want to know these things. You disgust me."

Sigi turns to me now. She's stopped crying. "One day you'll do it with someone. Will that make you disgusting to me? No, I don't believe so. Anyway, he wouldn't ever do it to me again. I tried to get him to, because I wanted to see if it might be better when you got used to it. But he refused. He said he was ashamed of himself. He also said he had another girl, he wouldn't say who, but his own age."

"What a bastard," I say.

Sigi comes over and kneels before me, placing her hands on my knees. I'm shocked and furious. But I look at her, and I'm amazed to see she looks exactly the same as always. Sigi's still Sigi. She has the same plain pale face, the same pink lips which have kissed mine, the same long fingers. Everything exactly the same.

Not a single sign of what she'd done. She puts her head in my lap and I lean down toward her. She even smells exactly the same. She's just my Sigi still.

But she doesn't feel the same. When she takes my hand and kisses me, she's a stranger. She knows something I don't know, and that transports her somewhere far beyond me, off in a distance I don't immediately know how to close.

17

IN THE EARLY SPRING of 1945, Fräulein Mumelter's lovely breasts become boundless.

It's amazing, yet it's plain for all to see. And everyone but Sigi does, even after Traudl starts draping a loose cardigan over the crisp white blouses that have always been her classroom uniform. The older boys, imagining a silky new heft, are forced to cover their hard-ons with books. The older girls compare her ripening womanly roundness to their own fresh swellings, with poor results. Fräulein Mumelter writes vigorously on the blackboard. She produces ranges of motion we have never seen before. Especially when she writes equations.

Of course, she couldn't have expected to keep her secret for too much longer, hope as she might. Her blooming is definite and unmistakable.

But Kaspar quickens her disgrace. We've been spying on the teacher's growing bosom for more than a month when Kaspar smuggles chalk from the classroom and sketches pairs of prodigious tits on barn doors all over, all of them labeled "Mumelter." Between dusk and dark one evening in late March, he manages to do six of these portraits without being seen. By eight-thirty the next morning, mothers in pairs, trios, and quartets are standing along the road, with arms folded across their chests, glancing at the schoolhouse and talking rapidly with one another. The men gather outside the bar with Mayor Ausserhofer and then go inside for a schnapps. I can see all this from the classroom window. We are all trying to look out the window. Fräulein Mumelter, who seems miraculously unaware that drawings of her breasts now decorate the village, has stopped writing and is rapping her ruler against the edge of her desk. This rapping introduces us to yet another new motion. She has about three-quarters of the class in close attention when Mayor Ausserhofer appears in the doorway and asks to have a word with her in private.

Moments later she comes back into the classroom with a clenched jaw and all the blood gone from her lips. She's followed by Ausserhofer and Pabst the gendarme. They are frowning officially. They are looking around at all the older boys, none of whom will meet their eyes. Kaspar's staring at his desktop with the unaccountable but identical expression pigs have when they see a full trough.

"One of you has done something impudent and obscene, really nauseating," Mayor Ausserhofer announces. He's using his speech voice, resonant, like he's practicing to be on the radio. "No one is going to leave this room until the culprit is found. We will stay here all day and all night and all the next day if need be. Whoever did this loathsome thing will be found out." Some of the little ones begin to cry.

"It was Kaspar," Andreas says almost instantly. There is still a thin white scar on his upper lip from their last encounter. "I saw him doing it last evening."

The mayor sways as if he had tensed himself for stubborn resistance and hit none at all. He's dubious of the ease of this. He looks at Andreas, puzzled. But Pabst knows boys better. At once he strides over to Kaspar's seat and reaches for his ear, planning to march him to the front of the room. Kaspar easily brushes off Pabst's arm and walks up to the mayor on his own. "Yeah, I did it. Only maybe I didn't make the tits big enough. Have a look at her, Mayor," he says.

Simon, later, names it the "Ausserhofer Reflex." As soon as Kaspar's spoken, the mayor's eyes shift instantly to the teacher's chest, linger longer than they should, then recoil, leaving his face with an expression of deep embarrassment.

Fräulein Mumelter bursts into tears and flees the room, clutching her cardigan. She runs like a girl past the groups of mothers and up the steps to her apartment. For a moment she doesn't seem able to open the door. Her head bows. Then the door gives, she slips in and slams it behind her.

We all watch her flight. No one says anything. When we turn away from the window, we find Kaspar, his back to Pabst and the mayor, smirking repulsively. Suddenly the mayor smacks him as hard as he can on the ear with his open palm. Kaspar collapses like an axed fir. "You are expelled from the school immediately, Kaspar Hufnagl. Get up and leave at once," the mayor says. No one knows if he has the authority to do this. Wouldn't it be up to the inspectors of the school district? But for the moment the mayor has the strongest voice in the room. He's knocked any fight out of Kaspar, and Kaspar obeys, holding his reddening ear.

"Did what? What? What's all this going on? Everyone's going crazy. Where's Fräulein Mumelter?" Sigi whispers loudly to me. Ever since her birthday night she's been behaving as if nothing had changed between us. But I'm all torn. I'm not the same. It disappoints me that Sigi, who knows me so well, can't feel this and honor it a little in the ways she approaches me now.

"Kaspar drew pictures of Traudl's breasts on everyone's barn," I reluctantly whisper to her.

"But why?"

"They're growing," I say.

"Growing?"

"She's getting fat too," I say.

Oh Traudl, Traudl, I'm thinking. Those beautiful breasts, that swelling belly. Did you have to be bad? Did you lie on your back and receive what most of the men in town would've loved to give you (and most likely did in their dreams)? But who was the one lucky one? Who had the privilege?

"Why didn't you tell me?" Sigi hisses.

"Nobody's said she's knocked up yet," I say. "But she's showing for sure."

Sigi starts to cry a little but wipes the tears away roughly with the back of her hand. "How could she? How could she?" she mutters to herself.

"Same way you did," I say. It's cruel, deliberately.

"That's a terrible thing to say."

"But it's true."

"It had to be Gregor. That rat," Sigi says.

"Yeah, who else?" I say.

But then I remember the way Traudl took my father's hand near the barn at four in the morning, how they disappeared into the dark together. I thought of how I turned my face to the wall, hoping to dream. I remember how she seemed to know about the Jew before we told her. I feel like sticking my fingers in my ears to shut out the noise, but I know that would only seal it inside my head. He didn't do it, he didn't do it, I say to myself over and over.

"It was most likely Gregor," I tell Sigi as firmly as I'm able. "It had to be Gregor, nobody else."

That starts her tears all over again. "Oh no, oh no," Sigi says. "It can't be. It's disgusting even to think of it."

"Now you know how it feels," I say. I've never been this rough with Sigi in my life.

"Niki," she says pleadingly, which is the way I want to hear her, "you've either got to forgive me or keep me away. You've got to stop throwing it back at me. It hurts too much. It's cracking my heart."

"Gregor's a swine. I hope he rots," I say, seeing her flinch and not feeling bad at all. She'd left me desolate. My hurt and anger were so cold they felt almost holy.

Yet all I really wanted was for everything to be the same again. I wanted to go back. Knowing we could not tortured me.

AT SUPPER that night, I even began wishing I had never been born. My mother was spooning up her soup with sharp, vengeful motions. My father saw this sign. He tried to damp things down. He told us that if the schoolteacher was pregnant, she was bound to be dismissed and sent away from Sankt Vero. Then the disturbance would disappear. My grandma said, "That's the best thing, if it just goes away."

"Maybe the father will have something to say about that!" my mother said, too loudly, I thought. "Maybe the father won't want his little piece to go away and will make some arrangement for the slut. She and her brat will probably haunt us here."

"Oh, I wouldn't worry so much about that," my grandma said.

"Easy for you to say—your husband's dead," my mother snapped. My grandma looked like she'd been slapped. "My husband, meanwhile, can't keep his eyes in his head when anything with tits walks by. I've even seen him look at Maria Stocker."

"You're talking nonsense," my father said. It was clear that he was having trouble remaining calm. "You're being ridiculous."

"Am I?" my mother said. "You're up so early in the morning, Martin. You sneak around while the whole town's still asleep. What do you get up to, so early?"

"Oh dear God," my grandma said. "Will you stop this? In front of Niki you carry on this way? Have some respect."

"I had some once," my mother said. "Martin married me for it, didn't you, Martin? I was respectable as they come. But the years beat it out of you, when your husband can't keep his fly closed."

"That's insane, completely insane. Are we going to have to get the doctor up here again?" my father said. He sounded almost desperate.

"I knew it!" my mother shouted, standing up from the table and moving to the door. "I knew you'd threaten me with that. And then you'll try to get them to put me in an asylum someplace, so you can get up to all the dirtiness you want. Well, it won't work, I'm telling you."

And that night she moved out of the room she and my father had shared all my life and up into a little spare bedroom adjacent to the attic, the same room where the Jew had spent his one night in our house years before. She speaks only to my grandma and me. I wish she wouldn't speak to me, actually. I feel embarrassed for her, but she doesn't sense this at all. She's not ashamed of anything she's done.

TRAUDL COMES BACK to teach the day after Kaspar's expulsion. She still sees us some evenings. And now she isn't shy with us, in our private world. She tells us how she vomits each morning, how the thought of certain foods makes her stomach flop at any time of day. And it's with us at her side that she speaks to the Jew of her new situation.

"I'm pregnant, Dr. Weiss," Traudl says.

"Good for you!" he replies. He sounds as cheerful as I've heard him, as cheerful as he was that time he described his affair with the nurse in Venice, walking hip-to-hip along the canal in the fog.

"But I don't want to be," she says.

"Nerves. It's common. You'll get over it," he says.

"No, not nerves. I can't be pregnant. Don't you understand?"

"I understand that you are certainly not the first girl to get herself pregnant shall we say . . . inconveniently? And I swear you will certainly not be the last."

"What can I do?"

"You can't marry him?"

"No, it's out of the question."

"Because there's no love, or for other reasons?"

"For every reason. It's simply impossible. I've got to do something."

"There's nothing you can do. Nothing, understand?" Dr. Weiss says.

"There are supposed to be ways," Traudl says.

"Which are dangerous, illegal, immoral. Gypsy women with knitting needles, doing butchery. There is nothing, I repeat, to do."

"I'll lose everything—my profession, my place. They won't let me teach. I've nowhere to go."

"Hold your head up, Traudl," Dr. Weiss says. "You've done no wrong. You've simply had bad luck."

"It's killing me," she sighs.

"You may have a hard time for a while, but you will survive it and you will flourish. Just sit tight here until the war ends. Then we'll see. Then there'll be chances, opportunities we can't know as yet. There always are after wars. We learned that in '18. Or some did. The ones with the stiff necks who wouldn't let go of the past, they sank without a trace."

"Oh God, Dr. Weiss, can't you help me? I cannot have this baby. I cannot."

"For now, I can't give you anything but my best hopes," he says.

Traudl and Sigi slip down the ladder from the loft, but I remain. I think I hear Dr. Weiss whisper, "God, why couldn't it have been me? Such a lovely girl. Just once, just once. And I'd have looked after her ever after."

"It's sad the way the world works," I say.

"You still here, Niki?" he says. He sounds as if he is just coming out of deep prayer, or is already half asleep.

"Nothing seems in proportion. People don't normally get what they deserve, do they?" I say. "But so few complain or fight. 'That's life,' they say. 'That's life.' "

"Ah, Niki, there's nothing to fight. It would be like punching fog. That's the mystery of life, the things we cannot know, aren't meant to know. If it was all clear, everyone would be like one of Pavlov's dogs, doing the same things the same way, to get the same things, over and over."

"Pavlov's dogs?"

"Russian dogs, naturally," he says wearily.

"Of course," I say, although I don't know what he means at all.

I caught up with Sigi just after Traudl had dropped her at her front door. "He's horny!" she said after I told her what I'd heard the Jew say about Traudl. "The dirty old man. How could he think that way about Traudl? She could be his daughter. I bet he does masturbate in there, even if he swears he doesn't. He's definitely going to hell."

I go home. I go straight up to my room. I get undressed. I look at myself in the mirror for a while. I only do this when I'm feeling braver than usual, or when my father has slipped some schnapps into my cup of chamomile. Sometimes I even take off my eye patch. I used to think I was good-looking in a boyish sort of way. That's spoiled. I was also used to thinking of scars as only thin pale lines, slightly raised, like the one on my belly. It's always shocking for me to see how deep and jagged the one in my eye is. They say it will fade over time. But it will stay deep, a permanent reminder of penetration. Violent like the scars soldiers get from bullets and shrapnel, not pretty and peaceful like women by nature all have in that one special private place.

I'm getting good at feeling sorry for myself. I put my eye patch back on and slip between the cold, coarse sheets. I'm ready to wallow. First Sigi breaks my heart, and now Traudl. I'm reeling. I'm rejected. I'm practically an orphan in this world. I want to be closer to both of them in ways I can't name, or describe, but feel deep in the center of my body. They're physical, but they're more than that too. With Traudl I am more realistic. But Sigi is different. We belong to each other. She'll do anything for me, as I would for her. I've never asked her for a thing, but now I feel I've got to. I've got to close the gap Gregor placed between us.

And then I think it can't be done, it won't work. I think I would like to give up. But I'm afraid of the cold ground, the photos on the crosses, the candles. And they'd have to move my brother's bones to make room for me. I couldn't do that to him.

Once upon a time I thought the pretty ones had it too easy in life. Now I look at Traudl and Gregor and I'm not so sure. Are they happier than others? Certainly not at the moment. Do their looks make life sweeter for them in any but the most superficial ways? It doesn't seem so. They seduce people like me and Sigi, and we learn eventually to distrust (and even hate) them for it— for making us think that a pretty face means a lovely soul. It's a sort of comfort to know their beauty doesn't give them immunity from fate.

Gregor could go rot. But Traudl I care for too much. I would like to help her, if I could.

ON SATURDAY MORNING Kaspar has to scrub away all his chalk drawings. As additional punishment, he is ordered by the mayor to whitewash certain municipal walls and doors under the supervision of Pabst the gendarme, who is actually wearing his sidearm for the occasion. Sigi follows Kaspar from one drawing to the next, taunting, and then on to the whitewashing. Pabst gently tries to shoo her away but can't cope with her persistence. I'm skulking in the background, unwilling to walk with Sigi in my usual way but also unwilling to let her go unwatched. Sigi begins asking Kaspar if he misses his friend Otto. She says it so innocently. She suggests he could use a sausage like a friend. Pabst doesn't seem to be getting this. He's just looking blankly at Kaspar whitewashing a door. And he stands frozen when Kaspar whirls and swipes his paint-laden brush down Sigi from her forehead to her waist. Then he makes another swipe across her breasts, just as Gregor turns the corner from the bar.

"You little shit!" Gregor shouts as he hurries over. Kaspar throws the brush at Gregor and swiftly wrenches the crutch out from under his arm. Then he swings the crutch against Gregor's good shin. Gregor goes down. Kaspar beats him around the ribs and face before Pabst finally comes unstuck and tackles him. It looks like Kaspar will outwrestle Pabst, but Big Ignatz rumbles over from his sawmill and kicks Kaspar in the ribs. You should have heard the thunk! That's it for Kaspar. He's lying there in the street, vomiting up something putrid yellow. Gregor's bleeding from the nose and a deep gash under one eye. Probably he's got some cracked ribs too. I come over and take Sigi's hand. She doesn't want to go, she's afraid of what's happened, but I lead her home. Let Pabst and Ignatz help Gregor.

The mayor and Pabst insist that Kaspar be locked in his father's cellar that night, so he can be taken down to Fussing in the morning and charged with assault. But Kaspar doesn't find it too hard to get out of his own cellar. He heads over the pass to Kaprun. He sends his parents a card from there: he's joined the Volksturm (claiming to be sixteen) and is marching east to stop the Red Army.

That's the last anybody in Sankt Vero ever heard of him.

I can't say Kaspar was ever much missed. Not even by the Hufnagls, I think. Once the war ended they were very quick to claim state compensation for the death in combat of their soldier son and actually won some small pension they seemed pleased to spend.

18

"NOBODY'S EVER HAD sex in Sankt Vero," Big Ignatz bellows in the swarming schoolroom. Most likely he's inflicting the aroma of cheap schnapps on everyone near him. "ALL the goddamned kids in Sankt Vero were Immaculate Conceptions, *nicht wahr?* Especially the illegitimate ones. Speaking of which—naming no names—there are at least four little bastards in class here every day. And one more who probably is, though his father doesn't know it."

"He knows it well enough," says a farmer from somewhere in the crowd. "He just doesn't want to admit his wife is a slut."

"Such slander! And you, Ignatz, shame on you. You should bite your tongue," cries Frau Stocker from across the room.

"Oh, *ja*, I should," Ignatz calls back, laughing. "But tell me first, has that pimply soldier knocked up your little Maria yet? Are you looking forward to being grandparents at such a young age?" Herr Stocker stands, fists clenched as if he is thinking of moving on Ignatz, but his friends restrain him. They don't have to try very hard.

"To get down to business: All I want to know concerning Fräulein Mumelter is who's the lucky man?" Ignatz says. Many of the husbands are laughing now too, but they're being elbowed and hushed by stern-faced wives.

"I could tell you something about that," shouts my mother just before my grandma, who's been watching her closely for any signs of agitation, can spirit her out the schoolroom door.

"Stay and do!" Ignatz calls out.

"Drop it," my father growls, and Ignatz sits again.

"Ladies and gentlemen," says the mayor, "please be more correct. Let's observe the amenities. Let's behave in an orderly fashion." He raps sharply on the teacher's desk with a little shoemaker's tack hammer, since there's no proper gavel.

They're all crammed in the school, the whole town practically, to talk about what's happening in Traudl Mumelter's belly. I'm lurking outside with Simon and Andreas, eavesdropping the way we always do. Sigi and Traudl are with the Jew. Later they'll be going to Sigi's house. I'll meet them there, if this meeting doesn't go on too long.

Ignatz turns serious suddenly. "Listen, just let the teacher teach, dammit. Who cares what she did with who? You think these kids haven't seen a pregnant woman before?"

"We can't have this immorality flaunted in front of the children," says Frau Fischnaller.

"Now, Trudi, your Egon boasted to all of us that you were no virgin when he married you," Ignatz says. "Hell, the older kids are already fooling around a bit with each other, I'd bet. And the little ones don't know anything anyway. So where's the harm?"

"Ignatz, you're going too far," the mayor says, rapping with his hammer. I imagine there are going to be tiny dents all over Traudl's desk. "I'll have to have Pabst expel you if you keep this up."

"Oh dear me," Ignatz says.

"One moment, please," says Herr Egger. "Ignatz does have a point. There are bastards in this town, we all know it, and we don't treat them any different from the other children, do we? We'd be ashamed of ourselves if we did. What's one more? And what's it matter if it's the teacher's?"

"You think your dad might have done it to her?" Andreas whispers to Simon as we crouch there outside the school.

"I don't think he can do it. I hear my mother swearing at him about it," Simon says.

"The teacher is supposed to set the good example, not the bad one," says Frau Hutter. "She's been up to mischief she shouldn't have been. Send her away!"

"The whole town would have to go if everybody who got into a bit of trouble was banished," says Herr Egger.

"Are you trying to imply I've been up to no good myself? Because if you are, Karl, I'll break your bones for you," Frau Hutter says. She is a very big woman, with hard red hands.

"I didn't mean anything personal, Katherina. I was speaking in general terms. You know, 'He who is without sin, let cast the first stone,' that sort of thing," Herr Egger says.

"What sort of sin are we talking about here?" says Herr Stocker.

"Ask your Maria for the details; I'm sure she knows them by now," Ignatz calls, and the mayor starts rapping his tiny hammer again.

THEY'RE TALKING, talking, talking. One thing leads to another. That's the way these meetings always go, with all these people who have known each other forever: misunderstandings and hurt feelings, taunts and gibes. But if there were even a single stranger in that room, not one of them, not even Ignatz, would say a word. They'd all just sit there looking grim and let the mayor make his speech, which they'd bitterly criticize at home later.

I'm still listening through my glass. I'm not missing a thing, but I've stopped peeping up through the window. Instead I'm watching a quarter-moon hook itself on the very tip of the Kirchspitz, a yellow moon on white snow. It's the sort of thing I've seen all my life, but lately I'm thinking there must be a meaning to the inexpressible effect a moon and a mountain provoke.

We don't even know who named these mountains, it was so long ago. I think those first people understood at once that the mountains are a sort of being, more present and more permanent than any of us or anything we do. We graze our cows up there, but the grass always grows back. We paint stones white and slash them with red to mark the trails, but the paint always fades. The mountains ignore us; they're like God that way. Sometimes, like God, they overwhelm us: blizzards and avalanches, rains and rock slides. But it's nothing personal. So it's conceited of us to name them, probably. At least we in the Alps never, ever, name mountains after people, as I've heard they do in America. That'd be begging for trouble, like spitting in the holy-water fountain in church. And after a few generations, a Mount Pabst or Mount Stocker would only be absurd. But the Kirchspitz is always and forever the Kirchspitz.

LATELY YOU'D THINK our Jew, fit and free and twenty years younger, had scaled the very peak of the Kirchspitz. He's displaying that sort of climbing euphoria, or as close as one in his circumstances might come to it. He's cold and dirty and worn out, but you can't shut him up, just like mountaineers in the bar retelling their ascent. He's seen the end of his imprisonment. It's plainly there on the horizon of his imagination. He says this. He says the winners will not harm us but may actually help. Where he gets these notions is beyond us. Maybe his daughter wrote him lots of nice things about the Americans before it all went to hell for him in Austria, and he believed her. My dad and Ignatz and most of the veterans would prefer the Americans to the Red Army, but either way, they expect it will be rough on us, very rough.

Not our newly euphoric Jew. He's so different from the dull, deathly soul of last autumn. He's moving in his mind, he's hurrying toward the beginning of life again. Linkages start to vanish when he speaks of his past. He seems now to assume that we must be personally acquainted with everyone in his past, as if we've lived with him from boyhood until middle age. He says things like: "You remember Major Musil of the Sixteenth Regiment, the doctor with dueling scars on both cheeks he got in Heidelberg?" We've never heard of this duelist before!

We learn how he once deliberately made a minor surgical procedure more painful than it should have been because he despised the patient. "A filthy plutocrat," he called him, a man who made a fortune out of the war and insisted afterward, in the hard times, on wallowing in it before everyone. "I made him scream for mercy on that operating table," Dr. Weiss says. "Of mercy he got none. If that bastard is alive, I'd guess he still has nightmares about it."

And we learn more of the details, good and bad, that give vitality to any life that's really lived: a little cheating on taxes, some flirtations with waitresses and shopgirls, embarrassing sexual thoughts about one or two of his daughter's prettier girlfriends, the free treatment for several veterans of his regiment whenever they were ailing, a particular summer picnic along the banks of the Inn, at which he ate one too many pickled eggs, the embarrassing moment when his daughter (at twelve), accidentally saw him naked in the bath with an erection, the fear he felt when the yellow stars were ordered to be worn, the way he tried to deny that he was a Jew to certain brown-shirted men who stood so close to him on an Innsbruck street he could smell their sour anger.

He wants to be let out of the box. But we can't. It still isn't safe. It won't be safe until the war is truly over and the Allies come to Sankt Vero.

But anyway: high hopes. Our Dr. Weiss has high hopes. Maybe he'll even go to America to join his daughter. He'll learn English and practice his profession. A surgeon can operate anywhere, he says.

Sigi isn't as much diverted by these revelations as she once would have been. She would have demanded details. She would have asked if he had wet his pants in fear when he was surrounded by brown men. But now Sigi's main preoccupation is whether it was Gregor who made our Traudl pregnant, and if not him, then who? She's planning something, I can tell, for the violator. That's the way she sees whoever it was. When Traudl's not with us, Sigi leads the talk around to her condition. She's quickly disappointed in Dr. Weiss. He offers no ideas, no leads, no theories. He could care less, beyond a slight curiosity. A healthy, strapping girl like that Traudl should be made pregnant by someone, in his opinion.

The Jew speaks so often of leaving his box, is so bright-minded and cheerful as spring advances, that he is getting on our nerves. Mine especially.

Mine especially, yes. Because mine are not good. If you were my friend and I were ever to say, "Put me in a box," you'd know not to believe me, wouldn't you? You'd know it was just nerves talking. You'd know I could never endure what the Jew has. But even knowing that, wouldn't anyone once in a while long for the helplessness of it, the absolute lack of responsibility? That same peacefulness and safety Gregor said he felt in the hospital? I do long for that sometimes, a little.

But that's not my present portion. I've got to worry about everybody: Sigi, Traudl, Dr. Weiss, my crazy father and mother. The world is turning upside down, everyone can feel it, and it's impossible to say what's going to happen to us. I haven't much confidence in anyone, except perhaps my grandma. She always keeps her head. The radio mainly plays Beethoven and Wagner; news bulletins are few. People are talking about storing food up in the *Heustadel*, the little hay barns in the high pastures, well out of sight of the village, and going there to hide if the foreigners come. As if those soldiers wouldn't find us up there if they wanted to. As if Ignatz is going to hold them off with his old hunting rifle. There's a lot of stupid talk. It feels almost panicky in the village some days. Arguments suddenly break out on the street between men who've been friends for years. Certain families have stopped speaking to other families.

So I worry. What's going to happen to poor Traudl? Who is her man? Will he step forward and look after her? Is it Gregor? Is it my damned father? I wish they both were dead, to tell the truth: beautiful Gregor and my too charming parent, who never showed that side of himself in our household. Traudl and Sigi and I could look after ourselves very well without them. These are the things that are constantly on my mind. I am even finding it difficult to concentrate on my lessons. More unsettling are certain yearnings, which seem to saturate me. I'm full of a strange obsession that shames me. I'm always wondering what Traudl looks like naked, and then disgusting myself by picturing her doing it with my father, or even Gregor. And it's pointless anyway, because it's really only Sigi I want to be with, though I can't muster any images of that.

"WELL PUT, WELL PUT," I hear the mayor say, trying out his speech voice and apparently finding just the resonance he likes. The moon is still over the Kirchspitz; the peaks of Mangart and Kanin look sharp and clean as dogs' teeth.

"As a practical matter let's ask ourselves one thing," the mayor says. "While none of us can condone the condition of Fräulein Mumelter, while her condition is certainly not ideal for someone in her position, where are we going to find another teacher to finish the term? In present circumstances, I think finding a replacement would be very difficult. Secondly, we may form our opinion, but we really have to leave any final decision up to the district education authorities in Schwaz.

"Therefore I propose to write a formal letter to the district superintendent, explaining our situation with respect to Fräulein Mumelter and asking for an inspector to come here as soon as possible to adjudicate the case.

"In the meantime," the mayor concludes, "I propose we do nothing to disrupt the precious education of our children. I propose we permit Fräulein Mumelter to continue to teach her classes, as she has these last few days. Although some of you have refused to let your children attend, I urge you to let them return."

"Mayor, Mayor!" Ignatz calls. "Just one question: Are we going to make her confess who did the cooking when she gets really fat?"

The men all laugh, their wives mostly frown or roll their eyes. The mayor shakes his head as you would at a big dog who won't behave no matter what you say. He calls for a vote. Clusters of hands pop up around the room. To me it looks close. Ignatz, Egger, my father, and a lot of the men vote yes. Only a few of the women do. The mayor makes a show of counting, and declares his proposal has passed. There would be plenty of arguments in bedrooms that night, I reckoned.

I slipped away from the school before the crowd filed out, and went down to Sigi's house. The moon had come unmoored from the Kirchspitz and was drifting slowly west. I could hear the echoing voices of people leaving the school and heading home. But at Sigi's I found that Traudl had already gone home herself.

"She's so sure they're going to send her away. She said she'd rather face that hard fact after a good night's sleep. But I doubt she's going to get one," Sigi said. "She's so nervous, Niki. All the time she was here, her foot kept tapping."

"But it turned out all right, for now at least," I said as Sigi's mother poured me a cup of weak peppermint tea. "The mayor's going to write the district commissioner of education and ask for some inspector to come up here. But in the meantime, Fräulein Mumelter's to keep teaching."

"So she'll at least finish the year," Sigi said excitedly.

"Looks that way," I said.

"Poor girl," Sigi's mother said. "It could happen to anyone. You fall in love, you give in. That's why, Sigi, I always tell you that no matter what, you must wait until you're married, no matter how much you like the boy and how hard he tries to persuade you."

"Nobody tries to persuade me into anything, Mom," Sigi said. "But I am getting beautiful breasts, aren't I? I can tell without even seeing them. I can tell by how heavy they are and how they move."

"Oh, Sigi," her mother said. "Don't talk like that. Those things are private. You've embarrassed poor Niki now—just look at that blush."

But it's Sigi's mother who's turning red, not me. I've had certain ideas in my head for long enough now that they don't make me blush anymore. They just make me feel warm. I finished my cup of tea and said good night.

Outside, in the drifting moonlight, stars as thick as can be, I decided to run over to Traudl's. I knew it would seem strange for me to turn up out of nowhere so late, but thought how pleased she'd be with my news. I hoped a little bit also that she, perhaps already in her nightgown, might invite me in for a moment. She'd have her hair down, her feet would be bare. But twenty meters from her stairway, I saw my father standing on the landing in the light from the half-open door. He was speaking to Traudl. Her hair was down. He had one hand resting on the edge of the door, as if any moment he would push it open and walk in. So familiar, that hand on the door. I spun and tore off home.

I went to my room and crawled into bed with my clothes on. I felt for some reason that I needed to be ready to rise at any moment, to go racing off through the snow to I don't know where. I felt this way until I heard my father come home, not ten minutes after me.

19

THE TIME'S COME. I don't feel I can wait anymore. I've got to try. I'm plotting and planning, desperate not to offend. I'm thinking it's going to be so difficult. It isn't.

All it takes is some kisses up in Sigi's bedroom. All it takes is placing my arm around her waist when we walk, instead of just holding her hand. All it takes is hovering near her when she feeds her bird, making sure my leg touches hers when we sit side by side on her bed, reading our lessons. I accidentally brush her breasts lightly with my arm, then once with the back of my hands. And one day in May, all it takes is saying, "I think you're so beautiful, Sigi. Could I see you naked?" She smiles at the air and murmurs, "Sure, why not?"

Is that so terrible? We wanted to be closer to each other. We were both fifteen. We weren't ashamed. Sigi wasn't even a virgin anymore, though we both were innocents still. We all come to this point innocently. Every boy and every girl has to have a first time sometime, don't they? Usually it's not perfect, but it's at least simple.

Not for us. It wasn't a matter of awkwardnesses or inexperience. It actually had a sort of perfection to it. But it was mortally flawed, because I knew one thing that Sigi didn't. She forgave me when she found out. That only made it worse for me.

I must have known on some level that what I longed for could only happen once, that there would be just that moment, unrepeatable. I thought that for it to be real, for it to be something I could hold forever as a part of me, there had to be a witness. There had to be living proof that I didn't dream a dream. But it had to be someone who could never speak of it to anyone, someone familiar but also entirely outside our lives.

The weakness of me, for confessing these things. The pitiful weakness of me.

IT BEGAN WELL. Once Sigi said "Sure," it was as if every burden I had was lifted. I wasn't worrying anymore. What was coming toward us we didn't know, but nothing could be done about it anyway. It was up to my father and Ignatz and the other adults to face it when it arrived. For the first time in a long while I felt carefree. I asked my grandma to cut my hair short for the warming weather. She did. She made me a trim new eye patch out of a mourning band, too, and a plaid kerchief to tie around my neck. She knitted me a new light cardigan out of the last of last year's wool, with horn buttons. Only a single burden remained: my feelings about Gregor. I would not speak to him. He knew why and kept out of my way.

I only noticed one unsettling change around this time. My father still got up earlier than anyone, but he had started sitting in the kitchen for a hour or so, drinking coffee, instead of heading right out to the barn, as I had seen him do one morning to meet Fräulein Mumelter. He'd start his chores just when the others started theirs, in the first full light. And he and I didn't seem to have very much to say to each other anymore, except the usual business of the day, such as what deliveries I had to make from the store.

But I had some fine talks with Dr. Weiss. He advised that I go on to gymnasium next year and then consider pursuing medical school. It seemed insane. Almost no one from Sankt Vero went down to gymnasium in Schwaz; maybe one or two boys every other year or so. And nobody we knew had ever gone to university, let alone become a doctor.

"Why not, Niki?" he'd say. "It's worth a try. Tell your father I said so. He'll understand what I mean."

I didn't say anything, of course. My father would only have laughed. I told my grandma, though, and she nodded seriously. It would be so fine to have a doctor in the family, she said. Sankt Vero could use a doctor.

"The first thing I'm doing when this is over is going to Innsbruck and moving back into my apartment, if it's still standing," Dr. Weiss told me. "Then I am going to haunt every authority I can find, like the most remorseless ghost, like an implacable shade of Vlad the Impaler, until I can learn where my wife was sent. And then I am going to find her and bring her home. When you come to study medicine, Niki, you can live with us."

"But she could be anywhere in Europe. How could you even start to look?" I said.

"The Nazi bureaucracy, the God-cursed Nazi bureaucracy," Dr. Weiss said. "They're demons for details. I'm sure they have records of exactly what happened to everyone."

"But they'll destroy them when the Allies come, won't they?" I said.

"Niki, no German bureaucrat would willfully destroy an official document. Of this I am certain. All the files will be handed over to the victors in good order. And surely the Allies will allow me to search."

"I'll help you," I said. "I'll tell the Americans what the Germans were going to do to you and why we had to keep you in this box."

"Thank you, Niki," he said.

Dr. Weiss was becoming sentimental about us. Sometimes when he talked, it seemed that he was on the verge of tears. His voice had that unmistakable sound, that quavery quality. One night over his thousandth bowl of boiled potatoes with butter and salt, he said we would be listed in the special book the Jews have, where good people's names are written. I doubted that any such book would benefit me in my life. It would probably get me in trouble with the authorities if they found out. But our Jew seemed to think it was something serious.

"There is a Book of Life, Niki," Dr. Weiss insisted.

"Who writes it? A rabbi?" I said.

"Of course not. God writes it. He's the only one who knows what each of us has done."

That's an idea I've always hated. I'd thought it was mainly a Catholic matter that you never had any privacy. That all you ever did was seen and noted, and that if you didn't confess to the priest, things would go badly for you later on. Now I learned that the Jew's God was like this too. Between the two, how could we ever get away with anything? I wanted to have my secrets stay secrets. At that age, I still almost believed it was possible.

Traudl was keeping hers, it seemed. There was never so much as a hint from her on the man. Of course, there was speculation all over the village. Names were flying every which way, but she never by word or gesture showed that she'd ever heard any of them. Even prying Sigi, even lovely but devious Sigi, could not worm anything out of her. Sigi would sit holding Traudl's hand up in the loft in front of the Jew and say things like: "Isn't there some risk of complications if the father isn't examined by a doctor?" The Jew knew what Sigi was up to and told her straight out such ideas were ridiculous.

A defeated Sigi finally resorted to pleading. "None of your business," Traudl said sharply.

One day Dr. Weiss made Traudl stand by the post where the old bridle hung. First she had to face his knothole, then she had to turn in profile. "I'd say four and a half to five months, Traudl," the doctor said. "You look splendid, healthy as a horse. Any complaints? No bleeding or anything?"

"Nothing at all," Traudl said. "Except that I feel too big for myself."

"Wait a few more months and you'll know what big really is." Dr. Weiss laughed.

WE SNUCK UP into the loft early on a sunny Sunday afternoon. The Jew would never expect us then, I told Sigi. We had to be very quiet. I told Sigi we'd sneak down to a corner at the far end of the loft, away from the Jew's box. She liked the danger of it, actually. "Imagine if he saw us—what a shock he'd get!" she whispers. "The shock of his life, probably."

I don't think so, but I keep that to myself. I am basking in Sigi's good mood, in her broadest smiles.

"Niki," the Jew suddenly whispers loudly.

We freeze. Sigi has to stifle a giggle. She seems so light-hearted, so eager, not at all nervous, like me. After a few moments we hear him mutter, "Shit."

I lead Sigi around a bit, but we end up on a bale of straw straight in the sight line of the Jew's knothole. It's unusually mild for May; the straw is warm and parched. Dust wafts through beams of sun into shadows. Sigi looks striped, like a tiger, as she sits there on the bale and begins to pull her sweater over her head.

In a moment she's nude. Her breasts are round, with small

high nipples almost like a boy's. There's just the slightest swelling of her belly below her navel, then a wisp of golden hair. She's perfect, she sits there perfectly still, smiling at me as if she could see me. I'm glad she can't. I'm a bag of bones, really. My hands and feet are too big. My mouth's a little sloppy, lips too big and not always willing to stay together. I smell a little musky to myself, even when I've just bathed.

But Sigi has no ragged edges at all. She curves, she's abundant exactly where she should be, she is so smooth. She takes my hand and places it in the midst of that yellow patch of hair. She guides one of my fingers to her center, and inside. When I take my hand away later and sniff my finger, it smells sweet. "Now you," Sigi whispers.

"Oh no," I say.

"It has to be," Sigi says. "I want you to."

"You can't see me," I say. I want some way out of this.

"But I can see you the way I see your face," she says. "It's what we agreed."

Are the Jew's eyes on me? Are his thoughts extreme? I'm afraid. But he never makes a sound. I feel I must slip out of my clothes and lie down next to Sigi on the bale of straw. It's scratchy, but we don't mind. We have our arms around each other, we're kissing, her skin is so creamy I want to cry. Then Sigi touches me between my legs, the tenderest touch in the tenderest spot. I can't control my quivering. She whispers to me that this is where she touches herself sometimes. Then, "This is how I touch myself," she says.

And with the tips of her fingers, Sigi sweetly ravishes my certain, fallow world.

20

EARLY NEXT MORNING I'm adrift, musing on the remnants of my dreams. I rub my eyes. I can smell Sigi on my hands, and the scent makes me desolate. I want to cry. I know something precious is already gone from my life. My mind roams. But instead of remembering a sweetness or searching for what's been lost, it retreats, it goes back to an unremarkable day last fall.

In the autumn everyone takes a pig or two to the butcher for slaughtering. That's how we get our winter bacons and hams. The first Saturday in November is usually the big day. I can remember at least a dozen of them.

Pigs don't go dumbly to their end like cows or goats or sheep. They know they're going to get it. They're intelligent beasts, and they're overcome with fear. They scream bloody murder as they're led to the execution spot, and the others hear them and tremble.

All day long the Jew in his box could hear this screaming. The village began to reek of blood. "That's the way it is for us," the Jew said when I took him his dinner. "That's the way it is."

"Yes, it's nasty," I said. "Really disgusting to watch, but it has to be done."

"I'm speaking of a people, Niki, not swine. That's the way it's been for Jews for centuries, of which you know nothing."

"I don't believe that," I said. "You sound like an Italian, the way you exaggerate."

"Ah, Niki, your ignorance is vast," the Jew said on that darkening November day. He sounded resigned.

But now I'm awake. I do know very little, that's plain. Though I know clearly what the Jew saw yesterday, what I made him watch. It's insupportable. I feel I ought to fill my pockets with rocks and jump into the stream. It's deep enough, in May, to drown a grown man. It's fast too. It would sweep a body down and away from the village in seconds. Even if anyone saw you go in, he could do nothing.

I get dressed. My grandma has some tea and bread and a spoonful of prune jam waiting for me in the kitchen. It's my fault that the Jew saw. But the act of seeing is irrevocable, isn't it? You can't somehow take it back, or deny it, like a bad word.

After I finish my breakfast I put on my new light cardigan of last year's wool, the very one I wore yesterday, and leave the house. The May sun is hot on my face, though the air's still cool enough so that I can see my breath. I don't walk down the street. I cut behind the buildings and go along the stream bank. I can't bear to look at the water; it's too loud and insistent. And then I sneak around a building and into the little office of Pabst the gendarme. He's sitting behind his desk, wearing dark-green suspenders, eating a slice of black bread with *schmalz* smeared on it. "Well, Niki," he says as he chews, "good morning to you."

"We're hiding a Jew," I say. It sounds like a line I've memorized for a play but don't know how to deliver properly. "We had this Jew in a box up in our barn for a couple of years now. I take him his food and everything; he's up there in the loft. You should arrest him."

Pabst stood up very fast for such a bulky man and slapped me hard across my right cheek. I reeled. It looked like he was going to hit the left one too, but I guess the sight of my eye patch stopped him.

"Get the hell out of here," he said. "And keep your mouth shut or I'll be telling your father what a damned little liar you are. There's no Jew in Sankt Vero."

III
It Could
Have Been
Worse

21

HERE'S THE present truth: Nothing happened in Sankt Vero during the war, as everyone knows. Life was usual except for the rationing. Somebody got the schoolteacher pregnant. There were those who wore brown and those who didn't. Probably no more casualties than motor and logging accidents and sickness usually claim. Gregor could just as easily have lost his leg at the sawmill. And the dozen or so who never came back from Africa or Russia or the Arctic? And fat Kaspar, who disappeared? A bad few years for accidents, that's all.

But later, when the time of guilt comes, even those who never knew a thing—even those who would have informed if they knew—will say: "We saved a Jew in our village. Imagine the risk, in those times!"

Oh Sigi, I wish you could see the flames of the bonfire I could make with all my boxes of memories. You'd understand. You'd be the only one who'd grasp the why of it. You would feel it down the whole lovely length of you from your brow to your toes. And for me there would once again be the beautiful smile on your face, which you imagine is like an angel's, even though it's plain as bread.

None of us saw the way it would be. The end was all questions, no answers. Wasn't it, Sigi?

▪   ▪   ▪

WHAT'S TO BECOME of Traudl Mumelter, teacher of the Sankt Vero school, once a fresh and secret lover? What to do with this conspicuously expectant twenty-four-year-old? The authorities must act, mustn't they?

They do. On the first of May 1945, Mayor Ausserhofer received a reply to the letter he wrote to Herr Doctor Professor von Starnberg, district superintendent of education. The district superintendent is pleased to inform the mayor—the mayor proudly tells everyone—that the chief inspector of schools, Herr Doctor Kurowski, will presently arrive in Sankt Vero to conduct a thorough investigation of the moral fitness of Fräulein Teacher Mumelter.

Everyone is well pleased. Our famous efficiency, no? But Herr Doctor Kurowski never arrives. The Americans come instead.

This is the news that rouses the mayor to lope, panting, from house to house. The Amis are in Innsbruck, Salzburg, Schwaz, even Berchtesgaden. They're coming to Sankt Vero tomorrow! The mayor had this personally, by telephone, from the Gauleiter of Schwaz, just before he was arrested. Details are scarce. Rumors are staggering. A whole battalion of combat-hardened troops will come to seize control of our pass and imprison us in camps. Perhaps, God help us, there will be black troops. The Americans use Negroes in combat.

On the morning of the next day I see the aircraft-spotting sergeant and his four troopers stack all their weapons in front of the mayor's office and simply sit down on the steps to wait. Kaspar's grandpa, old man Hufnagl, wobbles by, stops in alarm, and spits at them. "Cowards!" he shouts. "What a disgrace. I'd shoot myself before I'd surrender."

"Go right ahead, pops," the sergeant says. "The war's over."

Big white sheets (the oldest, the ones worn beyond use) are already flying from the school's flagstaff and hanging from the windows of the houses near the entrance to the village. This is where the crisp, fresh red-and-black flags used to fly on national days. I see Pabst the gendarme making his usual rounds, without his sidearm. Officially, he disapproves of the white flags, so he pretends they are not there. I see the mayor carrying his portrait of the Führer down near the stream to burn it. Officially, he's against the flags too, but he's no fool. At least two dozen teenage girls, with knapsacks and sleeping bags, start hiking up to the high pasture hay barns, on orders from their parents.

The Americans don't show.

We wait all day. Finally people drift off to their homes at suppertime. They look back over their shoulders at the curve where the road comes up from Fussing, listening for the roar and clank of trucks and tanks. There's nothing, just the cawing of crows in the blue dusk under the firs, just the clang of bells as cows lay themselves heavily down.

They're tricky, these Amis. They do come, but just before dawn, when most everyone but my father and the farmers up the valley are still in bed. I can see them from my bedroom window. They pull up in front of the school in two jeeps. There's just enough light for them to set up their little gas cookers and begin making breakfast. There are seven of them. One walks over to the German weapons stacked in front of the mayor's, checks the magazines, then walks back to his meal. Sankt Vero wakes up, occupied not by gunfire or tanks but to the overwhelming smell of Americans frying eggs and bacon.

In the light of day, the Americans look tired, dirty, and irritable. They eat their eggs without much enthusiasm. Most of them have their helmets off. Their boots are badly scuffed. Their rifles are leaning against their jeeps. By now everybody's watching them through their shutters, but nobody wants to come out.

Finally a young officer walks into the middle of the street, along with an exceedingly tall and thin soldier, who shouts in oddly accented German, "Anybody home?" It isn't a phrase we use. No one's exactly sure what it means, though everyone hears it; the soldier has a big voice.

The sergeant and the four soldiers come marching out of the mayor's office with their hands clasped correctly over their heads, followed by Mayor Ausserhofer, waving a white pillowcase. The Americans don't even reach for their weapons. A few are still eating. The officer and the tall soldier, who has a submachine gun draped casually over his shoulder, wait for the German sergeant to reach them. They look at the soldiers' papers. They pay no attention to the mayor.

Then, through his tall soldier, we hear the officer order the German sergeant and four soldiers to march themselves down the mountain to Fussing and turn themselves in to the first troops they meet. The Germans look stunned, as if they've been deprived of some customary drama. The tall soldier laughs at them. "You poor bastards don't think we're going to give you a ride, do you? Heinies can walk all right. *Alles klar?*"

The soldiers are looking at their sergeant. He slowly lowers his arms and orders his four to fall in behind them. "Hey," the tall American says. "You gotta clean up your mess first. Take those weapons and throw 'em in the river." The German soldiers do it at once. It's a shocking gesture, the most shocking of the war. That's what some people said afterward. Then Sankt Vero's very own Werhmacht unit—one tired sergeant and four teenage boys—shuffles off, unarmed and unguarded, down around the curving road to Fussing.

The sun's barely up, and already it's an unforgettable day.

Next, the officer has three soldiers drag Fräulein Mumelter's desk out of the school and place it in the middle of the street. Pabst the gendarme has appeared and is told to muster the entire village. Everyone must show his papers. The officer and his tall soldier write the names of all the Party members in one column on a long sheet of yellow pad, and seize their papers. Everyone else's name goes into another column, and these people's papers are returned. The Americans don't do anything to anyone. They tell everyone to go about their business.

That's when my father and Big Ignatz approach the desk for the second time and try to explain about the Jew in the box.

The officer stares at my father while he tells the tall soldier our story. The officer's eyes are a soft, weary brown, as if he has listened to so many explanations and excuses already in his life. The tall soldier's German is too poor for him to understand my father exactly. He seems to realize we have someone confined in a barn but can't make out whether that's good or bad, whether the person is a dangerous Nazi or some poor anti-Nazi we've hidden. The officer decides to have a look. Sigi and I trail along.

THE AMERICAN OFFICER and his soldier, cradling his submachine gun, watch my father and Ignatz use heavy pry bars to wrench away the thick planks that walled the Jew in. "Get these kids out of here. Why're they here?" the officer says to his soldier, who asks my father. "Because they've been part of this all along," my father says. "They helped save this man's life."

The officer still isn't clear. "But is he armed?" he asks. When the private translates this, Ignatz loses his patience. "Shit no, he isn't a Nazi, he's a *Jude.* Jew, get it?"

The thick planks fall, we're coughing in billows of dust. Then the Jew's revealed, huddled in the farthest corner of his box. The lieutenant seems to comprehend at once; you can see a flicker of recognition in his eyes. But there's also a suspicion, a mistrust. He starts asking Dr. Weiss a stream of questions through his tall soldier. The Jew looks confused and amazed; he answers as best he can. He hands over his papers, livid with the Star of David. Then he shakes Ignatz's hand. He embraces my father and kisses him on both cheeks. My father flinches. The Jew looks at me and winks. I look away. He looks at Sigi and begins to cry. "Never mind," Sigi says, taking his hand and petting it as if it were a small animal. "Never mind."

The Jew hasn't seen scissors in two years. Masses of black-and-silver beard tumble down his chest; his hair's as long as Jesus'. He's bony. His skin looks like thin old paper, almost transparent and dangerously brittle. His eyes are wet, but he is grinning like a fool. The American officer mutters something to himself. The tall soldier automatically repeats it in German. "Probably you Krauts think you'll get a medal. What the fuck are we going to do with him?"

The officer mulls over his problem for a moment. He's so young. Probably younger than Gregor. He turns to my father and says, "You kept him this long, keep him a while longer until I get some orders. I'm also naming you the new mayor in place of that Nazi Ausserhofer. But Jesus, give this poor Jew a bath and a decent bed, okay?"

"Fucking Krauts," the officer mutters as he's climbing down from the loft. Of course, I don't know what that means until much later, when I've heard it a lot more.

Ignatz and my father have to carry the Jew down the ladder. He's weak; he has trouble walking. Yet his eyes are bright and his head swivels rapidly from side to side, as if he's trying to take in the whole world in a moment: the mountains, the pastures, the houses, the astonished people in the street standing under flapping white sheets, staring at him.

So now we have the Jew in our home. My grandmother carefully cuts Dr. Weiss's hair and trims his beard to shaving length. Then she shaves him with grandpa's old cutthroat, leaving a neat little mustache at his request. His only other request is a long hot bath. It's the longest anyone's ever taken in our house. He's in there for at least an hour. He's singing Austrian lieder in a poor cracked voice, while my grandma stands outside the bathroom, yelling at him to use plenty of lye soap. We put him in the extra bedroom. My father gives him some trousers, a jacket, and a few shirts, which swim on him. His neck is as thin as a chicken's. This is something my grandma can't bear to see, Jew or not. She stuffs him at dinner and supper with masses of potatoes, dumplings, polenta, kraut. He won't say no to slices of ham or sausage, and even boiled turnips meet his approval.

But it's all useless. It's all gone to hell. The Dr. Weiss who just days ago seemed so confident and optimistic in his filthy box vanishes in a single day of freedom. Instead there's a shriveled old man huddled in oversized clothes, given to staring at his hands. Sometimes when he's spoken to, he even flinches, like a dog that's used to being beaten. Sigi and I spend hours with him alone in our kitchen, coaxing him to tell us what he knows, asking for his famous stories. But he'll no sooner start one than he chokes and sometimes sobs. We even tell him he can stay with us always and we'll look after him, but he says, "That can't be. That's finished now."

He brightens a bit when Traudl comes to see him, but it's only that she distracts him from himself with the glow of her obvious motherhood, I think. And also with the worries he has over what will become of her. "You must leave here," he says to her. "And wherever you go, you must always say that the child's father was killed in the war. Use a name of one of the Sankt Vero boys who was killed. No one will know."

The Jew knows the extent of his own damage. He seems to know he must treat it. He makes such an effort to talk with us at supper, but my father is shy. He'll answer any question but won't ask any. My mother and grandma keep mum, and I can't look him in the eye for fear our secret will suddenly become visible to all. Sigi comes to supper and tries her best, but she fails too.

"You're among the blessed now," the Jew says once. "Not because of me, Robert Weiss. But because of what you did for a human being, whose name doesn't matter."

"Mumbo jumbo," says Sigi. "I don't believe there's any sort of balance like that in the world. If God gives a reward for every good deed, then He's just training us the way you do dogs."

"Ah, Sigi," the Jew says. "I've been feeling that God stepped out of the picture a good while ago. But that's a hard thing to admit, that your faith may be useless."

And none of us wants to admit what all of us can feel: a tension as if the Jew had really been a prisoner and we his jailers, a bitterness and pain that will follow him implacably into his freedom.

One night Dr. Weiss makes a foray to the bar, forcing himself to leave our small kitchen and try to be among strangers. But it doesn't work. Some of the farmers there make it clear to him in a robust way that a Jew is not welcome, and only the presence of Ignatz prevents something rougher. Ignatz escorts him home to our place.

How could this happen, when at last we are all so safe? Our situation is beyond luck or prayer. It's the most excellent turn of fortune's wheel. We've escaped destruction. We are occupied by a handful of soldiers who seem to have no wish to punish us for being enemies. They rape no women, they arrest no one (drunks and the like are left to Pabst the gendarme), they torture no men to find mythic caches of Nazi gold. They give me and Sigi chocolate bars sometimes. One or two gaze overlong at Sigi's body, but there doesn't seem to be any threat in it. They feel sorry for the blind girl. And anyway it isn't long before I see Maria Stocker sneaking into dusky barns with one American or another. I wonder if Maria feels what I felt that time with Sigi, if that's the reason she keeps going off with young men. Sigi tells me not to be so stupid. "Of course she comes," Sigi says. "She's crazy about it. Otherwise why bother?"

Sigi wants to bother. She wants us to lie naked together in the straw and touch the way we have. She kisses me just the way I like, she strokes me. But I can't go further. It's all different now. I want to feel that feeling again, but I can't do what Sigi wants. You know how it is watching small birds, the way every movement's so quick you can barely follow? Sigi and I are like that now; we flit together and flit apart, sparrows in the snow.

Why then does my heart feel so empty without her and the future seem so blank? "You'll understand when you're older," my grandma always says when she senses I'm brooding. She says that now. Yet I know it's not true, for sometimes still I see pain and the sorrow of unanswered questions in her ancient eyes. There are some things we will never know. Sigi's one of my mysteries.

MY GRANDMA also always said, as part of her store of handed-down wisdom, that whenever one leaves, watch for another to leave soon too. In June Dr. Weiss goes from us. But not to Innsbruck to start a search for his wife. He must go to a camp for Displaced Persons in Zell am See, gathered and recorded as one of the horde of people who finished the war far from their homes. It's a bureaucratic carnival, this counting and classifying, Dr. Weiss says. Everybody in his assigned place, under his assigned name, with papers to prove it. It reminds him of the days of the Emperor, who even listed himself as a civil servant for the census. The Nazis relished the process too. But Dr. Weiss doesn't mistrust the Americans' motive. The young American officer sympathizes with Dr. Weiss, even drives him down to Fussing to argue the case with his superiors. But it's a snafu, as the Americans like to say. The Jew's bound for the DP camp.

It's a morning full of sun, the sort that makes you feel life is long and sweet. The village has been noisy with the songs of mockingbirds since four A.M. By seven, there is quite a little crowd gathered to see Dr. Weiss off. Big Ignatz is there; so is Pabst the gendarme; he never told anyone about my betrayal. There's my father, of course, Sigi and her mother, Herr Egger and Simon, my grandma, Fräulein Mumelter. My mother is at home but surely peeking through the curtains.

Our poor ruined Jew, the surgeon Dr. Robert Weiss of Innsbruck, is settled in the rear seat of the Americans' jeep. He beckons me over, puts one hand tenderly on the back of my neck, and pulls me close until our foreheads are touching. I'm weeping like a child. I can't seem to control myself at all.

"I never saw you that day," he whispers. "I heard you, but I didn't look. It was just you and Sigi, and it was all right. Remember that. Remember, too, that you gave me life."

My grandma was right this time. Two days after Dr. Weiss drove off in an American jeep down the curving road to Fussing, Fräulein Mumelter disappeared. She left her apartment spotless, no trace of herself at all. She did not even leave a note, which I think broke Sigi's heart as much as Traudl's going. Sigi spent the day in bed, mostly crying. When I went up to sit with her and stroke her hair, she told me to get out.

Fortune's wheel made another turn. My father announced at supper one night that he was sending me to gymnasium in Schwaz in the fall. He said Dr. Weiss had recommended it urgently. I'm going to live with an aunt and uncle I've met two or three times. I won't be entirely alone, my father told me, because Herr Egger is sending Simon to Schwaz too. I am excited and shocked, and also afraid. For a while I feel like I've got mice living in my stomach. It doesn't help that one night a rock bursts through our kitchen window while we're eating and a piece of glass gashes my mother's forearm. It's not easing to hear some of the talk around, that my father is a traitor for hiding a Jew, that he endangered the entire village. Some of the men from the bar are saying openly that my father and Ignatz were paid a fortune in diamonds by the Jew and that they're now getting rich off the Americans too. Some people even boycott the store. It was rank and surly in Sankt Vero that summer. Leaving in September was not as wrenching as I thought it would be. Sigi gave me one of her best smiles when we said goodbye. Love always, she said out loud.

ABOUT A YEAR AND A HALF after the Americans came and made my father mayor, he got a letter from Baltimore, U.S.A., which he forwarded to me at my aunt's in Schwaz. The Jew wrote that he survived typhus at the DP camp, where he was kept for a month. A bitter experience, he wrote, but not so bitter as what was to come. Dr. Weiss never found his wife, or her remains. He learned only that she had been taken to Theresienstadt and had most likely died there in 1944, with thousands of others. There was a job for him at Innsbruck hospital after he left the DP camp, and he could even have had his old apartment back. The Nazi family who had taken it over had been kicked out. But he could not bear it. He was able to get a visa to America.

Here I am, he wrote, in a neighborhood called Forest Park, living with my daughter and her husband. The houses are large, and they are all surrounded by gardens, but there are no walls or fences. I can't get used to America. There is too much of everything; it overwhelms you. I dream sometimes of my box, of talks with Sigi and Niki and Traudl. And not all of them are nightmares. The worst now is that I can't work. They won't accept my credentials. The fact that I've done thousands of operations, that I am a fine surgeon, means nothing to them. But I am hopeful this will change. That is the important point about America, he wrote. Things can change.

EVERY YEAR AFTER THAT, around Christmas, we got a card from Baltimore, U.S.A. My father would always forward them to me at Schwaz and, later, at Innsbruck when I started university. At first there were bits of news and well wishes, but later Dr. Weiss would just sign his name and add one thing: "Next year in Sankt Vero!"

For a long time I didn't know what that meant. There were no Jews around who I could ask. But finally I learned that Jews toast each other with "Next year in Jerusalem!" at every New Year's dinner. It is a solemn tradition. It has great meaning in their hearts, I was told.

Yet it's just a remembrance, a forlorn hope. Of course, they never go. None of us ever does.

Thomas Moran is currently a magazine editor. As a journalist he has reported from most countries in Europe and Asia. A ten-part series he wrote on the Mafia control of New York's garment industry was nominated for a Pulitzer Prize in investigative reporting. This is his first novel.